## Praise for *The Blameless*

"Christison takes the tropes of epic fantasy and strips them of their angst, crafting a feel-good page-turner. Brie is a likeable protagonist surrounded by good-natured, slightly larger-than-life companions. Flinton is especially striking with his bearlike size and caring nature, but even Vaylec—the villain—has a personality and depth beyond the genre's typical evilness for evil's sake. Christison refuses to manufacture conflict, focusing instead on a central premise and the characters that underpin it. Though the plot is simple and the book is long, Brie's story plays out with an endearing breeziness. As is often the case with series, the ending of this first novel comes as an interruption rather than a denouement. Nonetheless, there's a great deal here to ensnare young readers. A heartwarming and innocent upper-middle-grade fantasy."

—*Kirkus Reviews*

"A magical debut with strong writing and lovable characters. I rooted for Brie as if she were a member of my own family, and all the uncles were my favorite. As soon as my superpowers develop, I'm volunteering to be one of the Blameless. I'm anxiously awaiting the next book."

—Karen Amanda Hooper, author of *The Kindrily* series

## More praise for *The Blameless*

"Princess Brie's provincial life is shattered in one night as Aldestone falls at the hands of a brutal betrayal. Her family is gone, her life is irreparably unwound, and she is now swept away by three strangers of unknown intent. Her path to royalty is permanently detoured, or so it would seem. Magic, adventure, and new friendships await as she rises from the ashes to take her rightful place among the Blameless. In this series debut, Christison expertly transports the reader to a richly written fantasy world where self-sacrifice and honor are held above all. Well, at least for most. Fresh, original, and exhilarating, *The Blameless* is a must-have for your fantasy bookshelf."

—S.P. O'Farrell, author of the *Simone LaFray* series

"Reading *The Blameless* is the closest I've ever come to feeling the way I felt when reading *Harry Potter* as a child, which says a lot! I used to dream J.K. Rowling's world of magic would come true, because it felt so real. I'd never found a book again to give me quite the same feeling until *The Blameless*. E.S. Christison creates a realistic world full of excitement, terror, happiness, goodness, and hope. The characters are genuine and solid, with personalities just like people you would want to know in real life. They never become predictable or dull. Some of them would make such awesome friends! I found myself smiling, laughing out loud, and (almost) crying in several places throughout the book. I never wanted it to end! I don't remember *any* boring passages anywhere—how rare is that? This book is written for fantasy lovers who indulge in every part of a well-written story. If you are a bookworm like me, and always on the lookout for great stories, then snuggle up and get comfy. This is a book for you!"

—Bettina Ruhe, English teacher, grades 5-7

E.S. CHRISTISON

# THE BLAMELESS

BOOK ONE

BELLE ISLE BOOKS

www.belleislebooks.com

*This is a work of fiction. Any references to real people, locations, or historical events are used in a fictitious manner and should not be interpreted as fact. All other names, locations, or events mentioned are products of the author's imagination. Any resemblance to actual events, locations, or persons, living or dead, is entirely coincidental.*



ISBN: 978-1-951565-60-2
LCCN: 2020904717

*Cover and layout designed by Michael Hardison*
*Production managed by Christina Kann*
*Cover illustrated by Hannu Nevanlinna*
*The Blameless symbols and The Kingdoms of the Blameless map illustrated by Peter Cheetham*

Printed in the United States of America

Published by
Belle Isle Books (an imprint of Brandylane Publishers, Inc.)
5 S. 1st Street
Richmond, Virginia 23219

BELLE ISLE BOOKS
www.belleislebooks.com

belleislebooks.com | brandylanepublishers.com

*To the man who started my love of reading–*

*my father, Eddie Jay.*

*Thanks for a lifetime of selflessness, sacrifice, and love.*

*In my opinion, you're Blameless.*

# CONTENTS

The Kingdoms of the Blameless

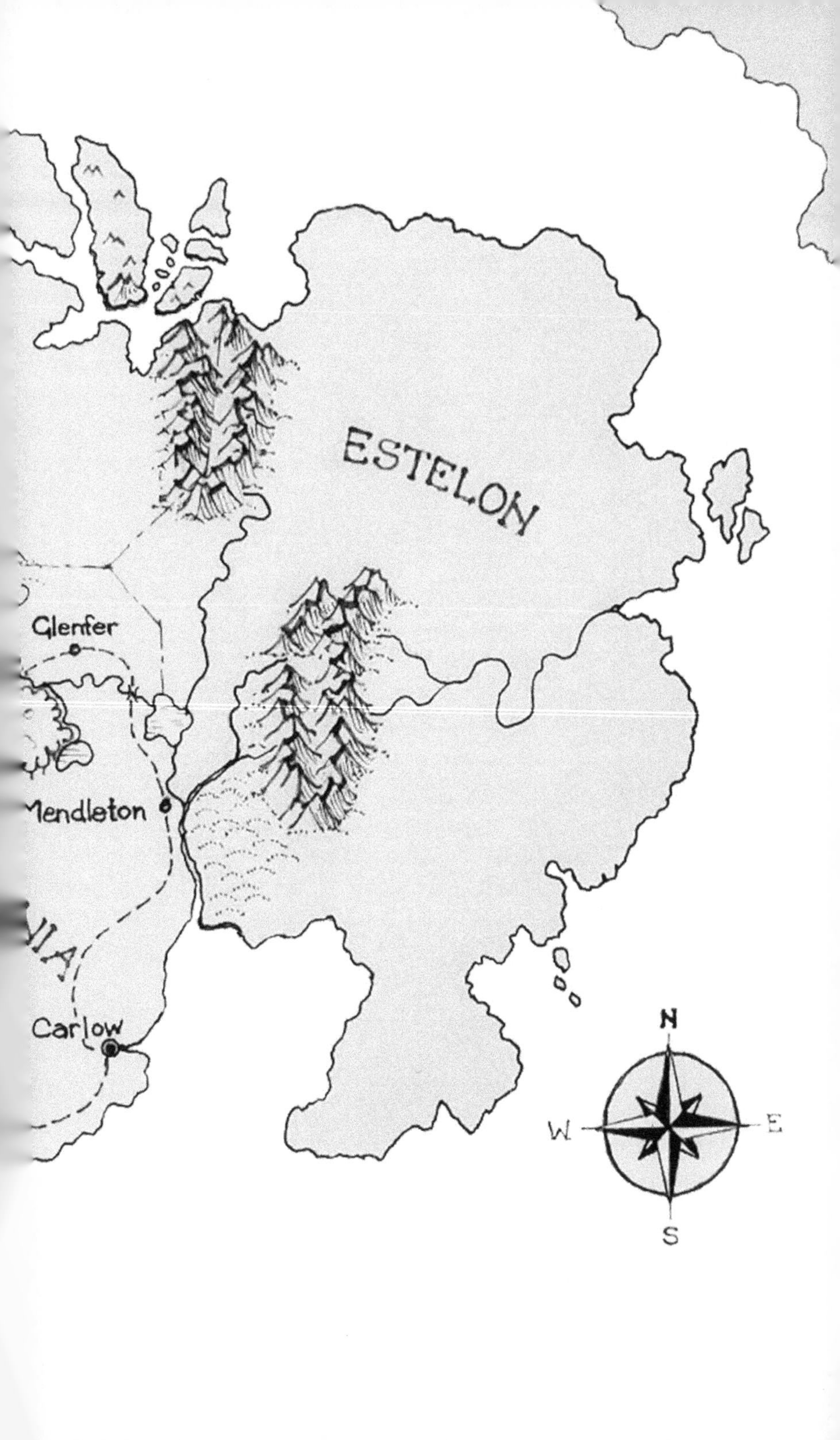
ESTELON
Glenfer
Mendleton
Carlow
N
W
E
S

# *A Savior in the Night*

Lightning flashed across the distant night sky. The roar of thunder that followed was so intense that the streets of Aldestone trembled beneath Princess Briana's slippered feet. Dressed only in her nightgown, she sprinted through her beloved city, surrounded by the sounds of her citizens screaming, soldiers shouting, and swords clashing. A group of enemy soldiers ran toward her in the street, but their eyes passed over her without recognition.

Fleeing further from the castle with every stride, Brie made a sharp left onto a street lined with shops and noticed a door swinging open on its hinges. Making a split-second decision, she dashed inside. She cleared the threshold, slammed the door shut, and secured the lock with her trembling fingers.

With her right hand fisted over her racing heart, Brie sagged against the wooden frame, and her eyelids fluttered shut.

The moment her eyes closed, the attack on her parents replayed in Brie's mind, and a wave of overwhelming grief nearly brought her to her knees. She'd seen it with her own eyes, but her mind couldn't accept it. It was too horrible to be real. She swayed on her feet for a moment, on the verge of yanking open the door and charging back to the castle to find proof that her life hadn't been shattered, but the sounds of battle in the streets stopped her.

Brie groaned and fisted her hair as a vision jumped to the forefront of her mind—her mother shouting for her to run. That shout had come just before the sword had brutally pierced the queen's chest. Her mother's last words were a command, a source of direction, and Brie clung to them with a consuming sort of desperation. The city was under attack, her parents and older brother had been caught in the raid, and she was being hunted, but obeying her mother's instructions became Brie's entire focus. Brie clung to the hope that her family would be taken to the castle infirmary and cared for by doctors, and then they would all be reunited, and everything would go back to how it had been before the invasion. Brie pushed aside worries over the amount of blood she'd seen. Her family *had* to survive, because she didn't know how she could possibly go on living without them.

Another bolt of lightning struck, closer this time, briefly illuminating the inside of the room through the window and snapping Brie back to the present. A quick glance around revealed she had taken refuge in a blacksmith's shop. It was messy, with tools and papers scattered all over the counter, and an overturned chair had been cast in the middle of the floor. A small fire still burned in the forge. It looked like the owners had left in a hurry.

Brie's eyes homed in on a doorway behind the counter as she heard galloping horses approach.

"Find the princess!" a shout came, sounding eerily close to the smithy. "Search every street and building!"

Brie rushed past the counter and through the doorway into a room that was shrouded in darkness. Blinking as her eyes adjusted to the dark space, she discovered she was in a small storage room with wall-to-wall shelving. She slipped past the first few rows and tucked herself behind a tall rack that was laden down with weapons. She settled on the floor, hugging her knees to her chest in an attempt to make herself as small as possible. The room was far enough away from the heat of the forge that it was cold, and after a short amount of time, the chill from the stone floor began to seep through her thin night-gown. Her lack of proper clothing, combined with the night's devastating events, set her teeth to chattering and caused her young body to tremble.

She wished Falen was with her. He made everything better. Why did her brother have to be in the corridor when the attack happened? Why couldn't he have been closer to her? They could have escaped together, and he would have known exactly what to do. Instead she was alone in a smithy, without a plan. She couldn't hide forever. If they were searching every building, they would eventually find her. She needed help. Fighting against the tears that threatened to break free, Brie wished for someone loyal to her family to find and rescue her.

Brie's thoughts were cut short as a rattling sounded at the door of the smithy. Her stomach clenched in fear, and she hoped the lock would be enough to keep the intruder out. The rattling stopped, but it was followed by clicking noises and the sounds of grinding metal. Preparing for the worst, Brie scanned the weapons on the shelf in front of her and grabbed one that suited her size: a knife with a curved blade. Grasping it firmly, she flattened her back against the wall and waited.

The commotion coming from the door ceased, followed by an eerie silence that stretched on for minutes or perhaps hours. It was impossible to judge the passage of time correctly in her current state. Brie sat perfectly still, hardly daring to breathe, waiting for the intruder to either move on or attack.

A bright lantern suddenly appeared out of thin air and blazed to life right in front of Brie. Her brain understood it was important to keep silent, but her mouth had a mind of its own. An ear-piercing war-cry ripped out of her as she swung her knife upward toward the threat.

In a blink, several things happened. The lantern was shelved, her wrist with the knife was seized, and a large hand smashed over her lips, silencing her. The hand was gigantic, covering not only her mouth but most of her face.

Brie tensed, preparing to fight, as her eyes traveled past the hand and up the exceptionally long arm. Her gaze finally landed on the face of a man easily six times her size, standing on the other side of the weapons rack.

The giant of a man peered through the shelving at her with his brows raised and a reassuring smile on his face. The light from the lantern cast shadows over his body, illuminating his face in a ghostly sort of way. His sudden appearance had set Brie's heart racing, yet the moment their eyes collided, hope blossomed inside of her. The man's eyes were deep, dark pools of kindness and warmth, and they contained no threat. Fear temporarily vanished, and hope that he had no plans to harm her took its place. Brie dropped her knife, and it clattered to the stone floor.

It seemed a savior had come for her.

The man's eyes made the biggest impression on Brie, yet the rest of him was equally remarkable. His curly brown hair was a floppy mess, and scattered chaotically over his forehead, curling around his ears and neck. His cheeks were sharp and defined, and his olive-toned face was tan and weathered. The thick muscles in his arms bulged as he released her wrist. He slowly lifted a finger to his lips, indicating that Brie should stay quiet, and removed his hand from her mouth, one finger at a time. Then his face split into a wide, tender smile.

"Hello, Princess Briana," he rumbled in a deep whisper. "There's no need to be afraid. I'm Flinton, and I'm here to help you."

He offered her his hand, and without hesitation, Brie took it, allowing him to pull her to her feet and lead her out from behind the shelving.

"We need to be very quiet." Flinton stated what Brie knew, despite her scream. "The enemy is all around us. I have friends waiting at the edge of the city who will help. We're going to take you to safety."

Brie nodded. She could hide with this man for a time until the threat in the castle was removed.

Flinton's eyes performed a quick scan of Brie's waist-length blonde hair, her purple satin sleep gown, and her bejeweled slippers. "Earth, air, and sun. We've got to cover you up, or they'll be able to recognize you for miles," he muttered, more to himself than to Brie.

Quickly, he pulled off his cloak and gently placed it over Brie's head, covering her hair with the hood. Though Brie was thirteen years old, she was small for her age. Flinton's oversized cloak fell past her feet and onto the floor. Reaching into a satchel at his hip, Flinton took out some coarse yarn and quickly wrapped it around her waist, creating a makeshift belt to keep all the fabric in place.

"Good enough for now. Let's go," he said.

As quietly as possible, they moved through the smithy toward an exit at the back of the building. Passing the store windows, Brie saw more riders approaching and quickened her pace. When they reached the exit, they found the door bolted shut and secured with a large iron lock. Flinton used his huge hands to attempt to open the lock, but he was unsuccessful. He tried again, but it wouldn't budge.

"We don't have time for this," he grumbled.

Opening his vest, Flinton reached his right hand inside, over his heart. When he withdrew his hand from his chest, he held a tool that was sharp and knife-like. It sliced through the iron lock as easily as if it were made of butter. As soon as the lock was broken, the tool vanished. Brie blinked and wondered if her eyes were playing tricks on her, but Flinton quickly pushed the door open and grabbed Brie's hand, and together they ran out into the night.

Leaving the smithy behind, they silently weaved their way through the cobblestoned back streets of the city. Brie was devastated by the destruction she saw. The beautiful brick homes and shops of Aldestone had been ransacked and searched. Windows were shattered, doors were smashed or simply pulled from their hinges, and whole streets were in flames.

As they ran, Brie's smaller frame, burdened by Flinton's oversized cloak that dragged on the ground, presented a problem. She tried to keep up, but she just couldn't match Flinton's longer strides.

It didn't take long for Flinton to notice, and he pulled to a stop. Squatting in front of her, he asked, "Can you climb onto my back, Your Highness? If I carry you, we can travel much faster."

Brie didn't need to be told twice. She jumped on Flinton's back, wrapped her legs around his enormous waist, and grasped his neck tightly with her small hands.

"Good girl. Now let's move!"

Flinton took off running. He was amazingly swift and agile for his size, even with Brie's added weight. As he ran, the chaos and noise of the city began to grow quieter, and fewer people could be seen in the streets. Flinton kept to the shadows and sprinted like a madman.

As they reached the outskirts of town, they passed an inn. They were approaching the stables when two figures in foreign uniforms stepped out into the street ahead of them. The uniforms were the very same ones worn by the soldiers who'd attacked Brie's family. Fear seized Brie's heart once again. Each soldier held a torch in one hand and a sword in the other, and they stood directly in Flinton's path.

Without breaking his stride, Flinton swerved to the left to avoid them and kept running.

The soldiers raised their swords, and one of them shouted, "You there, stop!"

Flinton and Brie were almost past the soldiers when, on instinct, Brie jerked her head toward the shout. Her hood slipped, exposing her golden hair, and the soldiers' eyes widened.

"It's Princess Briana!" one of them shouted, and he took off in pursuit. "Don't let them escape!"

Brie felt Flinton's muscles tighten beneath her as he mustered a fresh burst of speed. She closed her eyes briefly and said a prayer to the Three that they would make it to safety, but their luck ended as three more soldiers came out of the stables ahead of them with swords drawn.

They were cut off.

Flinton slowed his pace, and the soldiers behind began to quickly close the distance. Flinton's weight shifted, and from over his shoulder, Brie saw him reach inside of his vest. When he withdrew his hand, a massive sword appeared miraculously in his grip.

Before Brie could process where a sword that size could have been hiding during their flight, Flinton roared, "Hang on tight, Princess!"

Brie squeezed her hands more tightly around Flinton's thick neck, hoping she wasn't blocking his air flow with her chokehold.

Seemingly unaffected, Flinton spun around, extending his sword arm. Steel met steel twice in quick succession as he landed a solid blow to each of their weapons, disarming them with the force of his swing. Before the soldiers could recover from their shock, Flinton's empty hands seized their heads and smashed them together. The soldiers' knees buckled, and they dropped to the ground one by one, passed out cold. Their torches fell onto the street and continued to blaze on the ground, their light illuminating Flinton and magnifying his strength.

Flinton turned around to face the remaining three foes, who were advancing on them cautiously. He spoke in a voice low enough for only Brie to hear. "Get down, and run to the door of the inn. Stay there until I come for you."

As instructed, Brie slid down Flinton's back onto the street. Then she ran straight for the inn. She watched Flinton flick his gaze toward her, as though he was ensuring her safety. His eyes no longer radiated warmth but were hard and determined. Flinton nodded, the gesture reinforcing his desire for her to stay put.

Turning back toward their foes, Flinton wasted no more time. He held his sword in his left hand, and once again reached into his vest over his heart with the right. Removing his hand, he now held a long, thin, metal chain. Flinton was a formidable sight as he advanced on the three soldiers, and for a moment Brie questioned her blind trust in him. He was obviously a force to be reckoned with and a very real threat. His thick, muscular build was just as impressive as his incredible height. One of the three approaching enemies came to a halt and appeared to second guess their attack.

Flinton released one end of the metal chain, which soared away from his body and wrapped around the opponent's sword. He jerked the chain swiftly, and the sword flew out of the man's hands, leaving him weaponless. The man's eyes widened in fear, and he bolted.

Flinton advanced next on a female guard, who held her weapon poised and ready. He charged and swung his sword, striking the blunt edge across her shins, causing her to collapse onto her knees in pain. He quickly circled the woman's body with the metal chain, effectively tying her up, then turned his attention to the one remaining soldier who stood frozen with fear.

From a short distance away, Brie watched as Flinton walked up and peered down at the wide-eyed coward. Then Flinton took his fist and smashed it into the man's nose. The soldier's eyes rolled back in his head, and he fell backward onto the street.

Flinton turned around toward the inn, weaponless once again, and he slowly walked toward Brie. She watched him advance with his arms out, palms up, like he was approaching a wounded animal. He probably thought Brie was now afraid of him. And maybe she should be. She'd just witnessed him fight five soldiers without a scratch to his body, and he wasn't even out of breath. But he was offering her protection, which was far better than trying to kill her. Her options were limited, and a small piece of her battered heart continued to assure her that Flinton was trustworthy.

"I'm sorry you had to witness that," Flinton said softly, "but those soldiers would have taken you and hurt you." He knelt in front of her. "I did what had to be done to keep you safe."

The hood of Brie's cloak was back far enough for Flinton to have clear view into her hazel eyes. She bravely met his gaze and answered, "I understand why you fought them. Thank you for protecting me." She dropped her voice to a whisper and forced out the next words. "But I still need your help. Please don't leave me."

"I'm not going anywhere," Flinton confirmed.

Brie held Flinton's gaze and sniffed, trying her hardest to hold the royal composure she had been so thoroughly taught to maintain by her mother. But her resolve became shaky as she suddenly realized the man before her was helping her fulfill her mother's command to run, and his protection meant more to her than he would likely ever know. Her lower lip began to tremble, and throwing royal composure to the wind, she launched herself at Flinton. She threw her arms around his neck and held onto him like a lifeline.

After a brief pause, Flinton raised his arms and returned her hug, engulfing her tiny frame.

The embrace only lasted for a moment before Flinton gently untangled her arms from around his neck. Clearing his throat and blinking rapidly, he said with the gentlest of voices, "We need to keep moving, or my friends will send out a second search party. Come on, little lady; up you go."

Once again, Brie climbed onto his back.

Without further delay, Flinton and Brie traveled to the north edge of the city, where three horses awaited them. Two of them, one chestnut and the other black, bore unfamiliar riders, causing Brie's gut to seize with immediate worry and suspicion. The third horse was a mammoth-sized black Shire with white leg markings. The size of the beast and the empty saddle were clear indicators that the horse belonged to Flinton.

A lean, dark-skinned rider with a shaved head started speaking as soon they approached. "If you came all of this way without her, I swear I will strangle you."

"Relax, Derek. She's right here," Flinton said, turning slightly to the side and allowing Brie's hooded head to peek around his shoulder.

"Thank the Three." Derek's shoulders relaxed, as well as his tone. "Hello, Princess Briana," he said as Brie slid down from Flinton's back. "We don't have the time to chat, but I'm Derek." He motioned vaguely to the other man at his side. "This here is Kove. We're taking you out of Aldestone to safety. We promise to explain more as we go, but trust me when I say we're your friends. Our top priority right now is putting as much distance as possible between you and this city."

The other rider, Kove, stood in his saddle, raised his arms, and bowed with a flourish. "It is an honor to meet you, Your Highness." His shoulder-length blond hair was tied back at his neck, and it swayed as he bent over and searched through his saddle bag. When he sat up, he held a yellow rose—part of her family's crest—which he extended to Brie with a kind smile.

Brie's eyebrows raised in surprise. "Thank you," she said quietly, accepting the rose. Although she trusted Flinton, she wasn't sure about the other two.

Brie turned to Flinton with a furrowed brow, wondering how best to explain that traveling as far away from Aldestone as possible wasn't a good idea. Her family needed her. They'd been severely injured, and she wanted to be with them as they recovered. She simply needed to hide away long enough for Aldestone's army to fight off the invaders and restore order.

Brie opened her mouth to explain this, but Derek continued to speak. His gaze toward her was firm but not unkind. "We know what happened tonight, and we offer you our deepest sympathy. We were friends of your parents, and losing them and your brother is an unspeakably great tragedy." He moved his gaze to Flinton. "We need to start riding before we're noticed and followed. Mount up."

Brie's already fractured heart cracked open so wide, she wondered if it would ever recover. She shook her head, trying to make them understand, everything inside of her resisting his words. "No, I was there. They can't be dead, but they're hurt. We have the best doctors in all of Predonia in the castle. Once the enemies are captured, I need to get back to them."

The three men cast worried looks among themselves.

"Flinton," Derek sighed quietly.

Flinton placed his hands on her shoulders, gently but firmly holding her in place. "They're gone, Princess Briana. They didn't make it. The castle has been overthrown, and the city is taken. You can't go back."

Brie shook her head again, denying the words.

"We have to leave. I'm sorry, Your Highness."

Without asking permission, Flinton lifted Brie and placed her in the saddle of the Shire, then swiftly mounted behind her. Then the trio of riders urged their horses forward, and they galloped off toward the north highway that exited the city.

Brie continued to shake her head numbly, denying what she knew was right in front of her. For the first time on that horrible night, she was finally safe. Yet with her newfound safety came the freedom to remember, and flashes of the night's horrors began to run through her mind. . . . Evil men breaking into the royal family's rooms as they readied for bed . . . The terrifying sound of her brother's strangled cry being cut short . . . Her guards slain in the doorway . . . Her mother yelling at her to run . . . Her father stepping in front of her mother to protect her, then both being pierced through with swords . . . Running through the hidden passages of the castle alone.

The truth slammed into Brie with a force that took her breath away. It was real. Her family was gone.

The pain was too much to keep bottled up inside, and a lone, victorious tear escaped, rolling down Brie's cheek. It was followed by several more, and her resistance crumbled. The dam finally broke, and her tears were unleashed like a flowing river. They poured down her face, and her body shook with the force of them.

Flinton wrapped one arm around Brie, cocooning her against his chest as she sobbed. "There, there, Princess Briana," he said gently. "Let it out. It will be okay. You're safe with us, and we will never leave you."

They rode their horses hard, leaving the killings, the evil men, and the distant storm behind them.

Vaylec stood in the throne room, surveying the aftermath of his victory, and he smiled. It was a beautiful sight. He wasn't referring to the destruction and mess; they were just a means to an end. He would have his servants clean it up soon enough. But, standing in the throne room of the castle and knowing it was his—now *that* was a thing of beauty. At last, after years of scheming, he had accomplished the first phase of his long laid-out plan. He had slain King Eyrhill, and the great city of Aldestone was now in his control. In time, the entire country of Predonia would be his.

But he wanted more than a castle, lands, and wealth. To-night, almost everything had gone as intended. Everything except for the princess escaping. His smile faded, and his face darkened. He would tear the country apart, piece by piece if need be, and he *would* find her. His plan had taken years to mastermind, and if it took a little longer to accomplish, he could wait.

# Friends or Foes

Brie woke up with a scream, her heart beating out of her chest as it tried to recover from the terrible nightmare. She sat up in bed, her hair and nightgown damp with sweat despite the chill morning air. Pushing aside her blankets, she looked around the small tent in confusion and froze when she saw the yellow rose next to her pillow.

"No," Brie whispered. "No, no, no!" she repeated, her voice growing stronger. In a panic, she glanced down at her nightgown and found it hidden underneath a thick cloak. Flinton's cloak. Looking around the small, confined space, Brie's eyes landed in the corner on her lavender slippers, which were covered in mud.

It hadn't been a dream. Her nightmare was real.

A wail of agony escaped Brie's mouth, and she crumpled onto the small bed. Curling into a ball, she sobbed, her body shaking with grief as everything inside of her rebelled against the truth. How could this have happened? Predonia was a peaceful kingdom, and her parents were loved and respected leaders. Kings and queens were not supposed to die. They were supposed to be indestructible. They were meant to pass away peacefully in their sleep when they were old and gray, after having lived long and happy lives. But not this way. Not *murder.* And her brother—Brie wept harder at the thought of never seeing Falen again. He was six years older than her, but he was her favorite person in the entire world. Brie couldn't fathom her life without him. Her body rocked back and forth, trying to comfort itself as she soaked her pillow with her tears.

"Princess?" A familiar voice broke through her haze of pain and denial with concern.

Brie didn't look up as the flap of the tent opened and a dark shadow fell over her.

"We only stopped for a short rest. I know you're hurting, but you're still in danger and we need to keep moving, Your Highness. Please join us by the fire so we can eat and tear down the tents."

Brie opened her eyes and met Flinton's kind gaze. She was surprised but grateful that he hadn't tried to offer words of comfort, because there weren't any. She focused on his request and nodded as a few more tears leaked out and drew a pathway into her hair. After an assessing glance at her face, Flinton stepped back and closed the tent.

Wiping her eyes, Brie sat up again and reached for her dirty slippers. The memory of when she'd first received them assaulted her, making her pause. It had only been two weeks ago. Her father and Falen had just returned home from several weeks on the road, visiting the courts of the other three kingdoms. Brie loved sweets with unparalleled intensity, and Falen made it a tradition that whenever he traveled, he would find the most unusual and delicious candies to bring home for

Brie to try. They would spend his first evening back in Aldestone together, sampling the sweets and deciding which were best, eating until their teeth hurt and their bellies ached from all the sugar they'd consumed. When Falen and her father returned from their last trip, Brie had been bedridden with a fever and a cough. Falen saw how ill she was, kissed her forehead, and promised her they'd eat the treats another night, much to Brie's dismay. Then, he ran to his room and returned with the slippers, which he'd purchased for her from a "quaint shop" in Estelon. He'd bought them because they were lavender, Brie's favorite color, and he'd planned to give them to her for her birthday. But because he felt sorry for her, he gave them to her early.

Brie's birthday was still two moons away. She couldn't imagine celebrating it without Falen and her parents.

Brie put the slippers on her feet, loving them and hating them, as hot tears dripped off her chin. She cried for several more minutes, until the tears eventually stopped and her breathing settled. Falen had been the heir to the throne, and as Brie came to the realization that her brother would never be king, she suddenly realized something else. She was officially the rightful ruler of Predonia now. But the thought made her angry. She didn't want to be queen. The only thing she wanted was for her family to come back.

Feeling unprepared to face what was waiting outside of the tent, Brie parted the canvas and peered through the opening, taking the opportunity to study the men and her surroundings without being noticed. There were three small tents, including hers, and one larger one set up in a clearing in the middle of a forest of pine trees.

Perhaps because the man was so gigantic, Brie's eyes found Flinton first. He sat on a log by a blazing fire, stirring a sizzling pan of food. He was just as extraordinarily large this morning as he had been the night before. Maybe even more so. Despite the cool autumn morning, he wore a sleeveless shirt that revealed his muscle-bound arms. A shield was strapped to his back, and his large sword lay on the ground by his feet.

Beside Flinton, Kove stood with one foot propped on a log. He held a knife in one hand and a piece of flint in the other, repeatedly striking them together. His blond hair swung loose around his shoulders that morning, and his green eyes flashed toward Flinton as they talked quietly. Kove was average in height with an athletic build, clothed completely in black. In addition to the knife he was sharpening, Brie noticed several other blades attached to his belt, and even more strapped to his legs, running from his thighs clear down to his boots.

Derek was tending to the horses, which were tied to the trees at the edge of the clearing. He was tall, though his height couldn't compete with Flinton's. He wore a high-collared hunter green jacket that belted at the waist, brown trousers, and knee length brown boots. He was lean but fit, with smooth brown skin and intense dark eyes framed with black eyelashes and brows. A cloth headband with an unusual symbol on the front was tied at the back of his shaved head. Moving with confident strides, he removed a large bow and quiver of arrows from his back and secured them to one of the saddle bags.

Brie swallowed and involuntarily shivered. All of them looked impressively dangerous. If she'd come to the realization that she was the rightful ruler of Predonia this morning, she was sure these men had pieced together the same thing. Maybe they were only temporarily protecting her, and they were planning on eventually ransoming her off to the highest bidder. Doubt and worry gnawed at her stomach, but she realized she had nowhere else to go, and no means to get there. For the time being, Brie was safe, but she made the decision not to trust anyone. Well, except for maybe Flinton.

Taking a deep breath, Brie finally opened the flap completely and exited the tent. Her feet made no noise as she stepped out onto the fallen pine needles that covered the ground, but three pairs of eyes immediately snapped in her direction.

"Come, sit down and warm yourself," Flinton urged. "Breakfast will be ready soon."

Joining them at the fire, Brie chose the log closest to Flinton, seeking comfort from his familiar presence. She numbly watched him stir the food over the flames and blurted out the first thing that came into her head. "You are the most humongous human being I have ever seen."

Flinton released a small, deep chuckle. "And you're the tiniest princess I've ever seen."

Derek passed Brie on his way to a seat across the fire. He placed a firm hand on her shoulder, giving it a squeeze, which caused Brie to jump in fright.

"I didn't mean to startle you. I'm sorry. How are you this morning, Princess Briana?" He seemed like a direct sort of person.

Brie didn't have the energy or desire to put on a false show of strength. She was sure they had already heard her crying, anyway. "I don't understand what happened." Her voice wavered, but she continued, "It just feels like a horrible dream."

Kove took a plate, and Flinton scooped a pile of scrambled eggs and ham onto it. Holding the food out for Brie, Kove spoke. "You're right," he said softly. "It doesn't seem real." He paused and cleared his throat. "I don't mean to sound heartless, but maybe eating will make you feel better."

Brie shook her head. "No, thank you. I'm not hungry."

"Come on, Your Highness," Flinton prodded. "We have a long journey ahead of us, and you're going to need your strength. Try to take a few bites."

Sighing heavily, Brie took the plate. Flinton seemed to know what to say to put her into action. She forced herself to take a bite of food, which tasted surprisingly good to her nauseous stomach, especially considering it had been prepared over a campfire.

"Please, just call me Brie," she said, not wanting to be addressed repeatedly as "Your Highness" or "Princess." "It's what my family calls me." She swallowed. "I mean, it's what they called me." She put down the fork and stared into the fire, willing herself not to fall to pieces all over again. In that moment, a faint buzzing started up in her ears. It distracted her enough to prevent another meltdown. She glanced around, trying to find the source of the noise, but there didn't seem to be one. Perhaps it was a woodland insect.

Kove nodded and shared a look with Flinton and Derek. "We would be honored to call you Brie," he said.

Brie picked up her fork and took another bite as a question came to mind. "You said you were friends with my parents, but I've never seen you in the castle," Brie tried not to let her suspicion show. She reached up and tugged on one of her ears as the buzzing persisted. "How did you know them?"

Derek answered, "We've done undercover work for your father over the years, which is why you've never seen us in the castle. He's called on us regularly to help the Crown with tasks like delivering top-secret messages, squelching small rebellions, or gathering information. Our connection with your parents developed because of Adira, your father's advisor. She's our very close friend. It was Adira who sent the message to us last night about the attack on the castle. She let us know you had escaped, and she begged us to find you."

Brie felt a measure of relief, knowing it was Adira who had led them to her. A bit of suspicion toward them lessened as a small piece to a very large puzzle was put in place, but her nausea had returned in full force. She loved Adira like an aunt or an older sister. "Is she all right? Do you know if she's safe?" Brie had been so consumed by grief, she hadn't considered the wellbeing of others in the castle who had been left behind: her maids and her favorite guards; the cook's granddaughter, Delia, who was one of her closest friends; and Adira.

The men glanced warily at one another, which did nothing to settle Brie's stomach, before Flinton answered. "When we heard from her, Adira was alive and well. She was within the castle, however. According to Adira, many servants have been taken captive, and we believe she's one of them. If that's the case, it will be very difficult for her to send any further messages to us at this time. Don't spend time worrying about Adira," he added. "She can take care of herself."

Finishing his meal first, Derek got up from the fire and

went to his horse. After retrieving a bundle from his saddle bags, he came back and held up a pair of black leggings, black boots, and a thick blue tunic for Brie. "It's probably best that we disguise who you are, and I didn't think a dress was suitable. These will be more comfortable traveling clothes, and much warmer."

Brie felt relieved. She wanted to rip off her purple satin nightgown and burn it, along with the memories that would forever be tied to it. Grasping the clothing to her chest, gratitude filled her. She would likely be dead or captured if it wasn't for her rescuers, and she found herself hoping they were truly good men. Her voice wobbled as she quietly said, "Thank you for your help."

Soon, they were saddled up and riding at a brisk pace along a small road heading north. Derek and Flinton were on the alert, continually scanning the path both in front of and behind them, as well as the surrounding landscape, which was hilly and scattered with trees.

Brie sat in front of Kove. As they rode, he tried to interact with her by pointing out various animals in the hills and birds in the air, but Brie didn't feel like talking, and she couldn't muster up the energy to appear interested. Eventually he switched tactics and passed the time by attempting to entertain her with stories of his travels.

"Once, we were in the south of Predonia by the coast, in the town of Carlow, on a mission for your father," Kove began his second tale. Pain knifed through Brie at the casual mention of her dad. "He'd received many complaints from the citizens in the area regarding a certain spice merchant. Everyone who bought the merchant's goods became gravely ill, so we were sent to investigate why."

For the first time, Brie found herself paying attention. She rarely got to see this side of her father's rulings as king. Now that her father had been taken from her, she wanted to hear any story tied to him, even if it hurt.

"With our amazing investigative skills, we were able to uncover the source of the illnesses. You see, this poor excuse for a merchant was diluting his spices by adding straw he had ground down to a very fine powder. This straw came from the loft of his barn, which just so happened to be the home of hundreds of pigeons. Hundreds of diseased, pooping pigeons."

Brie cringed. She was horrified at the thought of eating diseased pigeon poop. "That is disgusting."

"Yes, it certainly is, and that isn't even the best part of the story," Kove continued. "When we were searching the barn for evidence, I came across a two-headed pigeon in the rafters."

Brie glanced back at him with an incredulous look on her face.

"I'm not lying, am I, Derek?" Kove asked. He leaned forward and muttered quietly, "He likes to call me out on my bluffs."

"No, you're telling the truth," Derek confirmed.

Kove raised his eyebrows and gave Brie an "I told you so" nod.

"What happened to the merchant?" Brie couldn't help asking.

"We put him in jail and then burned down his barn to contain the disease," Kove answered. Then he added wistfully,

"I wanted to keep the two-headed pigeon as a pet, but sadly, Derek wouldn't let me. He spouted off some nonsense about the diseased pigeon being a health risk," Kove added, "but to this day I just think it creeped him out."

The morning passed swiftly, thanks to Kove and his stories, and the temperature warmed as the sun rose higher in the sky. They stopped for a quick lunch, eating bread, ham, and fruit, then resumed their steady pace.

As the afternoon wore on, Derek appeared more and more uneasy. His eyes continuously scanned the countryside around them with concern. Suddenly, he hissed, "Something isn't right! Get your weapons out!"

As soon as the words left his mouth, an arrow sailed toward them, grazing Flinton's arm.

Simultaneously, the trio armed themselves. Flinton's sword appeared in his hand, Derek drew his bow, and Kove had a knife ready to throw. Flinton and Derek pulled their horses up next to Kove, flanking him on both sides in what Brie assumed was an effort to protect her. Brie's chest began to burn, and her hands began to itch.

"Why didn't you see this on your scan?" Kove shouted at Derek, the easygoing manner he'd exhibited during his storytelling no longer present.

"I don't know. Something isn't adding up," Derek answered. "I've been able to sense Adira approaching since we stopped for lunch, but she hasn't answered me. I was hoping she had escaped from the castle and was coming to meet us. Now, I'm not so sure. Adira is here and there are soldiers with her, but I can't tell how many. She must be blocking them from me."

Brie became hopeful at the thought of seeing Adira, but Derek's words made no sense to her. How could he sense Adira approaching? His hearing couldn't be that good. And where were the soldiers Adira was supposedly blocking?

They approached a small forest, and a group of horses with riders emerged from either side of the road. Brie performed a quick count and came up with a total of ten soldiers, plus at least one archer hidden from their view. As they drew closer, Brie's heart leapt as she recognized Adira, her auburn hair in its signature braid, among them. "ADIRA!" she shouted with relief and waved.

Recognition and joy were evident on Adira's face as she met Brie's gaze and caught sight of her friends. Adira opened her mouth to speak, but no words came out. A look of frustration swept over her, but it was swiftly replaced by anguish. Her eyes glazed over, and she stiffly raised her arms into the air, holding them high above her head, her palms facing toward the sky. As she sat there, rocks and pebbles rose into the air and hovered, causing Brie to blink in amazement. Then Adira pointed her arm right at Brie, and the rocks zoomed toward her, pelting her, Flinton, Derek, and Kove all over their bodies. Several small pebbles hit Brie's arms and chest, the pain resembling that of a bee sting. Behind her, Kove cursed.

All at once, the nine riders raised their swords and charged, with Adira right alongside them.

Brie was stunned by the assault, and she winced as rocks continued to bounce off her legs and arms. What was happening? A loud humming filled her ears, and the burning in her chest intensified.

Brie's rescuers were momentarily caught off guard by the attack, but Derek was the quickest to recover. He touched his right hand over his heart and raised his left hand, making a fist with a jerk. The rocks and pebbles stopped their onslaught as though they had slammed into a wall, then dropped to the ground.

Goosebumps broke out over Brie's entire body. She had witnessed what could only be described as magic.

An arrow appeared in Derek's hand. He nocked it and let it fly toward one of the horsemen, hitting him squarely in the chest and forcing him from his saddle.

Kove followed Derek's lead and let his knife loose with a deadly throw. The blade met its mark in the heart of a soldier. In a flash, Kove had another knife out and ready.

"Wait!" Brie screamed. "Don't hurt Adira. She's here to rescue me!" She didn't understand what was happening, but Adira was her friend. The only explanation that made any sense to Brie was that Adira was attempting to save her. But weren't Derek, Flinton, and Kove supposedly Adira's friends too? Why was she attacking them, and since when could Adira use magic? Brie had never witnessed Adira or *anyone* else using magic before, but she knew the old tales. According to history, magical people had disappeared centuries ago.

Kove yelled to Brie, "Lean forward, and hold onto the horse's neck! I don't know what she's doing, but you're not going anywhere with Adira. Look at her uniform."

Brie leaned forward, hugging the horse as her eyes focused on Adira's clothing. She gasped in confusion at what she was seeing. Adira was wearing a uniform that bore the same crest as the soldiers who had attacked the castle. The very same one as the men who'd killed her family. Her eyes took in the other men and women who were fighting alongside Adira. Every one of them had on the same green tunic and breastplate, engraved with a fox.

Flinton spurred his steed toward a group of four soldiers to the right. He attacked with his sword. His arm span and strength were unmatched. Blow after blow, he skillfully took enemies from their horses.

Derek dropped another soldier on the left with a well-aimed arrow as Adira raised her arms and launched another attack. Small twigs and pinecones began to assault them. Brie's leg stung as a branch made contact.

Another arrow from the right whizzed between the small space separating Kove and Brie, missing its mark. With lightning fast reflexes, Derek twisted and stood in his saddle. He aimed and released an arrow in the direction of the threat. In the distance, the archer collapsed.

Derek looked at Kove and shouted, "I'll take Brie. I can't keep shielding all of us from Adira's attacks. You have to stop her."

Nodding, Kove loosened Brie's hold on the horse and grabbed her upper arms. Putting his bow in his left hand, Derek extended his right arm and circled Brie's waist. With a yank, Brie went soaring off Kove's horse and into Derek's chest, landing side-saddle in his lap. Derek's horse put on a burst of speed, and they galloped forward, veering away from the fight and toward the forest. Stopping a short distance away behind a cluster of trees, they watched together as the fight continued.

Kove took his feet out of his stirrups and stood up on his horse's back. Crouching with both arms out to the sides, he launched himself off of his horse with a backflip, landing gracefully on the ground. He grabbed one of the attacking branches and launched it at Adira. The branch hit Adira in the face, and her head snapped backward. The glazed look left Adira's eyes and was replaced by relief, and her attack stopped.

Kove and Adira locked eyes. Adira's mouth moved, attempting to form words, but no sounds could be heard. With pleading eyes, she looked at Kove, like she wanted to relay some kind of message. Then she forcefully shook her head back and forth.

Despite Adira's apparent distress, she and the two remaining soldiers resumed their charge.

In the blink of an eye, another knife appeared in Kove's hand, and he threw it with perfect aim, hitting dead center between the eyes of one rider. Then Kove sprinted toward Adira, reaching up to drag her from her horse. But in that moment, Adira and the one remaining rider stopped their advance. They jerked their horses in the opposite direction and rode off at high speed toward the hills where the archer had been, leaving Kove in the dust.

Derek and Brie came out of hiding, and they and Flinton urged their mounts toward Kove. Breathing hard, the trio of men wore grave expressions, and their frustration was palpable.

"Is anyone hurt?" Derek asked. "Brie, were you injured?"

The others shook their heads, and Brie answered, "Not really. A few of the stones and branches hit my arms and legs, but I'm fine."

"What in the name of all that is Blameless just happened?" Flinton demanded, wiping sweat from his brow.

Kove shook his head and began to look among the slain soldiers for any survivors. "I don't know, but we're going to find out."

One man with an arrow in his chest was still breathing. Kneeling, Kove propped the man up, causing his eyes to flutter open.

"Was it Vaylec who sent you?" Kove asked.

The soldier weakly shook his head.

"He's lying," Derek stated.

"Your time's almost up, friend," Kove pressed. "Do something honorable before you leave this earth. Did he send you to capture the princess?"

The man swallowed thickly, then shook his head and weakly corrected, "All of you."

"Why?" Kove asked.

The man's eyes began to dim and close. His head rolled back, and he let out his last breath.

# *Secrets of the Blameless*

Brie needed answers, but so far she had been left alone with her wild imagination to dwell on what had happened. Why had Adira attacked them? What type of people were her rescuers? Unless Brie had suffered a mental breakdown since the death of her parents, she was sure she had witnessed magic. What else could it be? Derek promised to answer all her questions once they stopped riding, whenever that might be. He insisted they first needed to put as much distance as possible between Aldestone and themselves.

As it turned out, riding such a distance took a long time. Several hours later, after no food and little conversation, they finally pulled their horses to a stop. Flinton dismounted and lifted Brie off Derek's horse. Instead of putting her down, he embraced her, his body so tall, her legs dangled high above the ground.

"You've been through a lot in the last twenty-four hours. How are you managing?" he asked, his question causing Brie's eyes to burn and threaten tears yet again. Putting Brie down, Flinton began to examine her, searching for signs of injuries.

But most of Brie's pain and injuries were inside, where eyes couldn't see.

Brie shrugged. She didn't want to talk about the death of her family or the devastation she felt over Adira's betrayal. She wanted to keep her feelings to herself. However, she did want information about the ambush. She swallowed, evading Flinton's question, and spewed out some questions of her own. "What happened back there? Why did Adira attack us? Who is Vaylec?" Then she dropped her voice and whispered the last question. It was easier to ask quietly. "Was everyone using magic?"

"I think it's time for us to have an open discussion," Flinton answered. "We have a lot of explaining to do."

Derek and Kove dismounted, and Kove went to work tying up the horses. Derek closed his eyes, covered his heart with his right hand, and raised his left hand high in the air.

"What's Derek doing?" Brie whispered.

"He's performing a perimeter check," Flinton answered. "Making sure there are no threats around us."

Brie nodded, though she did not understand. But it did sound like a very smart thing to do with magic, if that's what was happening.

Opening his eyes, Derek announced, "The scan is clear. We're safe for now. I don't know how Adira managed to ambush us, but we won't be blindsided again. Moving forward, we need to be more cautious and maintain a shield for our safety. The dying soldier confirmed that for whatever reason, Vaylec wanted to capture all of us, not just Brie."

Before Brie could make sense of what Derek had said, Kove

finished with the horses and joined them. He swept his arms around the clearing with a flourish, and four wooden chairs appeared. Brie gasped in surprise at the open display of magic, but the three men sat down, making themselves comfortable, like chairs popped out of thin air every day. She prodded the nearest seat suspiciously with her foot. It felt solid enough. Then she carefully lowered herself onto it and looked around at the men in wide-eyed wonder.

Flinton took a deep breath and began, "Let's answer your easiest question first. Yes, Brie; as you have just now witnessed, all of us perform magic."

"*That's* the easiest question?" Brie asked, her eyebrows raised in surprise.

"Well, it's the question with the easiest answer," Flinton explained. He paused and swallowed. "We're members of the Blameless."

All of them eyed Brie cautiously, awaiting her reaction.

Brie gawked at Flinton, her jaw dropping open. "The Blameless?" she asked incredulously. If she hadn't seen their magic with her own eyes, she might not have believed him. "The same Blameless who brought peace to our world over a thousand years ago?" Brie had studied history very thoroughly. Even though Falen had been the heir, their parents had required that Brie study all the same subjects as her brother. It was the type of thing that was required of any member of the royal family.

"We aren't the same ones who lived a thousand years ago, but yes, our powers are the same as theirs," Kove confirmed.

"The Blameless were heroes," Brie said. "That's why we

honor them at the Gifting. Their stories are so amazing, even my tutors used to question what was fact and what was legend. Could they really control the weather, heal the sick, and end wars with their magic?" Brie shook her head in amazement, struggling to believe what she had seen and heard; yet she forged ahead before any of the men could answer. "I was taught that, after bringing peace to the earth, they disappeared." Although, over the years, whenever something incredible happened, like an unusually plentiful harvest, or a speedy recovery from an illness, whispers began. People often gave credit to them: *It must have been the work of the Blameless. . .*

"They didn't disappear," Kove clarified. "They simply wanted everyone to believe they had. In reality, they blended into the background, but continued to work in secret for the Three as peacekeepers and protectors of humankind, all throughout the ages—and now. We are among the select Blameless alive today, and the same duty given to the original Blameless has fallen on us."

Brie's mind was exploding with questions. "Were you born with magic? Are your parents Blameless, too?"

"We weren't born with magical powers, and it isn't inherited," Kove explained. "If a parent is Blameless, it doesn't mean their child will be, but it's possible. My father is Blameless, but neither Derek's nor Flinton's parents are. The Three ordained that magical gifts are given to individuals who perform an act of extreme selflessness. It's the deed that makes them worthy, not their family or their status."

"Explain what you mean by magical gifts." Brie requested. "What kinds of gifts?"

"Every Blameless has their own unique set of powers," Derek explained. "Our primary tasks are to protect the innocent and uphold the peace, so for this purpose, there are certain things we all have in common. We can each create weapons for protection, but the types of weapons vary. During the ambush, you may have noticed that Flinton produced a sword for protection." Brie remembered Flinton's mammoth sword that kept appearing and disappearing. "I carry my bow and summon arrows quicker than I could draw them. Kove prefers knives. He carries plenty on him, summons them through his power, and creates more as needed."

"Our powers come from the Three and their three creations," Flinton continued. "Terren, Solis, and Cael have gifted us with the ability to harness the energy of the air, earth, and sun. A Blameless normally draws power from just one of these sources, but occasionally a Blameless is created who can harness a combination of two, or even all three."

"What about the three of you? What can you do?" Brie asked.

"My power comes from the air and the sun," Derek answered. He pointed to his headband, and Brie noticed a small sun and a swirl of wind woven into the design. "I can form shields and deflect attacks, which is how I stopped Adira's onslaught of stones. I use the wind to move objects—for example, I can increase the speed of my arrows. I can also communicate without speaking, but only with someone else who has the same ability. It's called telepathy. Simply put, it is sending our thoughts through the air to one another. Adira and I share this gift. It's how she notified us of your escape from the castle. She and I have very similar talents."

Brie thought about Adira and tried to recall clues from her childhood that might have indicated that Adira was Blameless, but she could think of none.

Derek continued, "I can draw on the sun's heat to produce fire. I can also hear a person's thoughts and motives, if I choose to. I can discern when an individual is telling the truth or lying. Adira also has this gift, which is the main reason she was your father's advisor. She was very helpful when the king negotiated deals with other leaders."

Brie winced to hear him speak about her father in the past tense.

Kove interjected. "It's a pain in the backside. You have to watch what you say around them. And it's very, very challenging to pull off a surprise . . . but not impossible." He grinned like he had experience in the matter.

"You made these chairs, Kove." Brie pointed at their seats. "What else can you do?"

"Some call their magical skills gifts," Kove said. "I call them flairs. Most of my magic comes from the earth, but I have a little magic from the air, which I use for summoning. My main flair is creating. The wood from the earth gave the energy to make these chairs. The rose I gave you came from the power of the soil. I can create cotton clothing because it is grown from the earth, or leather because it comes from the animals that roam the fields. The clothing Derek purchased for you, I altered to fit perfectly. There's an endless amount of creating that can be done from the earth. I can summon as much gold, silver, or jewels as I wish from the mines of Predonia."

Brie gasped, but Kove went on, "But remember, it can only be done for non-selfish purposes. There has to be a good reason for it, and wanting to be rich isn't one."

"What's an example of a good enough reason?" Brie couldn't help but ask.

"To feed the poor." Kove flicked his wrist and held out his hand, dropping a delicate ring with a square yellow gem into Brie's palm. "Or to ease the pain of a brokenhearted young girl."

Brie's chest burned with warmth at his kind gesture. Through learning about the Blameless, any suspicions she'd had regarding Kove and Derek had disappeared. She slipped the ring on her finger and smiled as a few tears snuck out of her eyes. "Thank you."

"Ahh, a genuine smile. It looks good on you, short stuff," Flinton said as he patted her shoulder.

"Short stuff?" Brie shook her head, feigning offense, but secretly she liked that he'd given her a nickname. "What about you, big guy? What can you do?"

Flinton grinned as he answered, "My magic comes from the sun and the earth, but it manifests itself differently than it does in these two," he motioned toward Derek and Kove. "All of the Blameless can sense each other, but I have a special gift with tracking and protecting. The sun illuminates the energy of a person I am seeking. It's nearly impossible to hide from me, which is how I found you, hidden away in the smithy. I've also been graced with unusual strength and speed."

"And just look at him," Kove added. "It's like he's had

his own personal sun shining on him, growing him as tall and enormous as possible."

They all laughed.

"There may be truth to that," Flinton agreed with a shrug of his behemoth shoulders. "I can also conjure as many weapons as I need to fight and protect others."

Brie was listening intently to everything that was said. She decided to ask another question. "Did my father know about Adira and the Blameless?"

"Yes, your father and your mother both knew," Derek confirmed quietly. "But they were the only ones in the castle. Serving the Crown is part of our duty. Historically, kings and rulers have had at least one Blameless on their staff because of their value in giving honest advice, and sensing deceit among servants, advisors, and generals. The peace that your kingdom and the surrounding kingdoms have enjoyed for hundreds of years can be directly linked to help from the Blameless."

"If they are so important, then why have they been kept hidden?" Brie asked.

"While many humans could be trusted with the knowledge, there are those who could not," Flinton answered. "We would be bombarded with requests to help improve the lives of those around us. Even if we have pure intentions, we couldn't guarantee the requests of others would be harmless. We could selflessly help one person, and it might backfire and cause life to become more difficult for another. And apart from that, there are men who would be envious of our powers and want to harm us. It's been discussed at length throughout history, as well as by our current leader and the Elders, but for now, they've decided it's best to continue to keep the existence of the Blameless quiet."

"You have a leader?" asked Brie, her hazel eyes filled with wonder.

"Yes," Kove answered. "His name is Lord Renolt. He appoints a trainer to each new Blameless. We have a stronghold, a city for the members of the Blameless, called Mount Elrad, where we live together and receive training and advice. That's where we are heading. We need advice, training, and protection, and we'll find it there."

The more they explained, the more fascinated Brie became. But the mention of protection brought her back to the memory of the attack and sobered her up. "Why did Adira attack us, and who is Vaylec?"

All the men looked troubled by these new questions, but it was Flinton who answered. "Your question about Adira is hard, because we're just as confused as you. She's never raised her hands and used her gifts against us. It's unheard of, and it shouldn't be possible. What's even more bizarre, she looked upset while it was happening, like she didn't agree with what she was doing."

"Yes, but that didn't stop her," Kove responded with a bite, before he reluctantly agreed. "You're right; I could see she was upset. She looked me in the eye and shook her head like she was attempting to send me a message. I just couldn't understand what she was trying to relay. The whole thing is a mystery."

Derek gazed into the trees and spoke like he was thinking

out loud. "It is against all of the laws of the Blameless. We do not use our gift to inflict harm on others, unless it is to defend ourselves or for a greater good. It should not have been possible, and yet it happened." Derek turned and focused on Brie, sitting up straighter in his chair. "Vaylec Spaur is at the center of this. We don't know much about him. He's from Predonia, and he comes from a family of Blameless—though he is not Blameless himself. He attacked the castle, killed your family, and is searching for you. We can speculate, but so far, we have no solid evidence for his motivations. But I have my suspicions. Brie, you are the princess, but not just any princess. You are very special and extremely unique. I wonder, do you have any idea why that is?"

Brie thought about it, and piece by piece, understanding slowly settled inside of her. She thought back to the terrifying moment when her mother had yelled for her to run. Her exact words had been, "Briana, run! For Predonia, save yourself!" Brie's instinct had been to rush to Falen and her parents and attempt to pull them to safety, even if it meant dying alongside them. Fighting an internal battle, she'd thought of the many times her mother and father had emphasized the importance of her duty to her country. After hearing Falen scream from down the hall and watching her parents be struck down with swords, she'd turned her back on them. This act had sealed her fate: she would forever wonder if she could have done something to save them. And though, in the heat of the moment, it hadn't occurred to her that she would be destined to rule, she'd fled for the sake of Predonia. If this was her act of extreme selflessness, it was horribly bitter, not sweet.

Brie met Derek's gaze. "I've felt different since my escape from the castle." She remembered the buzzing in her ears, the burning in her chest, and even the itching in her hands. She'd never experienced these things before, and just thinking about them made the sensations return. "But I've been too sad to think about why."

Slowly, accompanied by Derek's nod of approval, Princess Briana Rose Eyrhill lifted her right hand and covered her heart. It was instinctual; she did it for reasons she could not explain. Heat flared in her chest at the connection. She closed her eyes and concentrated, making a wish. There was a rustle of wind and a brief flash of light. Suddenly, a familiar weight landed on her head. She opened her eyes and yanked it off. Sure enough, the crown she had left behind during her hasty retreat from the castle was in her hands. The royal crowns of her father, mother, and brother had also miraculously landed in her lap. Brie was shocked at first, but then determination lit her face.

"This may sound stupid, but I hated that he had our crowns," Brie said fiercely, eyes flashing.

There was a brief moment of stunned silence, and then Flinton threw his head back and roared with laughter. Derek and Kove joined in. Brie couldn't help it; another genuine smile spread across her face.

Lord Vaylec sat on his new throne, swirling a goblet of wine in his hand. His jet-black hair was perfectly styled and parted under his golden crown; his beard was neatly trimmed. His cream trousers and scarlet top, embroidered with gold stitching, were spotless and wrinkle-free, and he was flanked by his most trusted guards. Everything seemed to be in order; yet as Adira and the general stood before the throne, giving a full report of their failed mission, Vaylec's good mood transformed into rage. Vaylec's gray eyes narrowed as the report came to an end, and his hand clenched the metal goblet hard enough that his knuckles turned white.

"So you're telling me," Vaylec said in a deadly, quiet voice, "that I sent out ten of my best soldiers with a Blameless to recover the princess and her kidnappers, and instead of completing this task, nine of my soldiers were killed—*and the princess managed to escape?*" He flung his goblet to the ground—it clanged loudly, spilling its contents—and stood up, swiftly striding down the throne steps.

Vaylec stopped in front of Adira.

"Yes," Adira confirmed, boldly meeting Vaylec's eyes, her back stiff and straight. Her leggings and boots were dusty from traveling, and some of her hair had escaped its braid, framing her scratched face. Adira's breastplate, emblazoned with Vaylec's fox crest, bore a small dent. "We followed your orders exactly. We turned around when we were down to two survivors. We really didn't have a choice in the matter, did we?" She kept her voice level, but her nostrils flared, and her eyes flashed with anger.

"What good are you?" Vaylec seethed, ignoring Adira's lack of respect. "You had the advantage of a surprise attack, and yet you still failed."

"Your Grace," Adira continued, "the princess's rescuers are a force to be reckoned with. Their skills are unmatched, even among the Blameless. The ambush was nothing but an inconvenience for them. They are unstoppable."

Vaylec reached out, wrapped his long fingers around Adira's neck, and began to slowly squeeze. Stepping closer, he spoke quietly into Adira's ear. "Ah, you see, you are wrong on two accounts. Those were not Briana's rescuers. No, they were her kidnappers. She is *mine*. And those men, Blameless or not, will never be unstoppable, because I will find a way."

Adira's face was turning a deep shade of red, and she began to claw at Vaylec's fingers.

"I need to rethink my strategy, and you *will* help me," Vaylec said, releasing Adira with a small shove, causing her to stumble backward.

Adira drew in several ragged breaths as she regained her footing. She rubbed her throat, her color slowly returning to normal. "Yes, Your Grace." She stood up straight once again, and she raised her eyes to meet Vaylec's, glaring at him while clenching her hands at her sides.

Watching the proud woman in front of him bending to his will brought a smile to Vaylec's face. "It's killing you to do what I say, isn't it?"

Adira lifted her chin but didn't speak.

"Answer me!" Vaylec demanded, his eyes narrowing.

"Yes, *Your Grace*. I hate it."

Vaylec's eyes gleamed, seeming pleased by her answer. "Maybe one day, you'll change your mind."

As he turned to his general, ready to address the man's poor leadership, the heavy weight of Vaylec's crown suddenly lifted from his head.

Vaylec's expression changed to one of confusion as he reached up and touched the top of his head, feeling for the crown. He turned in a complete circle, searching the floor by his feet, but found nothing. His hands grabbed at his hair. His confusion remained, but his anger resurfaced with a vengeance.

"WHAT. JUST. HAPPENED?" Vaylec roared in fury, directing his question at Adira, who appeared just as confused and shocked. "Are you responsible for this?" he demanded.

"No, sire," Adira managed. "I don't understand it. I . . ." She was cut off when Vaylec dealt her a backhanded slap to the face.

Vaylec wanted to take the life of the Blameless woman, but he hollered in frustration instead. "You couldn't have done it. It's not possible, and I still need you." Instead, in a rage, he drew his sword and drove it into the general's chest.

He shouted at his guards, "Get them out of my sight! Everyone, leave me, NOW!"

The guards rushed forward in obedience and seized Adira by the arms. They lifted the general from the floor and quickly exited the throne room.

Vaylec paced the floor like a caged lion, furious over the failed mission and the disappearance of his crown. It brought back his old insecurities.

Vaylec had felt inferior his entire childhood. As the son of two Blameless, he was constantly exposed to his parents' talents despite lacking his own. And if that wasn't torturous enough, fate decided to twist the knife even further, and Vaylec's twin sister became Blameless as well on their sixteenth birthday. Everyone in the family was gifted. Everyone except for Vaylec. He had grown up surrounded by their effortless magic, receiving plenty of love and reassurance that he was special just as he was: without power.

So, Vaylec had thrown himself into becoming the best "ordinary" human being he could be. He trained for countless hours with a sword, excelled in sports, and exercised his body into perfect shape. He was honored and looked up to by all his peers, and it didn't take long for him to collect a group of followers. But it wasn't enough. Every time he saw his family wave their hand and create something, all his hard work seemed futile. It mocked him, and eventually drove him to seek a way to become equal to the Blameless. *No, not equal,* he'd decided. He was more powerful than the Blameless because in all his seeking, he had found a way to harness their power and control them.

As Vaylec paced, he thought of all he had accomplished, and slowly his anger subsided. *Of course, there will be challenges along the way,* he reasoned. He would just have to overcome them to accomplish his plans. Obviously, a Blameless was out there playing some kind of mind game with him by taking the crown he had rightfully earned. He wouldn't cower to their tricks. He would simply dip into the royal treasury and have a crown crafted that was much more impressive than the last one. The crown he'd taken had been too plain for his taste, anyway. As for the princess, his ultimate prize—he would need to secure the help of more Blameless.

Vaylec left the throne room and marched toward his private chambers, nodding briefly to the guard stationed outside his rooms.

“Are they both inside?” Vaylec asked.

“Yes, my lord.”

“Wonderful.”

Vaylec entered the room and walked to an older couple seated at an elegant table, eating dinner. He bent over and kissed the woman on the forehead.

“Good evening, Mother,” he said.

Vaylec turned to the gentleman and gave him a nod of acknowledgement. “Father, find and bring me your copy of the Registry of the Blameless. I need a map that contains the location of each member. You may finish your dinner first, of course.”

Vaylec’s mother dropped her head into her hands, and when she lifted it, there were tears in her eyes. Vaylec ignored her. He couldn’t give into sympathizing with her feelings. It would weaken him.

Vaylec’s father looked up and tried to refuse. Vaylec watched with detached interest as his father’s face turned red with the effort. Eventually, his father released a pent-up breath. “Son, please rethink this. There has to be another way. Isn’t it enough that you have us and your sister under your control?”

“You know nothing about what I need,” Vaylec replied. “You will keep your opinions to yourself and do as I say. I have no desire to hurt you or Mother, but I won’t hesitate to do so if you try to interfere with my plans.”

Vaylec exited the room while his parents looked after him, their jaws agape in disbelief.

Vaylec made his way to his study, feeling better as new plans began to swirl around in his head.

# The Appropriate Use of Gifts

Brie sat in a chair by the fire and observed Flinton, who sat beside her. He held a ball of yarn and two needles, and was steadily knitting away. Two weeks had passed since the ambush, and their group had encountered no other distractions. They were nearing Mount Elrad. If their travels went as planned, they would arrive the following day.

They were deep in the heart of the Predonian mountain range, and with the change in altitude combined with the approach of fall, the weather was getting cooler by the day. Flinton had decided that Brie should have a scarf with matching mittens to help ward off the cold.

Brie grinned. "Isn't knitting a delicate hobby for such a giant of a man?"

"Yes, it is!" Kove laughed. "I've been trying to convince him of this for years!"

"It's a relaxing pastime that I enjoy," Flinton said to Brie, briefly scowling at Kove, "At least, I *usually* do. But if this fool doesn't stop teasing me—" He jerked his head toward Kove. "—I'll throw down my needles, pull out my sword, and challenge him to a duel. Just because I like to knit, doesn't mean I'm not a force to be reckoned with."

"Seriously, Flinton," said Kove, holding his palms out in innocence, but wearing a smirk, "it would be much easier to stop this nonsense and just create the scarf, for pity's sake. I know you aren't nearly as skilled at conjuring as me, but you've got a little bit of the earth in you. I'm certain that whatever you could manage would look far better than the tangled mess you have in your lap."

Brie covered her mouth to hide her smile as Flinton glared across the fire at Kove. "Kove, some things are just more satisfying to make with my own hands. My gifts can be spared for when I really need them. I like knitting, okay? Leave it alone." With a sigh, he yanked on his roll of yarn a little harder than necessary and resumed the sharp clicking of his needles.

"Well, if you're reserving your gifts for when you truly need them, I would say there is a desperate need for them right now." Kove eyed the growing lump of yarn with suspicion. "Or better yet, let's get in touch with my grandmother and put in an urgent plea for help."

Flinton stilled his needles and began to lift his mammoth frame out of his seat. He looked like he was ready to strangle Kove with his yarn. Brie touched Flinton's arm and examined his work. "Flinton, *I* think it looks fantastic. I can hardly wait until it's finished!" She threw an arm around him and gave him a quick hug.

Flinton slowly turned his head in Kove's direction, and a smug grin spread over his face. He relaxed into his seat, propped his foot on a log, and continued with his knitting.

Kove rolled his eyes but got to his feet and began to sharpen his many knives.

Hoping she had diffused the tension, Brie walked several paces away to watch Derek create a target. Since discovering she was Blameless, Brie's travel companions had insisted that she participate in some form of physical exercise or magical training every evening after the day's travel. Brie knew it was important to learn how to use her gifts, and she was grateful for the training because it gave her a purpose. And right now, more than anything, she needed a purpose, and she needed to stay busy. Without her training, Brie was afraid she might lose her desire to live. Riding all day and practicing every evening had the benefit of exhausting her. When she finally collapsed in her tent each night, she was asleep within seconds, often before she had the energy to shed a single tear. With such full days, she could almost make herself believe her family wasn't gone.

Derek was responsible for teaching Brie self-defense. Thus far, he'd spent a lot of time demonstrating how to escape an attacker by aiming for weak spots like the eyes, throat, and groin. Practicing various scenarios, Brie learned that, if she were grabbed from behind, she should stomp on Derek's feet, or kick backward into his kneecaps. Once, Derek had even insisted she bend his pinky finger backward as far as possible to get him to release his grip on her. She'd done a fabulous job on that particular exercise; afterward, Derek had said with watering eyes that it wasn't necessary to try it again. Brie didn't like inflicting pain, especially not on someone who'd saved her life, but Derek had reassured her it was necessary, and he continued to praise her for each successful performance.

Kove had become Brie's personal fitness trainer; he had created varying combinations of nightly exercises for her. After squeezing her biceps on one of their first days together, he'd given Brie a pitying shake of his head and informed her, "You're too weak. We need to work on that." Since then, he'd guided her through nightly sets of push-ups and sit-ups in ever-increasing numbers, and every evening he accompanied her on a run. He'd also insisted they engage in various tree-climbing activities. Sometimes Brie didn't understand the reasoning for these exercises, but just as Derek had been adamant that she kick and hit him, Kove had insisted she jump through trees. They were surrounded by evergreens, and according to Kove, it was a great opportunity to work on her agility and balance.

It was Flinton's job to train her on how to tap into her magic. Because he was an expert tracker, he'd been explaining how to sense when another Blameless was near. "As magical beings, we send out high-pitched signals or vibrations into the air. This allows us to sense the gifts in each other so we can recognize when another Blameless is nearby. There's a network of Blameless strategically placed throughout Predonia, Westlor, Estelon, and Alderia. Each country keeps their own registry of its members' locations and gifts. Whenever we sense a new link, it's our duty to seek that person out to determine if they are a newly gifted Blameless. If they are a new Blameless and not someone else—for example, a Blameless visiting from another kingdom—then we are obligated to report the information back to Lord Renolt, and he appoints a trainer for them."

In addition to gaining new and fascinating insight to the world of the Blameless, Brie had finally discovered the reason for the periodic buzzing in her ears. She had yet to master the ability of tracking Blameless signals, but regardless, her practice had developed into extravagantly fun games of hide-and-seek. Flinton, Kove, and Derek would hide, and Brie would try to find them, either by tracking their magical signal, or—more often than not—simply the normal way: with her eyes and ears.

While Flinton continued to knit and Kove continued to sharpen his knives, it was Derek's turn to work with Brie. A few paces away from their camp was an open area with a stretch of relatively flat land. Instead of their usual self-defense training, Derek decided to introduce something new. He was teaching Brie how to shoot with a bow. For some reason, seeing Derek in action with his bow enthralled Brie. He'd not only saved her life during the ambush, but most evenings, he caught their dinner as well. Night after night, she'd watched him take down deer, rabbits, and various types of birds. She had questioned him about the bow repeatedly until he'd finally taken the hint and decided she could try her hand at archery.

Derek finished carving a large X into the bark of a tree to serve as a target. He held up his bow and showed Brie where to place her hands. He faced the target as he spoke, giving Brie a view of his profile. "Okay, Briana Rose, hold the bow with your left hand, placing it in the curved grip. You will use your right hand to nock the arrow and pull back the string. Every bow has its own draw weight. Get a feel for holding it and pulling back the string without an arrow first."

Derek turned and held out his bow. "Now you—" he started to say, but he stopped in surprise.

Brie focused on trying to hold up the enormous black bow

in her hands. She had to admit, it wasn't ideal. It was much too big, but at least it was something. She attempted to do as Derek had instructed and pull back the string, but the draw weight was far too much. Even though her arms trembled with effort, the string barely moved.

"Where did you get that?" Derek asked.

Brie glanced at him, continuing to yank on the string. She thought the answer was obvious. "I summoned it. Where else was I supposed to get one?"

"You've been Blameless for all of two weeks, and suddenly you can't think of a way to obtain a bow without using magic?" Derek said with a grin. He took the bow from her and examined it, noting the name carved into the lower limb. "Where did you summon it from?" he asked with a straight face, although Brie could swear she saw a twinkle in his eye.

A brief feeling of guilt passed over Brie, and she wondered if she'd done something wrong. "I really have no idea where it came from. I just called for the closest bow. But from the looks of it . . ." She paused and glanced at the engraved name. "It came from Sir Mudgeon, whoever he is."

Derek shook his head but bit his lip to hold back a smile. "Briana Rose, you need to return it to Sir Mudgeon at once. You can't summon things that aren't yours unless there's a very good reason. It's no different from stealing. Poor Sir Mudgeon could have been in the middle of catching his evening dinner. Imagine his surprise and confusion when his bow just disappeared out of his hands. Use my bow for now, or perhaps we can see how Kove's skills are at creating one for you."

Brie was horrified at being compared to a thief. Thieves

were put in dungeons, and dungeons were for evil people. They were no place for a princess. She'd never been in one before, and she hoped she never would be. She held her hand over her heart and tried to return the bow to its owner, but nothing happened.

Brie looked at Derek sheepishly. "I don't know how to give it back."

Derek nodded, as if he'd been expecting that response. "When you summon something, you're able to receive it because it's needed and wanted. To return an item that was summoned, you simply have to no longer need it or want it."

"But I still want a bow," Brie said in defeat. "I don't know how to un-want it."

"You want a bow—that's true. But think about it: Do you really want this specific one? You can't pull back the string, it weighs nearly as much as you, and it has someone else's name carved in it."

"You're right," Brie agreed. "And it's ugly," she added.

"It most definitely is ugly," Derek said with a small smile.

Brie closed her eyes and tried again, and this time she was successful. The black bow vanished, hopefully returning to Sir Mudgeon. "I didn't think about what I was doing. I'm sorry, Derek," she said.

"You didn't know any better," Derek said. "There's a reason why every Blameless needs to go through training." He turned his head and raised his voice. "Kove!"

Kove, who had been throwing his sharpened knives into a tree trunk, came to join them. He tossed one of his knives into the air and watched it twirl several times before catching it.

Then he asked, "How may I be of service?"

"Derek was trying to teach me how to use his bow," Brie explained. "He explained that if I summon one, I'm no better than a thief, and I should be thrown into the castle dungeons."

Kove arched an eyebrow and glanced at Derek. "He said that, did he?"

"Basically, yes, he did," Brie answered before Derek could speak. "And I don't want to be a thief. I'd rather just be a princess." She smiled at Kove. "Could you make one for me?"

Derek was overcome by a fit of coughing. When it subsided, his grin was enormous.

Brie peered upward into Derek's dark eyes. "Are you laughing at me?"

Derek's dark eyes twinkled, but he remained quiet.

Kove grinned, first at Derek, then at Brie, seeming pleased by her request. "Well, we can't have you living in the dungeons. It appears I have no choice but to help."

He closed his eyes in concentration. Brie tried to wait as patiently as possible, but Kove took an extra-long time with this particular creation. She bounced up and down on her toes and wrung her hands together as Kove touched his chest briefly over his heart and swept his other hand dramatically through the air. Finally, a small, delicate bow appeared on the ground. Brie let out a quiet gasp. It was beautiful. Made of a shiny, dark wood, it had intricate roses carved along the curve, reminding her of her family's crest. She loved it.

Picking the bow up reverently, Brie examined every inch. Tears glistened in her eyes when she finally met Kove's gaze. "It's perfect," she said.

Kove nodded with a swift jerk of his head. "Alright, let's see what you can do."

Brie assumed the stance Derek had taught her and though it was still hard, she managed to pull back the string of her bow. Once she became comfortable with the new weapon's weight, Derek introduced the arrow. After showing her how to aim, Derek fired a few shots into the target as a demonstration, and then instructed her to try.

Brie nocked an arrow and pulled back the string. Carefully eying the tree in the distance, she took a slow, deep breath and let the arrow loose. It sailed away from her, falling short of its mark. Disappointed, she nocked another arrow right away. She eyed the target, held her position, and paused.

Taking a deep breath, Brie lowered her bow. She glanced at Derek and examined his headband. He was the most impressive archer she had ever seen, and maybe it was silly, but she wanted a headband too. "Wait, Derek. I think I should have a headband like you."

Derek dipped his head down and pinched the bridge of his nose, but Brie would have sworn she saw him smile.

Kove, on the other hand, did nothing to hide his enormous grin. "What a brilliant idea. Why didn't I think of that myself?"

Kove circled one hand in the air and conjured up a headband in the same royal blue as Brie's tunic. Then he handed it to Derek, who quickly tied it around her forehead.

"Fire away," Derek said.

Feeling more like an archer, Brie aimed and shot. The arrow soared away from her in a beautiful arc and hit the very edge of the X on the tree, which felt like a victory.

Brie let out a shout of triumph and jumped up and down with her arms in the air while her guardians cheered and clapped. Determined to improve, she spent the remainder of the evening practicing until it was too dark to continue.

With a smile on her face, Brie lovingly placed her bow inside her tent and joined her guardians by the fire for a late dinner. Brie'd had so much fun with her bow. She loved archery! How she wished she could share tonight's experience with Falen. As soon as she thought of her brother, Brie's happiness started to wane, and she began to feel horribly guilty. Her family was dead, and here she was, cheering over hitting a target. It no longer seemed right for her to be happy. She hadn't let herself think about her family very often because it was too painful, but tonight, she craved their presence. The truth was, she *had* experienced joy, but she wanted to share her joy together with them. She felt their absence more than ever and she missed them. As she realized this, all traces of her good mood evaporated, and she was left feeling terribly lonely and sad.

Lost in her own thoughts, Brie looked up when Flinton sat his mammoth body down beside her, causing the log they now shared to precariously tilt in his direction.

"Don't be discouraged, short stuff. You did well for your first time with the bow. By the end, you were hitting the target nearly every time."

Brie shrugged. "I know. I think I did rather splendidly for my first time. I'm not sad about that. I just . . ." She paused and took a deep breath. "I don't have any family left to share it with. I wish I could run into my mother's room and tell her all about today. She would have hugged me and told me how wonderful it sounded. My father would've been proud of me too. And Falen was so competitive, he probably would have challenged me to a shooting contest." She sniffed. "I just miss them so much. I miss my family." The tears that she had held at bay for several days began to drip down her face. "It feels wrong to be happy without them," she added with a whisper.

Flinton put his arm around Brie's shoulders, causing their log to sink a few inches lower into the ground. "We can never replace your parents and brother, Brie. And I am more sorry than I could ever express about that. But you can't stop living *your* life because they're gone. It's okay to be happy. They would want you to be. And if it's any comfort, you can share your sorrows and your joys with us." He patted her back. "You know, tomorrow, when we arrive at Mount Elrad, you will get to meet my family."

"Really?" Brie's interest was piqued. She hadn't even considered the fact that her guardians may have families.

"I haven't told you my story yet, but I think now is the perfect time. My full name is Flinton Blackwood. When I was born, I was so large that my mother died giving birth to me." Brie's stomach knotted horribly, and she slipped her small hand into Flinton's. "A few years later, my father remarried a good woman, and together they had five daughters. They left the girls at home with me one morning while they took a trip to town. Unfortunately, my father and stepmother passed away in a carriage accident that day."

"Oh Flinton," Brie moaned quietly. "I'm so sorry."

Flinton cocked his head toward Brie and continued in a

gruff voice. "They died when I was eighteen, leaving me in charge of my five younger sisters. The youngest was just a baby at the time. I could have sent them to live with my aunt, but they wanted to stay with me, and I couldn't bear to cause them any more pain. I gave up my plans for my future, and with the help of my oldest sister, Ava, we managed just fine. This was my act of selflessness, and this was when my Blameless powers were revealed. When it came time for my training at Mount Elrad, I refused to leave my sisters behind, so the Elders didn't have much choice. They made an exception and let the whole lot of them come with me. We've been living there ever since."

Brie gave a watery grin at the thought of anyone trying to keep Flinton's sisters away from him. They wouldn't stand a chance.

Flinton continued: "I married a lovely woman named Milly. She's Blameless too. We met when she came to Mount Elrad for her training a couple of years ago, and we've been married for just over a year. My sisters live with us, and Milly runs the house while I'm traveling, bless her heart. One of my sisters is fourteen. Her name is Cassandra, and I think the two of you will get along splendidly."

Brie sat up, listening with rapt attention now. "I can't wait to meet them. Will I be staying with you?"

"Yes," Flinton confirmed. "The three of us talked about it." He nodded toward Derek and Kove. "My household is rowdy, but we think it's the best place for you. With so many girls, you'll fit right in. We can be like your second family, if you want us to be."

Brie's chest bloomed with guilt and longing. She didn't

want to replace her family, but she needed a home. "I think I would like that." She paused, and before she could talk herself out of it, she asked, "Flinton, would it be okay if I called you 'uncle'? I know we aren't related by blood, but it would make me feel like we're family." Her eyes began to water again, and she sniffed.

"Of course, you can." Flinton gave a sudden sniff of his own. He glanced at Kove and Derek, who sat listening across the fire, and added, "I realize I'm by far your favorite, but I don't think these guys would mind being called 'uncle' either." He gave Brie a quick wink.

Brie looked at Derek and Kove hopefully.

"Yes, you may call us 'uncle,'" Derek answered with an exaggerated sigh, followed by a smile. "We would be honored, Briana. But Flinton is wrong on one account. After teaching you how to be such an accomplished archer, I am quite certain I have secured the position of favorite." He crossed his arms over his chest with a grin.

Kove jumped to his feet, then reached behind his back and brought his arm forward, holding a bouquet of yellow roses.

"Kove!" Brie grinned, taking the flowers. "Why do you keep giving me roses?"

"Because I don't ever want you to forget your family and where you came from. And because the yellow ones remind me of your hair, which is as bright and lovely as the sun." After this serious statement, a cocky grin formed on his face. "Remember who created your bow, sunshine. Uncle Kove at your service. I do believe I have just been challenged to one of the greatest competitions of all time. May the best uncle win."

Their silliness accomplished what Brie realized was likely their intended goal, and she giggled. Her giggling turned into full-blown laughter, and they all joined in until Brie was wiping happy tears from her eyes.

"Let's get some sleep," said Derek. "Tomorrow's going to be a big day."

"Yes, Uncle Derek."

# Mount Elrad

"Here it is." Derek pointed out a strange protrusion of rock to Brie, who sat in front of him in the saddle. "The entrance to the tunnel that will lead us through the heart of the mountain. The other side opens up at Mount Elrad. Just a few more hours, and we'll be there."

"Hours?" Brie asked, slumping in her saddle. She'd thought they were almost there, and her backside was terribly sore from all the riding they'd been doing.

"Don't worry," said Kove with a sly smile. "Greatness takes time. You won't be disappointed."

Brie's heart pitter-pattered in both excitement and nervousness at the thought of finally arriving at Mount Elrad. After traveling for over two weeks, she was looking forward to their journey coming to an end, but at the same time, she felt jittery about what awaited her in the Blameless stronghold.

They'd spent the morning riding single-file along a narrow path that weaved up the side of the mountain. A wall of rock expanded straight upward on their left side, and on their right side was a steep drop-off. The traveling conditions certainly hadn't helped Brie's nerves. Since dawn, she'd sat, stiff as a board, worrying about the possibility of their horse losing its footing and plummeting over the side of the mountain into the abyss. Riding with Derek and his mind reading ability was somewhat embarrassing. He kept patting Brie and reassuring her that she had nothing to worry about.

They arrived at a point along the path where two large rock formations converged, creating a bulging overlap, which was the landmark Derek had pointed out. Derek carefully led them past the overlap in the wall of the mountain, and then swung his horse around to face it from the opposite direction. It was a tricky turn due to the narrow path; Flinton and Kove had to hold back and await their turns to advance. Facing it from this angle, Brie saw that the bulging rock formation was actually a narrow opening into the mountain, just large enough for a horse and rider (or two) to slip through.

Using a calm, soothing voice, Derek coaxed his horse through the mouth of the tunnel. Once inside, Brie breathed a sigh of relief. Kove and Flinton followed behind them shortly afterward. The passageway expanded, allowing the three men to ride alongside each other.

Derek snapped his fingers, and torches mounted on the walls blazed to life around them, illuminating the tunnel, which extended ahead of them as far as Brie could see.

"Wow! Where are we?" Brie asked.

Kove answered, "We're in a hidden passage, specifically built as a means of defense for the stronghold. This tunnel is the only entrance from the south."

"So why is the stronghold called Mount Elrad?" Brie asked to the pass the time.

"Mount Elrad is the name of the largest mountain peak in the Predonian mountain range, which overlooks the city of the Blameless," Derek explained.

"Which is more like a village," Flinton added. "But, like Kove said, you won't be disappointed. It's small but mighty."

Excitement was palpable in the air as they advanced through the mountain toward home. The men seemed to be sitting taller in their saddles than during the previous weeks of travel. Flinton began to whistle a catchy tune, which echoed and reverberated around them. Derek began to hum along with him, and Kove grinned.

"Excited about seeing all of your ladies?" Kove asked Flinton.

"Of course I am! The girls make it their mission in life to drive me crazy, but I've missed them. And Milly . . ." Flinton sighed, and a faraway look took over his eyes. "She is simply amazing. It's been too long. Any amount of time away from her is too long, really."

"I can't wait to meet them." Brie smiled.

Flinton grinned widely, seeming more than happy to discuss his loved ones. "They're a lively bunch. I know you'll love them."

"Derek and Kove, what about your families? Can you tell me a little bit about them?" Brie asked.

"My family name is Hawke," Derek began. "I was born an only child to a family with a long history of military service. I grew up rigorously training to follow in my father's and grandfather's footsteps. I planned to join the king's army, your father's army, and eventually serve as a general, but when my magic surfaced at age sixteen, plans changed. My parents weren't very happy about me turning my back on the military, but they didn't have a choice in the matter. I haven't seen them very much since I moved to Mount Elrad."

"I think a more accurate explanation for their disappointment has less to do with you turning your back on the military," Flinton said with a smirk.

"And everything to do with how you became Blameless," Kove finished.

Derek chuckled. "Yes, there is that small detail."

"What am I missing?" Brie asked. "How did you become Blameless?" She turned around in the saddle to look at Derek and was surprised to find him blushing. "*What?*" she pressed, grinning, the curiosity killing her.

Derek cleared his throat and reluctantly began. "My family has money."

"*Lots* of money," Kove interrupted.

"Shut up, Kove," Brie said, surprising everyone. "Let him tell the story."

"Anyway," Derek continued. "My parents live in Fendale, and they're quite well-off. When I was sixteen, I was given a portion of my inheritance money early and instructed to deposit it at the bank for safekeeping. As I walked through the city, the gold in the satchel on my back was heavy, and I decided to take a shortcut along some of the back streets to get to the bank quicker. This put me in the very poorest section of the city, down streets I had never been on before." He paused, taking a deep breath and letting it out. "A little boy, maybe five or six years old, came up to me and asked me for something to eat. He was filthy and dressed in rags." Derek's voice had grown more serious and very quiet.

Brie frowned, not understanding where the humor was in the tale.

"I didn't have any food with me, and I told the boy so. Then he asked me for a piece of copper so he could buy dinner, since he hadn't eaten yet that day." Derek shifted in the saddle behind Brie. "Here this little lad wanted a copper coin, not even a silver coin, and my bag was overloaded with so much gold, the seams were nearly bursting. I looked up and down the street and saw more children, mothers, and fathers, just as poor and emaciated as the small boy, and I realized how easy my life had been up until that point. I'd never been hungry a day in my life. My parents had two houses, servants, and more money than they knew what to do with. I decided these people needed the gold more than me. Not knowing if my parents would disagree or support me, I spent the rest of the afternoon walking through the slums of the city, handing out gold coins to as many families as possible. I went home later that night with my heart and my satchel feeling much lighter. I never made it to the bank."

Brie was stunned. She realized Derek's blush was likely him being humble. It took her a minute to respond, but then she said, softly. "I guess that counts as exceptionally selfless."

"Needless to say, my parents didn't agree with my decision. They kicked me out of their house and said I had disgraced them. It was during my argument with them that evening that my powers surfaced. I began to hear their thoughts, as clearly as if they were shouting at me. In their minds, I was a fool, a disappointment. They were worried about having an embarrassment of a son, but they didn't care one bit about the condition of the poor families I had helped. I didn't understand what was happening at the time, but regardless, emptyhanded, I left my family and title behind. Lord Renolt sought me out, and I was brought to Mount Elrad shortly afterward. Now, I serve the Crown, just in a different manner than my family had anticipated."

"A much more fun manner, might I add," Kove said, lightening the somber mood.

"I can't argue with that," Derek agreed.

"Plus, you've had the pleasure of having me as a partner in your service to the Crown, which has greatly enriched your quality of life." Kove smirked.

Derek sighed with gusto and muttered, "Kove, you never let up. You have the healthiest self-confidence I have ever seen. How you became Blameless is beyond me."

Kove grinned broadly at Derek's statement. "Confidence, not arrogance. If you want, I could always give you some tips to help you in the self-confidence arena. A new hairstyle might help." He cast a fleeting glance at Derek's head. "How does one feel confident with a shaved head?" He ran his fingers through his long blond locks.

Brie giggled.

Derek rolled his eyes and shook his head. "Don't encourage him. It will only make him worse."

Kove turned his attention to Brie and winked. "Let's give poor Derek a break, shall we? And I'll tell you more about the legend that is me. My last name is LeBlanc. My father is

Blameless. He's one of five Elders, which you'll learn more about later. He lives in Mount Elrad with my mother."

"Do you have any siblings?" Brie asked, thinking longingly of Falen.

"Yes," Kove answered, "I have two brothers, one older and one younger than me."

"How did you like growing up as the middle child?" Brie wondered. She'd always wanted a younger sister.

Kove shrugged. "It didn't bother me in the least. In fact, I think it's ideal. The oldest carries too much responsibility, and the youngest is never taken seriously." Brie nodded, acknowledging the truth in his statement. "Being in the middle allows for the perfect amount of respect and shenanigans."

Flinton guffawed as Kove continued, "My older brother is a horse breeder who lives in the south of Predonia, by the sea. My younger brother is the tender age of fourteen," Kove said with a wink, "and still lives at home with my parents. You'll meet him tomorrow."

Derek snorted. "Don't let the 'tender' comment fool you. He's inherited his self-confidence from his legend of an older brother," he said mockingly.

They continued to talk and tease one another as they rode, and time passed swiftly. A few hours later, natural light glowed ahead of them into the tunnel. They picked up their pace and soon exited the passageway into a large valley.

Brie's breath caught at the stunning view.

Snow-peaked mountains surrounded them as far as the eye could see, with one large summit towering over the rest of them. In a valley, nestled between the mountains was the village of Mount Elrad. The evening sun was beginning its descent in the sky, streaking a plethora of colors over the valley before them. A narrow road weaved from the opening of the tunnel where they sat and circled downward into the village. The homes, buildings, and shops, although various sizes, were all built out of stone and wood. Instead of being blemishes amid the beautiful landscape, they appeared like an extension of the mountains and forests, adding to its charm.

Brie and her uncles advanced together along the winding path. Villagers were outside, some chopping firewood, others sitting in their yards with drinks in hand as children ran and played. A few waved and called out warm welcomes as the riding group passed, and Brie's uncles shouted greetings in return. Halfway down the road, the horses pulled to a stop in front of a magnificent home.

Brie smiled as she took the building in. She had never seen such a unique place. It was three stories high and as wide as it was tall. The entire dwelling, except for wooden doors and open windows, was made of dark gray slate, textured and jagged. It was rough, yet magnificent in Brie's eyes. A stone walkway led to the front door and ended in a beautiful covered stone patio that extended along the front of the house. Wooden rocking chairs and benches sat next to slate tables on the patio. Perfectly placed pine trees and bushes dotted the yard. The place was so earthy and natural, it looked like it had grown out of the side of the mountain rather than been built by the hands of humans.

When Brie saw Flinton dismount, she was hit with the realization that this beautiful home belonged to him. She never could have dreamed up such a spectacular building, but after seeing it, she decided no other home could suit such a mountain of a man as well as this one did.

With an enormous grin on his face, Flinton cast a wink in their direction as he approached the front door. He pounded his fist on it, his grin still in place, and bellowed, "Is there an angel and five hellions inside?"

"Why on earth is he knocking on his own door?" Brie asked.

"Watch," Derek whispered.

Brie looked on in amazement as the door was flung open, followed by squeals and shouts of excitement. Flinton was attacked by a blur of five figures launching themselves at him. He roared with laughter and stood firmly in place like the giant he was, unfazed by the assault. Wrapping his enormous arms around his sisters, he hugged them, lifting the whole lot of them off the ground, and began to twirl them around and around.

Soon there were complaints as the girls yelled, "You're squishing me," "I can't breathe," and "I'm going to be sick." Flinton put them down, ending the group hug, then he proceeded to give a personal greeting to each of his sisters. A touch on the shoulder, a pat on the head, a peck on the cheek. Brie could see by the adoring looks in their eyes and the beaming grins on their faces that they were thrilled to have him home.

Flinton's gaze moved from his sisters to the woman leaning against the frame of the open doorway. She was exceptionally tall, with a sturdy build, and carried a little extra meat on her bones, which Brie thought only added to her appeal. She had a kind, beautiful face that was surrounded by a mass of curly red hair, which spilled over her shoulders and down her back. She was watching the reunion with her arms crossed and a fond smile on her face.

"Milly," Flinton breathed out, like a prayer.

He advanced toward her as she left the doorway. Meeting each other halfway, they stopped toe-to-toe and gazed lovingly into each other's eyes.

"Welcome home, handsome," Milly whispered as she raised her hands and placed them on his chest.

Flinton wrapped his arms around her with infinite tenderness and planted a kiss on her lips—a kiss that went on for so long, Brie had to look away in embarrassment, and the younger sisters began to serenade the couple with gagging noises.

Flinton and Milly broke apart, and Flinton beamed triumphantly at his family and friends. "It's good to be home! I'm sure Milly has a delicious meal nearly ready, but we have some introductions to make before we eat."

The girls finally swung their attention in Brie's direction, to the horses and riders. They extended excited hellos to Kove and Derek, while casting curious, but not unkind, glances at Brie.

Brie, Derek, and Kove dismounted and stretched their stiff limbs, then together they joined Flinton's family on the patio. Brie watched as a couple of the sisters squeezed closely together onto the benches. Flinton sat in one of the rocking chairs, close to Milly, and the two of them immediately reached for each other's hands. Another sister picked up the littlest girl and gave her a kiss on the cheek before plopping her in Flinton's lap and joining her sisters on the bench. The love among the family was palpable, and a pang of longing stabbed through Brie.

Derek placed his hands on her shoulders from behind, perhaps sensing her need for support, and led her to a spot on a bench between him and Kove.

"You must be parched from traveling," said the sister who appeared to be the oldest, still standing. "I'll bring out some drinks."

Once everyone was comfortably settled with cups of water in hand, Milly asked, "So, who is our lovely young visitor?"

"I think it's best to introduce the family first," Flinton said. He turned to Brie. "In case it wasn't obvious earlier, this exquisite creature is my wife, Milly."

The red-haired beauty smiled and blushed.

Flinton pointed to a young woman with olive-toned skin, shiny, straight black hair, and brown eyes, the one who'd offered them drinks. "This is the oldest of my sisters, Ava. She's nineteen."

Brie nodded and smiled while Ava blew her a kiss.

"The quiet sweetheart, who can usually be found with a book, is Nina. She's seventeen." Nina's long brown hair was pulled back in a clip, and loose curls fell over her shoulder. She smiled and waved.

"The freckled beauty, Emilee, is fifteen." Flinton pointed to a young woman with a scattering of freckles across her cheeks and long brown hair braided down her back. Emilee looked pleased, but responded with a surprisingly bored sounding, "Hello."

"The trouble-maker sitting beside me is Cassandra. She's fourteen, just a few moons older than you."

"My name is Cassandra Elane, but you can call me Cassie," the girl said. "There's almost no one in the village to hang out with, so I am thrilled to have you here, whoever you are." Cassie looked like a younger version of Ava, olive-toned, but her pin-straight black hair had streaks of red highlights, which seemed to compliment her outgoing personality perfectly.

"And this precious little munchkin is Adelaide, the baby of the family," Flinton said.

The "little munchkin" on Flinton's lap had huge brown doe eyes and ringlets of brown hair that fell to her shoulders, and she was grinning like it was Gifting morning.

"Hi. I'm eight!" she said proudly.

"And now it's time to tell you all about our guest," Flinton continued in an uncharacteristically somber tone. "It's been a very sad and momentous few weeks since we left home. You know we were stationed in Aldestone to help the King."

Brie noticed several heads nodding in understanding. Her heartbeat quickened, and a flock of butterflies took flight in her stomach, knowing the story Flinton was about to tell.

"It is with a heavy heart that I tell you: while we were in Aldestone, there was an attack on the city, and King and Queen Eyrhill, along with Prince Falen, were slain."

Several of the girls gasped.

"Oh, no!" Milly cried, covering her mouth.

Brie felt like vomiting, and her eyes began to water. Kove reached for one of Brie's hands, while Derek firmly grasped the other, providing Brie with some much-needed support.

Flinton kept going: "Adira sent us a message from within the castle on the night of the attack. She told us the princess had managed to escape."

Milly's eyes flashed to Brie, but she remained quiet.

"We were able to find her and take her out of the city to safety." Flinton swung his gaze to Brie and gave her an encouraging smile. "Girls, this is Princess Briana Rose Eyrhill. Please greet your future queen."

There was a stunned silence.

Brie pushed her tears away and gave a genuine smile as everyone in the family gawked at her. The attention didn't fluster her. As a member of the royal family, she was used to it. "I'm so happy to meet you, and I'm looking forward to getting to know you."

Milly and Ava regained their senses at the same time, followed shortly afterward by Nina. They sprung to their feet and curtsied in a rush. Different octaves of "Your Highness" were said hastily. Emilee stared at Brie in wide-eyed shock. Strangely, Cassie clasped her hands together underneath her chin and stared at Brie with a dreamy smile, while Adelaide merely looked around the room in confusion.

"Oh, for the love of the Blameless," Kove snorted. "Flinton, you're being far too uptight. This is the last thing Brie needs or wants. And here I thought you would have an inkling of how to do this, given your experience with women." He rolled his eyes. "It's a good thing one of us has some common sense. Ladies, please say hello to Brie. She's thirteen years old. She likes boots and leggings. She's recently taken an interest in archery, and she can play an impressive game of hide-and-seek. She's excited about joining our circle of family and friends."

Kove grinned and flung his arm around Brie's shoulder and added, "Oh, and I almost forgot. I'm her favorite uncle."

He looked at Brie and giggled. Derek reached behind Brie and smacked Kove on the back of his head.

Brie covered her smile. She was so relieved to have Kove break the tension that she let loose a giggle of her own. She looked around the room, and every pair of eyes were homed in on her. "Please, just call me Brie. Perhaps you can call me 'queen' and curtsey when I'm older."

"Thank *goodness!*" Cassie blurted out. "It would be so weird to curtsey to someone younger than me."

Laughter filled the patio, and everyone relaxed.

"Welcome to our home, Brie," said Milly. "We are sorry for your loss, and we are honored to have you here with us." She smiled kindly. "How about we move into the kitchen? Dinner is nearly ready."

Milly led them through a spacious entrance into an enormous living room, three stories high, with dark wooden beams exposed in the ceiling. The room was filled with couches, overstuffed chairs, dark wooden tables, a plush tan rug, and furs thrown about. A floor-to-ceiling stone wall featured a fireplace with a blazing fire, and a stairway in the corner rose up to the second floor.

The group moved on, past a small library and into the kitchen.

The kitchen was just as immense and impressive as the rest of the house, and the smell of herbs and spices hit Brie and made her mouth water. One side of the kitchen had marble counters covered with knives, cutting boards, potted herbs, bread, and fruit. There were also several ovens, which were cooking a scrumptious smelling dinner.

In the middle of the room was a massive black wooden table with black cushioned chairs. At the head of the table was an extra-wide chair, so large and sturdy that it resembled a throne. It obviously belonged to Flinton.

As soon as they entered, the girls fought to seat themselves around the table. Brie noted with keen interest that, while the other girls tried to seat themselves as close to Flinton as possible, Ava placed herself at the other end of the table next to Kove and gave him a radiant smile. His ears turned red, and he cleared his throat, but he uncharacteristically had nothing to say. Instead, he gave a weak smile.

Brie gave a quiet snort as Cassie plopped down beside her and said, "I'm so happy to have you here. I can't believe I'm going to be best friends with a princess." She sighed with a smile. "When do you turn fourteen?"

"Next moon," Brie answered, a little surprised by Cassie's bold statement. Brie'd had several friends back in Aldestone: daughters of lords and generals, and then Delia, the cook's granddaughter, who had been her closest pal. But Brie's very best friend had been Falen. Though no one could replace him, her lonely heart liked the idea of having another companion.

Milly served roast chicken with carrots, potatoes, and freshly baked bread. It was delicious. Brie glanced around the table, taking in everything. Flinton's sisters were all dark-eyed and dark-haired beauties, but each different from the rest. Cassie kept up a steady stream of conversation throughout the meal, impressively managing to breathe, talk, and eat all at the same time. She was bubbly and outgoing, and Brie found herself endeared to her instantly. Ava was bold, happy, and attractive both in looks and personality. Nina hardly spoke a word but smiled a lot. Emilee seemed to struggle between indifference to what was happening around her and excitement at seeing her brother again. It seemed excitement was slowly winning out, although her apparent happiness could have been a result of the chicken. Brie hadn't had a meal so enjoyable since leaving the castle.

And then there was Adelaide, who hadn't left Flinton's side—until now. She got down from her chair and walked over to Brie. With wide-eyed sincerity, she said, "I'm sorry about your family. My parents died too. But we're happy again. You'll be happy again someday, too." Then she opened her arms and wrapped them around Brie.

Brie's throat felt tight, and her eyes stung. "Thank you, Adelaide," she said. One of her hands involuntarily made its way to her heart, and she felt it burn in her chest. She grasped one of Adelaide's small hands in hers and gave it a squeeze. When she let go, Adelaide gasped and looked down. A chain with a silver, heart-shaped locket rested in her palm.

"Briana Rose, what did you just do?" Derek asked sternly.

Brie was shocked. "I didn't summon it on purpose, I promise! I don't know how I did it. It just appeared."

Kove got out of his seat and knelt beside Adelaide, examining the locket carefully. He fingered the necklace. "It's brand new and still warm." He shook his head and said, "You're full of surprises, Brie. I believe you created it."

"I did?" Brie's jaw dropped.

"*What?*" shrieked Cassie. "She's Blameless too? I can't believe it! I am *so* lucky!"

# *Resourceful Friends*

Brie woke up after a blissful night's sleep. She'd been given her very own bedroom, complete with a fireplace and her own bathtub. After spending two weeks riding on horseback and sleeping in tents, the luxury felt wonderful. Her body ached all over from traveling and training. She was sore in places she hadn't known could get sore, and she hadn't felt properly warm in weeks.

Last night, after Flinton and Cassie had given Brie a tour of the house, they'd led her to her room. Brie had taken a warm bath, dried off, and dressed in front of the blazing fire, and then she'd collapsed into bed. She was asleep shortly after her head hit the pillow.

Lying in bed this morning, Brie was in no hurry to leave her room. She was alone behind a closed door for the first time since her family's death, and her thoughts went to how much she missed them. For once, she let herself think about the night they died.

In a few shallow breaths, something terrible occurred to Brie. When the raid on the castle started, her parents had been in her bedroom, saying goodnight to her as they did every night. Falen had been on his way to join them when he was caught in the hallway, cut down before he could wish her his usual "sweet dreams."

Brie covered her eyes with her palms, and tears began to fall as she realized that it was her fault they were dead. She was thirteen, but she still liked being tucked in and wished good-night. If only she had been more mature and independent, her family would have been in a different part of the castle that evening, and their lives might have been spared. Brie sobbed into her pillow, wishing she could go back and change what had happened on that awful night. She cried until the sun rose and her eyes ran dry.

As Brie dressed for the day, her thoughts repeatedly went to Vaylec. What kind of person slaughtered an innocent family? Brie's grief was changing and turning into something deeper. She was angry at Vaylec, and she wanted him to pay for what he'd done.

Eventually, Brie made her way downstairs and followed the sounds of conversation to the kitchen, which she found buzzing with life. Milly was cooking bacon and eggs, and another loaf of freshly baked bread was cooling on the counter. Flinton sat at the table with Adelaide on his shoulders. He took a small sip of his coffee, holding his head perfectly still, while Adelaide ran small, wooden horses through his thick, floppy curls. Derek sat across from Flinton with his own cup of coffee, playing a game of cards with Cassie and Emilee. Nina sat at the foot of the table, reading a book with a small, contented smile on her face.

"Good morning, Briana Rose!" Derek smiled across the table.

"Good morning, Uncle Derek." Brie smiled back.

Flinton waved with his free hand. "Morning, short stuff. How did you sleep?"

"Like a baby. It was wonderful."

Flinton nodded. "Good."

"Hold your head still!" Adelaide shouted, yanking on Flinton's hair.

"Ouch!" Flinton winced, and his eyes began to water.

The other girls gave greetings of "Hello" and "Good morning," and Cassie sent an especially bright smile Brie's way.

Milly walked toward Brie and opened her arms. "May I have a hug, my dear? I could really use one this morning."

Feeling a little hesitant, but not wanting to be rude, Brie stepped into Milly's open arms and returned her squeeze. It felt surprisingly good, and Brie let out a shaky breath. Milly was soft and cozy and smelled like cinnamon. This wasn't a quick hug. Milly seemed to feel the need for a much longer one, so Brie went along with it and held on tight. The longer it lasted, the better it felt. Another shaky sigh slipped out of Brie's mouth as she thought about her mother. Brie hadn't been hugged by a woman since her mother's death. A few tears leaked out of her eyes and got lost in Milly's mass of red hair.

They broke apart. Milly said with apparent relief, "I feel much better. Thank you, Brie." She gave Brie's shoulder a final squeeze, then returned to her work at the stove.

As Brie took a seat at the table, she noticed Flinton's eyes were glued to his wife, and his coffee cup was suspended in midair, unmoving. His eyes looked suspiciously red and watery as he blinked rapidly. Eventually, he raised his mug to his lips and resumed sipping.

Ava breezed into the room, planting a peck on Brie's cheek. In no time, breakfast was served. Brie piled her plate high with eggs, bacon, fried potatoes, and fresh bread. All of it was perfectly cooked and seasoned. The eggs were fluffy, the bacon was crisp, the potatoes were spiced with a bit of heat, and the yeasty bread was soft and smothered in butter. It was absolutely mouth-watering. Milly was an amazing cook. If she needed a hug every morning to feel appreciated, then Brie would give her one.

There was a loud bang as the front door slammed shut. Kove entered the kitchen with a boy about Brie's age hot on his heels. The boy was only half a head shorter than Kove, with windblown, sandy-blond hair and the same athletic build. It could only be one person: the younger brother Kove had mentioned. And just as Derek had described yesterday, the boy carried himself with an air of self-confidence.

"Excellent! We're just in time for breakfast!" the boy said, rubbing his hands together with a crooked grin.

"Our perfect timing wasn't a mistake, Milly." Kove smiled widely. "Good morning, Blackwoods! Good morning, Brie!"

"Good morning, Uncle Kove!"

The boy's eyes landed on Brie and widened. He worked his way around the crowded table and stopped right beside her, staring at her expectantly.

Feeling obligated to stand, Brie did, and she said, "Hello, I'm Brie."

The boy surprised Brie by dipping into the most dramatic bow she had ever witnessed in her thirteen years in the royal castle. He said with reverence, "My name is Taeo LeBlanc. It is an honor to meet you, Your Royal Highness."

*Wow*, Brie thought, *this kid has a flair for the dramatic*. Taeo held his pose for a long time, his back bent down, one arm curled at his waist, and the other arm flared ridiculously behind him. Brie was tempted to tap her foot impatiently, but Taeo finally stood up and gave her a triumphant smile.

His reverence flew out the window as he pumped his fist in the air and shouted, "Yes! I have *always* wanted to do that!"

Cassie burst into gales of laughter. Derek groaned.

Kove walked over to Taeo and put him in a headlock, running his fist back and forth through his hair. "Rein it in, Taeo. Two of us are a lot to take in."

Something inside of Brie boiled up and reacted to his charade. It was downright disrespectful. "You need to work on your form, young man," she said stiffly, and sat back down.

"Lucky for me," came Taeo's quick reply, "I'll have plenty of opportunity to practice with you around."

Breakfast resumed, and the conversation and laughter flowed easily. In spite of Taeo, Brie found it refreshing to be among the close-knit group.

"This morning, we have a council meeting with the Elders," Derek announced. "They've asked Kove, Flinton, and I to give a report of Vaylec's attack and our rescue of Briana."

"Can Brie and I come?" Cassie asked, surprising Brie with her boldness.

"I'm sorry, but Brie is not invited, and neither are you.

Council meetings are not for children," Derek answered.

Cassie's eyebrows raised toward her hairline. "First of all, we are not children. We are lovely young women. Second of all, the meeting is about Brie. She deserves to be there."

Brie couldn't help but agree with Cassie's argument, but she decided to keep quiet.

Flinton spoke up and pointed his fork at Cassie, giving her a sharp look. "Not today. End of discussion. You girls can stay at home, or Cassie, you can use the time to show Brie around the village."

"Hmm," was all Cassie said. She waited a few moments until the conversation had moved on, and then she leaned over and whispered in Brie's ear. "We'll find a way in. Don't worry."

About fifteen minutes had passed since the men had left for the council meeting. Cassie stood up and casually suggested, "Well, should we take a walk through the village so I can show you the shops?"

Sensing a plan was underway, Brie readily agreed. "I've been wearing the same clothes for almost three weeks, so I would love to see the shops."

Milly looked horrified. "Oh, you poor dear. I cannot believe those men didn't think to provide a princess with more than one outfit." Her eyes flashed as she got to her feet, muttering something that sounded suspiciously like, "They'll hear about it later." Milly retrieved a bag of money and gave it to Brie. "Please, go buy yourself some new clothes, and have fun while you're at it."

"Thanks, Milly!" Brie called as Cassie yanked her arm, pulling her toward the door.

Once they were outside, Cassie huffed, "You aren't used to lying, are you?"

"Of course not!" Brie answered indignantly.

"Well, I find it necessary to color the truth every now and then," Cassie said. "Now we're going to have to allow ourselves the time to actually buy you clothes."

With a shrug, Cassie looped her arm through Brie's, and they took off at a brisk pace. "We'll worry about shopping afterward. For now, we need to get to that meeting. We've got just enough time. The first half hour, they cover things like updating the Registry of the Blameless, illnesses, the weather. You know, boring stuff. The important information comes after that."

They had barely made it past the Blackwood's front lawn when Taeo materialized from behind a pine tree. "You're going on an adventure without me?" he asked, crossing his arms and raising his eyebrows.

Cassie stomped her foot on the ground. "I *knew* you would follow us."

"And I knew you were up to no good," Taeo retaliated.

"We're going shopping. It's for girls only," Cassie said, waving her hand like she was dismissing him.

Taeo narrowed his eyes. "You are not. You're going to the council meeting. I can read you like a book, so don't even try to lie. We've been playing together since we were little. You are about to have an adventure, and you can't possibly leave me behind. Ava is too old to play with, Nina's nose is always buried in a book, Emilee has turned weird and doesn't know how to have fun anymore, and Milly is baking with Adelaide. I will die of boredom if I stay here!"

Cassie gave a frustrated groan. "We're wasting time, or I would keep arguing. Come on; let's go."

They resumed their speedy advance. "You won't regret it, I promise," Taeo said. "My presence will come in handy, especially if we're climbing into the attic." Clearly, the two of them had experience in the matter.

Brie, who'd been observing the entire exchange with surprise, couldn't keep quiet any longer. "This is not meant to be a fun adventure. We're trying to get information on why my family was slain. It's not a game to me. I want the heartless criminal who killed my family and destroyed my city to pay for his actions. If your presence will help, then you can come with us. But in the future, you need to ask my opinion and not just Cassie's."

Cassie stopped walking and grinned at Brie. "You're going to be an awesome queen."

Taeo looked thunderstruck, like he'd been clobbered over the head. He probably wasn't used to being put in his place. "Forgive me for my lack of sympathy, Princess," he finally said.

Brie nodded. "I forgive you. Now, come on."

They continued down the street that led into the very heart of the village.

"So, what should I call you?" Taeo asked innocently. It was too innocent, and Brie was suspicious that he was already up to no good. "Your Highness, Princess, Your Majesty, my lady, Your Worship?"

Brie narrowed her eyes at him. "One day you will address me as 'Your Majesty, the Queen,'" she said, sounding ridiculous, even to herself. She normally didn't like to rub her royalty in other people's faces, but something about Taeo ruffled her feathers. She looked at him sternly for a moment and then shrugged. "But for now, just call me Brie."

"Oh, no. I don't think I could ever call you that," was Taeo's mysterious reply.

In the center of town, the trio came to an enormous stone building with impressive marble pillars running along the front. On the face of the building, just below the peak of the roof, was a large replica of the same symbol Derek wore on his headband. The symbol was a circle divided into three parts. One section had an image of the sun; another had a small triangle with circular lines extending away from it; and the third part contained a circle with a cross through the center.

"What does that symbol mean?" Brie asked.

"It means we're here," Cassie said. "This is the Council Hall, and that is the sign of the Blameless." She pointed. "Those designs represent the earth, air, and sun. Come on." She motioned for Brie to follow. "There's a back door we can sneak in."

Brie took another look at the symbol and saw its likeness to the earth, air, and sun. She nodded to herself, soaking in the information. Then, picking up her pace, she followed Cassie.

They circled around the building until they reached the rear entrance. Cassie attempted to open it, but it was locked. She muttered a very unladylike word. Taeo pushed Cassie aside, shaking his head and rolling his eyes. The look very much said, "I told you you'd need me." Then he pulled a ring of metal gadgets out of his pocket and proceeded to pick the lock in a matter of seconds. Taeo and Cassie looked completely unfazed, like breaking and entering was an everyday occurrence for them.

Brie snatched the metal ring out of Taeo's hands before he could pocket it and examined it. The ring held curved and pointed instruments of various sizes, as well as several keys. "What kind of boy carries around tools for picking locks?" Brie asked in a whisper as they slipped inside the Council Hall.

"The resourceful kind," Taeo whispered, grabbing his ring back.

They entered a small storage room full of brooms, mops, and garbage bins. A door on the opposite wall exited into a dark hallway, which they followed until they began to hear voices. Brie tiptoed after Cassie and turned left into a massive room lined on all four walls with sturdy wooden shelves. Cassie waved at the shelves, which were laden with thousands of scrolls, and whispered, "These are the records of the Blameless. They contain the names of all of the Blameless who have ever lived in Predonia, along with their gifts and a detailed explanation of their good deeds." Then she pointed to a square up in the very far corner of the ceiling. "We need to go through that hatch door into the attic."

Brie gawked at it all. How Cassie had discovered there was a hatch door into an attic, in a room full of scrolls, in the Council Hall of the Blameless, was beyond her.

Cassie took the lead and climbed up the shelving first,

using them like steps on a ladder. Brie followed, the shelves groaning and creaking as she went. As she climbed, she noticed the shelves were labeled and organized according to year. There were dates from several hundred years ago, and part of Brie was tempted to curl up on one of the shelves to simply read through years of history.

Taeo came last, climbing up the shelving in no time. They reached the top shelf and stood. Several feet separated the tops of their heads from the attic door. Brie now understood why Taeo's presence would come in handy. He squatted down, and Cassie climbed onto his shoulders. With their combined height, Cassie was able to reach the hatch door. She pushed it open, then disappeared through the hole in the ceiling. Brie followed, although a little less gracefully. Coming last, Taeo jumped and grasped onto the frame of the opening. As quietly as they could, the girls pulled on his arms and hauled him through the door.

Breathing heavily from the exertion, Brie looked around the attic and whispered, "How does everyone else get up here?"

"They use a real ladder." Cassie said quietly, "but it's locked up down the hall. Our way is much quicker."

"Do I want to know how you figured all of this out?" Brie asked.

Cassie shook her head. "We've had lots and lots of free time."

Together, they crept through the dark, dusty attic, passing bins filled with more scrolls, until they reached a wall. The voices were noticeably louder in the attic than they had been in the hallway below. Cassie and Taeo clearly knew what they were doing. This suspicion was confirmed as they began to wiggle loose pieces of mortar in the wall.

"Wait!" Brie whispered, realizing something. "They'll be able to sense I'm here because I'm a Blameless."

"They're in a room full of Blameless," Cassie whispered back. "We're counting on their many signals to cloud yours."

Taeo glanced at Brie and added, "We should be okay. As little as you are, you probably only send out half a signal anyway."

Brie glared at him. Almost everything that came out of his mouth was an insult.

Cassie pierced Taeo with a pointed look. "You're the tag-along, so Brie and I get to look through the holes."

Miraculously enough, Taeo nodded and didn't argue. They slid the mortar out of the wall, revealing two separate peepholes, each large enough for one eye to see through.

Brie peered through one of the openings, taking in the council meeting below them. She and Cassie looked down into an enormous room with a domed ceiling. Three older men and two women sat around a large, round, wooden table, along with Derek, Kove, and Flinton. An amphitheater surrounded the table with additional seating for several hundred guests. The first row was occupied with approximately twenty to thirty additional people of various ages.

Kove's voice drifted up to the kids. It didn't hold any of its usual playfulness. It was deadly serious as he gave his report of events. "During our undercover work for the king, there wasn't a single leak about an attack on the castle. It came without warning. However, there was a lot of talk about Vaylec in the taverns. He seems to have developed an enormous group of followers in recent years. The attack wasn't an ambush from outside of the city, but rather a well-executed plan from within. Vaylec had an entire army, ready and waiting. They struck at dusk. Former royal guards and trained citizens appeared, fully armed, organized clear down to the detail of new uniforms with a 'V' crest emblazoned on their banners," he spat out in disgust. "They overpowered the loyal guards and civilians."

Murmurs from the Blameless in attendance rose up to the attic.

"That's what happened in the streets of Aldestone," Derek clarified. "What happened within the castle is more of a mystery, but we'll tell you what we've pieced together. Vaylec himself led the attack on the castle. He entered through the guards' entrance with a group of nearly fifty armed soldiers and moved directly to the royal family's chambers. He didn't have to search the castle; he knew exactly where to go, so it's likely he had inside help."

Hearing this made Brie shiver as visions of her parents' murders resurfaced in her mind.

Derek went on: "They killed almost every castle guard and anyone who put up resistance along the way. Since it was late in the evening, the normally peaceful city was caught completely unprepared. Adira discovered the attack when she sensed an unusual number of soldiers in the castle and she followed the sounds of fighting. She ran straight to the king and queen in an effort to protect them, but when she arrived, it was already too late. Prince Falen was spotted separated from the rest of the family, lying in the hallway. According to Adira, he was a feisty young man, so maybe he put up a fight, but we can only guess."

Brie's throat tightened, and her eyes burned, but she fisted her hands and listened to the tale of that dreadful night with determination.

"The king and queen were dead, and Adira heard Vaylec shout at his soldiers to find the princess," Derek continued. "After realizing Brie had managed to escape, Adira sent word to us telepathically. She was beside herself with grief and worry, and she asked us to find the princess. Shortly after that, our communication was cut off."

Flinton continued with the story. "Because of my gift with tracking, we agreed that I should look for Briana. I traced her into the heart of the city and found her hidden in a blacksmith's shop. We got her out of Aldestone with only one minor skirmish with some of Vaylec's soldiers."

They continued with a recap of events up to Adira's bizarre attack on them.

"In light of these events," Derek said, "I've drawn a conclusion. Adira's magic wouldn't have worked if her heart had become evil. She's still Blameless. She didn't join the other side. It was very clear she was attacking us against her wishes, like she was somehow being forced into it. I believe Vaylec was somehow controlling her, although I have no idea how or why."

His theory chilled Brie to her very bones. The cries of alarm in the room revealed that she wasn't the only one who was distressed.

Kove jumped in, "We questioned one of the soldiers after the attack. He told us Vaylec planned to capture all of us, not just Brie. Why would he want us?"

"Perhaps to control us as well," Derek suggested grimly, shaking his head.

"Earth, air, and sun," Taeo whispered.

One of the Elders, a female with snow white hair, spoke up. "Eldon Spaur has failed to respond to any of our summons or letters. It would seem he has forsaken the council, whether on his own or because his son has forced him to. It's a shame—Eldon was one of our keenest minds, and the council is not as strong without him. Vaylec may very well be holding both parents captive in the castle; no one has seen Cecily in moons, either. In light of this new information, I think it's most likely that Vaylec is involved. We'll send a scout to investigate, but until proven otherwise, we need to assume they are somehow being hindered by him. And if Vaylec is hindering his parents and making Adira do things she doesn't want to do, there's a strong possibility that he's involved his twin sister, Violet."

Derek's jaw clenched and unclenched. He seemed upset by this information. "I trained Violet. Her specialty is shields, and she has the power of persuasion. Her gifts are rare, and she's quite powerful. She can literally convince anyone to do her bidding." Derek paused briefly, then switched topics. "What do you know about Brie and her gifts?" he asked the Elders. "We were told she showed evidence of significant power as a young child, but she used her magic for the very first time just two weeks ago. There has to be a reason for

Vaylec's interest in her; otherwise, he would have wanted her dead and out of the way like the rest of her family. Could he have known about her powers?"

Another Elder stood to speak. He was stocky, with salt and pepper hair and a beard. Cassie whispered to Brie, "That's Lord Renolt, the leader."

Lord Renolt began, "The story I am about to tell has been kept secret among the Elders since the birth of the princess."

Brie gasped quietly. Taeo slid closer, smashing himself between Cassie and Brie with his back to the wall.

"When the princess was born, as is customary, the local Blameless presented themselves to the king and queen to offer congratulations and swear loyalty to the new child. Eldon and Cecily Spaur, along with Vaylec and Violet, were passing through Aldestone and stopped to visit the royal family. They were presented to the royals in their private sitting room. Queen Serafeen was holding Princess Briana, and Prince Falen was sitting beside King Thyron. When the Spaurs entered the room, a phenomenal thing happened. The princess vanished. In front of everyone in that small room, she disappeared from the arms of the queen. But amazingly enough, Queen Serafeen could still feel the weight and warmth of Briana in her lap. The baby had become invisible.

"I want you to appreciate the significance of this. The power of invisibility has only been given to a handful of Blameless over the years, and it takes years to master, yet the princess was one moon old when this happened. She had performed no act of selflessness. In that moment, Briana became the youngest person to have ever been touched by the gods. For that reason, she is anticipated to be the most powerful Blameless to have ever existed."

Kove let out a low whistle. Flinton shook his head in astonishment, and Derek nodded slowly, as though piecing together another piece of his puzzle. Whispers of surprise swept through the council hall.

Renolt continued, "It was a shock to the king and queen, as you can imagine. Queen Serafeen nearly fainted in fright. Thank goodness, Adira was in place as their advisor and was able to explain what had happened. The king and queen and Adira kept a vigilant watch on Princess Briana over the years. From Adira's reports, they've been cautious with her, limiting her exposure to situations that could cause extreme emotion, and there have been no other known displays of magic."

Derek spoke up. "Why do you think she was touched by the Three in that specific moment as a baby?"

A man who had the same sandy blond hair and green eyes as Kove and Taeo answered: "We discussed it at length thirteen years ago, and we reviewed the scrolls of the Blameless. Our best guess was that being in a room with so many Blameless could have been the cause, but we never came to a conclusion."

Taeo confirmed Brie's suspicions by whispering, "My father, Holden LeBlanc."

Derek continued to address the Elders. "In light of recent events with Vaylec, I have another theory. What if, when Vaylec entered the room all those years ago, he was already a threat? What if Terren, Solis, and Cael sensed that threat, and chose that very moment to bless her with protection and mark her as Blameless?"

Brie left the attic in a daze and woodenly made her way through the back rooms, back hallways, and back doors of the Council Hall, finally exiting into the back street. She'd never felt so backward in all her life.

Coming to Brie's rescue, Cassie grabbed her hand and pulled her through the village to a tavern a short distance away. Taeo held the door open for them, and, as they stepped inside, Brie briefly registered its clever name as the sign swung in the breeze above the entrance: the Guiltless Pleasure. It was perfect for a Blameless tavern.

Yanking on Brie's arm, Cassie picked out a table in the far corner of the room, while Taeo went to the bar and purchased three steaming mugs of hot chocolate. For a moment, Brie wondered if someone had told Taeo about her love of sweets—but that was impossible, because she hadn't shared it with anyone in Mount Elrad.

Taeo raised his eyebrows and shook his head after delivering their drinks. "So, a princess and the most powerful Blameless of all time." He seemed reluctantly impressed.

"This is *crazy!*" Cassie exploded, bouncing in her seat. "I needed a best friend, but I never thought she would come with so much excitement!" She took a large gulp of her hot chocolate, sighing happily. "This is amazing."

"What exactly have I been all of these years?" Taeo muttered. "A pain in your—"

Brie interrupted, "Wait a minute. This is hard to wrap my brain around, and I'm not so sure I'm happy about it. I don't mean to sound arrogant, but aren't you jealous of my powers?"

Cassie's expression turned serious. "Brie, I've grown up surrounded by the Blameless. Taeo has too." She motioned toward him. "It's a *lot* of responsibility. They are always being sent on new missions with an urgent obligation to save the world. I would hate that kind of pressure. I know I'll never be Blameless, and I'm perfectly fine with it. So to answer your question, no, I'm not jealous."

"How do you know you'll never become Blameless?" Brie asked curiously.

"I would break the rules right away because it would be too tempting to use my magic selfishly. Oh, don't look so horrified," Cassie said in response to the shocked expression on Brie's face. "I wouldn't do anything awful, but I'm sure I couldn't resist the temptation to cover Taeo's face with warts." She ducked as Taeo tried to smack her. "Or grow my hair extra-long overnight. See what I mean? I'm not cut out to be Blameless. I've accepted that. But that doesn't mean I'm not thrilled to be right in the center of all of this craziness with you!"

"Huh," Brie said thoughtfully. "I can see your point, but still, I don't have a choice in the matter, do I? I feel like I'm in shock. I can't keep up with everything that's been happening. First, my family was taken from me." She swallowed thickly. "And as if that wasn't enough, I was attacked by someone who was supposed to be my friend, then I found out about magic and the Blameless, and now I'm suddenly supposed to be the most powerful Blameless ever!" She was breathing hard. "This is ridiculous!" A very un-princess-like snort slipped out of her. "The two of you probably know more about the

Blameless than I do! I have *no idea* what I'm doing! How am I supposed to defeat Vaylec? I need to learn everything I possibly can if that's ever going to happen!"

"You're in luck, your Royal Brieness," Taeo said gallantly. "We are experts on all things Blameless, with absolutely nothing better to do with our time. Seriously, this place is so boring, you would be doing us a favor by letting us help." He fidgeted a bit in his seat and added, "Listen, I know I may come across as a bit of a jokester . . ."

"You mean a pompous, swollen-headed, arrogant, loudmouthed fool?" Cassie said with a smirk.

Brie couldn't contain herself: she burst into laughter. She had never gone from being on the verge of tears to laughter before. She already liked Cassie, and maybe Taeo would grow on her. Together, the two of them might be just what she needed. Wiping tears from her eyes, Brie looked at Taeo. "I'm sorry; what were you saying?"

Taeo put on a front, like he was offended, but his eyes were smiling. "Yes, as I was saying." He cleared his throat and continued. "I really am sorry for everything you've been through. I promise to do everything within my power to help."

"And so will I," Cassie added, grabbing Brie's hand and squeezing it.

"Thank you both. So, so much," Brie responded with a watery-eyed smile, feeling unspeakably grateful for their pledge of support.

Taeo raised his mug, sloshing a bit over the edge in his zeal. "Drink up! We've had enough soberness for one day. Here's to newfound friendships, and to defeating evil people!"

Cassie raised her mug. "And to an honest afternoon of shopping!"

They all clinked glasses and took a hearty drink of deliciously sweet hot chocolate, smiling conspiratorially at one another.

The door to the tavern opened, bringing a gust of cold air with it.

Cassie looked up, and her face paled. "Oh, no," she whispered.

Brie followed Cassie's line of sight to find Flinton, Derek, and Kove marching in their direction, their eyes narrowed beneath furrowed brows, looking murderous. She gulped. Flinton's face resembled a thundercloud. Grabbing chairs from neighboring tables, the men sat, surrounding the kids.

"Well, isn't this cozy," Cassie said weakly.

"Cassandra Elane Blackwood," Flinton growled, "you have some explaining to do. You went directly against my orders."

"Flinton, you told me to show Brie around the village. I didn't think you would care about us coming to the Guiltless Pleasure. We were thirsty. That can't be a crime," Cassie said, blinking innocently.

"Stop playing games, Cassandra. I know you were in the Council Hall. I could sense all of you. Have you forgotten my gift of tracking?"

"Or that I can read minds?" Derek added.

"You're lucky I didn't stop the meeting and bring your presence to the attention of the Elders."

"I can't believe we miscalculated!" Taeo said, looking disappointed.

Derek cut in and leveled his sharp gaze at Taeo. "And no, she doesn't send out half of a signal because she's so small. As her protectors, we are very in tune with her signal. It's as blaringly obvious as the sun."

Taeo's shoulder's drooped, and he looked even more forlorn at this news, but Brie sat up straighter in her seat and arched an eyebrow at Taeo.

Derek continued, directing his words at Taeo again. "Sensing you on my scan was equally easy. My ability to pick people up on a scan strengthens when there's a threat or dishonesty in the vicinity. Clearly, you met the criteria."

Taeo gulped, looking more upset at being caught than guilty.

Cassie barreled forward with another explanation. "Flinton, there comes a time when you have to make decisions for the greater good, even if it means going against orders. You are my brother. Brie is my *queen*. It was in her best interest, and she outranks you."

Kove whistled and raised his eyebrows, looking impressed. Derek pinched the bridge of his nose and closed his eyes, and Flinton ran his hands through his hair, lifting his eyes to the ceiling like he was at a complete loss for words.

Flinton finally recovered and asked, "Did Brie give you orders to take her to the council meeting in order to spy on us?"

"Well, not exactly," Cassie admitted. "But she had the right to be there."

"Why didn't you tell me?" Brie interrupted, feeling suddenly and irrationally angry. "We've been together for over two weeks, and you never mentioned there were rumors about my powers. I had the right to know."

Derek turned to Brie. "We didn't know all of the details, Briana. We knew you were special, but we didn't know why. Plus, you were already going through so much, we thought it was best to wait and speak with the Elders first. We would have told you soon, I promise. You need to trust us; don't resort to spying. *We* trust *you.* We let you stay because we think you're correct, Brie. You have the right to know."

"You just went about it in the wrong way," Flinton said.

Kove shrugged. "But I suppose this way, we didn't break any rules by telling you the details of the meeting ourselves."

Some of Brie's anger dissolved. It had been momentarily directed at Derek, Flinton, and Kove, but if she was being honest with herself, she was struggling with why she had never been told about what happened when she was a baby. Her parents had witnessed her being touched by the Three. Why hadn't they told her? Falen was six at the time. Did he remember what had happened, and had he been keeping a secret from her as well?

Brie sighed. "I'm sorry," she muttered.

"Well, that was easy," Cassie said with relief.

Flinton pointed his finger at her. "You aren't out of the woods yet, you little hellion."

# *Flair Ball*

Over the next few weeks, Brie settled into a new routine. She woke up every morning, often after nightmares of her family's death. In some dreams, she relived the night they died, but others were different—yet contained equally disturbing scenarios. In one dream, Brie stubbed her toe and was crying for help, and her family was chased with swords while they raced to bring her a bandage. In another, Falen brought her a piece of chocolate, and then he was stabbed by a shadowy figure while Brie ran away with a mouthful of sweets. Each scenario held a common theme: it was Brie's fault they'd died, and she would start the day with the same devastating feeling of guilt.

Brie wished she could change the past, but she couldn't. It made her want to be a different person, a better person. She didn't want to be weak or a drain to those around her. She wanted to be strong. She vowed to grow stronger every day so she could one day make Vaylec pay for taking away the people she loved the most.

Brie's days were bright, though, too. After mornings spent wallowing in memories, Brie's new routine continued. She ate breakfast with the Blackwoods and hugged Milly (a favorite part of her day); she trained during the day with her uncles; and she spent her evenings wandering around Mount Elrad with Cassie and Taeo. Her new friends fed her all sorts of information about the Blameless, sometimes useful and sometimes useless. She loved every minute she spent with them.

Flinton and Milly treated Brie like one of the family, even including her in the weekly chore rotation. Brie had begged and pleaded before Flinton caved and allowed her to join the dishwashers. She refused to be pampered just because she was a princess. Milly had to teach Brie how to wash dishes, since she'd never performed a chore before in her life. Brie finished the task with only one broken glass and the entire front of her tunic drenched, but feeling very satisfied with herself. However, when she turned around, she found all of Flinton's sisters staring at her like she had grown three heads.

Brie's Blameless training during the day wasn't quite as satisfying. Some aspects of it were amazing, like learning about various magical gifts. It wasn't so fun to try to figure out exactly what Brie's magical abilities were. When Brie had used her powers before, it had seemed effortless, but now that she was in front of an audience and expected to perform, it was a disaster. No one had the foggiest idea what she was capable of, so they resorted to having her try a bit of everything: creating shields, levitating, mind reading, forging weapons, manipulating water, starting fires, healing wounds, and conjuring items. They even had her try to recreate another locket, like the one she'd given Adelaide. To Brie's dismay, she failed at every single task. If her uncles thought she was going to be the most powerful Blameless of all time, they were in for a big disappointment.

Brie often had other Blameless observers, people who were interested in seeing how the princess's training was coming; even Lord Renolt occasionally came to watch. For the most part, though, Brie was grateful to be trained by Derek, Flinton, and Kove. She grew to love her uncles more and more with each passing day. They didn't seem concerned by her epic failures, but they assured her she would learn.

"You possess powers from all three of the gods," Flinton explained, "which is extremely rare for a Blameless."

"Why do you think that?" Brie couldn't help asking.

"Your creation of the heart locket for Adelaide was a talent from the earth. Your ability to summon your crown and Sir Mudgeon's bow was manipulation of the air. And becoming invisible as a baby was a gift from the sun."

This made no sense to Brie, and she said so.

"Blameless scholars have studied our gifts and researched these factors," Derek explained. "Their scientific understanding goes far beyond what the nonmagical world can comprehend. The human eye can only see visible light, but the sun emits a special light, a radiating wave of heat, that is invisible. For this reason, tapping into the magic of the sun allows invisibility."

Listening to Derek talk about "invisible light" made Brie's head hurt. Truthfully, she didn't care about the details of invisible waves of heat. She only cared that she was supposed to be able to harness it—and she couldn't.

Brie felt weighed down by the pressures of all she couldn't

yet do. She was relieved when, one day, Kove announced they were going to have fun and try something new.

After breakfast, Brie, Cassie, and Taeo hiked through the crisp morning air to the training arena, which was on the east side of the village, nestled in the valley between the mountains. The outdoor arena provided a large, safe meadow for weapons training, summoning, archery, and fire practice.

The trio crossed the large field to Brie's favorite uncles, who were standing next to an enormous pentagon painted on the ground. As soon as Taeo saw the pentagon, he whooped out an excited, "Aww *yeah!*" Cassie let out a high-pitched shriek of delight.

"We aren't going to train today, per se," Kove explained happily. Even Derek and Flinton wore smiles. "We are going to play a game. A little game I created called Flair Ball." Kove pointed to the pentagon, which was about one hundred feet in diameter; a large bullseye had been painted in the middle. Painted lines led away from the bullseye, dividing it into five equal triangles, and each triangle had lines running through it, making the pentagon look like a gigantic spider web.

As that thought ran through Brie's head, Kove said, "This is the Web." Brie smirked. At least she had gotten one thing right so far.

Kove continued, "The game is usually played by five Blameless. But today, Taeo and Cassie will form a team." Cassie jumped up and down, clapping her hands in excitement. "They will stand inside one of the triangles on the Web. The rest of us will occupy our own triangle. Go ahead and pick a spot on the Web."

They made their way onto the pentagon. Kove conjured up a smooth, brown leather ball about a foot in diameter and held it up for Brie to see. "The object of the game is to avoid being hit by the ball. It's stuffed with feathers, so don't worry, sunshine—it shouldn't hurt. If you're hit, you remain in the game, but you get one point. Points are bad. You do *not* want points. You may catch the ball or deflect the ball with your magical flairs, but you cannot use the same flair more than once per round, hence the name 'Flair Ball.'"

Kove tossed the ball from hand to hand as he continued his explanation. "In the first round, we stand in the outer edges of our triangles. Round one ends when someone has been hit three times and therefore gained three points. Everyone stays in the game, but we step forward into the next section of our triangles. The same rules apply in round two, but we add a second ball. We progress through each round, adding a ball each time, until we get to the very center of the triangle. This is round five, and there will be five balls at play all at once. It's my favorite round." He winked. "Again, when someone has been hit three times, the final round ends. The person with the lowest total points for all five rounds is the winner."

Kove tossed the ball to Derek, who held up his hand and stopped it midair, two inches from his face. He flipped his hand nonchalantly, and the ball went spiraling toward Cassie, who caught it.

"Any questions, sunshine?" Kove asked.

"Yes, just one," Brie said. "How is it possible to use our gifts in a game? I thought we couldn't use them to benefit ourselves."

Brie had wondered about this on more than one occasion. On one of her nightly walks with Taeo and Cassie, she had asked, "What would happen if a Blameless used their gifts selfishly?"

Taeo had come to a screeching halt and grabbed her arm. "Don't *ever* try to do it, Your Worshipfulness. I've seen it happen once, and I'll never forget it. It was horrible." He shuddered and put his head in his hands, like he was trying to remove the memory. "You'll explode! It took us a week to find and clean up all of his pieces."

Brie had stopped, frozen in horror, until Cassie rolled her eyes and Taeo's face began to twitch. He burst into laughter and collapsed weakly onto the ground. Holding his stomach, he'd wheezed out, "You should have seen your face."

"What *really* happens?" Brie had demanded.

Cassie had shrugged and answered, as Taeo continued to roll around on the ground in laughter. "It simply doesn't work," she'd said. "In some cases, you lose your powers."

Brie pulled herself back to the present as Flinton answered her question. "Is it selfish to play a game, short stuff? Since Kove's creation of the game, we use Flair Ball as part of our training, and it's also a boatload of fun. Don't worry about it. Just relax and have a good time."

"Any more questions?" Taeo asked with exaggerated slowness, raising his eyebrows up and down.

Brie glared at Taeo, trying to wipe the smirk off his face, but it only got bigger. He was likely remembering the joke he'd played on her the other evening, as well.

Of course, Brie had more questions, like *How am I going to play Flair Ball if I can't get my flairs to work?* But she kept those thoughts to herself. Feigning confidence she didn't feel, she said, "No, I'm ready to get started."

Derek raised a questioning eyebrow at her but said nothing.

Brie groaned quietly. *Curse him and his mind reading.*

Derek proceeded to raise both eyebrows at her.

*Darn it!* She'd forgotten again. Brie decided to do the only thing she could think of and stuck out her tongue. Derek shook his head and chuckled.

Kove put the ball in the center of the Web, on the bullseye. Each player stood in the farthest section of their triangle, staring at one another from about fifty feet apart.

"On the count of three, you may use your flairs to move the ball. Taeo, you can pick it up if you get there in time, but we all know that won't happen."

Taeo nodded quickly, his body frozen in place, ready to sprint.

Kove looked at Brie. "Remember, catch it or deflect it."

Brie gave him a thumbs-up and a fake smile.

"One, two, three—*go*!"

The ball rose up off the ground and levitated for a moment. Derek's hands were in the air. He sent the ball careening toward Flinton. And just like that, the game had started.

Flinton conjured a metal shield and used it like a bowl, catching the ball. He bounced it three times with the shield, high into the air, and then swatted it. The ball flew toward Cassie, who tried to catch it, but it bounced out of her arms.

"That's one point for you, Cassie," Kove said. "Your team moves the ball back into the game."

Cassie picked up the ball and gave it to Taeo, who threw it with all his might at Kove.

Kove caught it, tossed it in the air, performed a front flip, and kicked it in Brie's direction. Whizzing between her outstretched arms, the ball smacked Brie right in the forehead.

Brie picked the ball up and hurled it at Taeo's laughing face. Well, "hurled" may have been an exaggeration. It fell limply onto the Web barely inside Taeo's triangle. Taeo ran forward with a gleeful look on his face, picked up the ball, then volleyed it to Derek.

Derek lazily put up a protective shield, causing the ball to bounce and soar toward Brie again. She jumped as high as she could to catch it, but it sailed over her head, just nicking her finger.

"That's two points for you," Kove said unnecessarily.

Brie tossed the ball toward Flinton. He caught the ball in a yarn sling that appeared from nowhere, swung it around his body, and released it. It sped with lightning precision in Kove's direction.

Kove created a series of miniature geysers that sprayed water upward out of the ground. The ball splashed through them, each one slowing it down. The ball eventually landed in the last stream of water, where it levitated, bouncing around in the fountain. Kove picked the ball up, and the fountains vanished. With a knowing look on his face, he whisked the ball once more in Brie's direction.

Brie braced herself, preparing to catch the ball, but it bounced off her stomach and slid right out of her hands, still wet from the fountains.

"*Yes!*" Taeo shouted.

"Three points!" Kove bellowed. "Round one is over. Everyone, step forward. Come on, sunshine, flair up! You're better than this."

Kove and Taeo were goading Brie on purpose. And—*Curse them!*—it was working. Brie was getting angry. Obviously Kove, Derek, and Flinton weren't going to lose this game. It would be Brie or Taeo and Cassie. Brie would not be able to stomach the look on Taeo's smug face if he outplayed her, nor could she endure his teasing that would be sure to follow. Her hands began to tingle. She felt something stir inside of her chest, and her heart sped up. She would *not* let Taeo outplay her!

Brie picked up the ball and threw it with all her might. It shot like an arrow toward Taeo, who froze in shock. At the last second, he dodged to the left, and it blasted Cassie in the face.

"That's more like it!" Kove hollered. He introduced a second ball into the game by whipping it at Derek.

Brie gasped, "Sorry Cassie!"

"No problem!" Cassie said with a smile. Her face had a large red mark, which was already beginning to swell. "I was starting to wonder if I was even in this game."

Cassie shoved her way past Taeo and drop-kicked the ball to Flinton, who closed his eyes. With a smirk on his face, Flinton took two steps to the right and caught the ball.

"Show off!" Cassie shouted.

Flinton turned around, his back to the others, and threw the ball over his head, directly at Cassie. She caught it and curtsied, then turned around in imitation of Flinton, and tossed the ball over her head. Brie wasn't sure who the ball was intended for, but it went in Derek's direction.

Suddenly, it was windy. Derek had created a miniature funnel cloud. The wind rotated around his body, entrapping the two balls. At Derek's command, the tornado released the balls, which shot out in different directions. One sailed toward Brie, while the other dove toward Taeo.

Brie sensed the ball coming and willed herself to catch it. She opened her arms, and they closed firmly around one ball as the other ball hit Taeo.

"Ha!" Brie danced a little jig, then had a brilliant idea. Concentrating as long as she dared, she let the ball loose, shrieking in excitement when it sprouted feathers and wings. Looking very similar to an overstuffed turkey, the ball lazily flapped its way over to Kove, who was bent over, holding his stomach and laughing in astonishment.

Kove caught the ball easily but was surprised by a well-aimed second ball from Taeo. He ducked his head, but the ball grazed the end of his long hair.

"That's one point!" Brie, Cassie, and Taeo shouted in unison.

"That long hair isn't quite as helpful as you thought it was," Derek teased.

Taeo sat down on the ground, thoroughly occupied with laughing at his brother. With perfect aim, Kove threw four knives in quick succession toward him. They pierced Taeo's shirt sleeves and embedded them into the ground, two on either side of his wrists, locking his hands in place. Taeo's eyes widened in fear as Kove wound up both balls and released them. They met their mark in Taeo's gut, and knocked the wind and laughter right out of him.

"That's three points and the end of round two," Kove announced.

And so the game continued. As more balls were added, it became more challenging. Brie was amazed at the speedy reactions of Kove, Derek, and Flinton, as well as their precision and creativity. She, Cassie, and Taeo racked up the most points, but as the game progressed, they hit the uncles a few times as well.

Brie found she was able to use her flairs whenever the ball came her way. She caught one ball in a net. She propelled one across the web with wind. She hit one to Flinton with a wooden paddle she summoned from his home. He called her a little thief, which horrified her until she saw him laugh. She was being exposed to more joking and teasing with her new friends than she had been in her entire life in the castle. It took some getting used to, but she liked it.

Round five lasted all of ten seconds. Derek blasted three of the five balls at Taeo and Cassie all at once. Derek was the winner of the game, finishing off with only two points. Kove and Flinton each had three, Brie had nine, and Taeo and Cassie were in last place with ten. The whole experience had been so much fun that there were no hard feelings, but Brie was secretly thrilled she had done better than Taeo.

As Kove began to magically repair the damage that had been done to the paint of the Web, Brie overheard Derek say to him, "Good call, Kove."

"She had it in her. She just needed to be fired up," Kove replied.

# *Birthday Surprises*

Early one morning, Brie was awoken by giggles and thumps coming from the other side of her bedroom door. She stretched and rolled over, pulling the covers up snugly beneath her chin, and tried to go back to sleep, but the sounds continued.

Brie lazily opened one eye and looked toward her window. The sky was just barely beginning to lighten. It was awfully early for there to be such a commotion in the upstairs hallway. Flinton's home was a lively and noisy place, but not usually until after the sun had fully risen. It was one of Brie's favorite things about living there. Instead of servants prodding her to get out of bed and begin her lessons, she was left in peace in the mornings. She half-heartedly wondered about the reason for the disturbance, but eventually she decided she didn't care. She shut her eye. She'd worry about it later.

The racket persisted, and Brie's sluggish brain began to slowly wake up. Hearing her doorknob wiggle was the trigger that finally reminded Brie what day it was. She bolted into a sitting position and grinned. It was the sixteenth day of the eleventh moon. It was her birthday!

Shoving her blankets aside, Brie jumped out of bed and

hastily dressed in a new rose-colored tunic and brown leggings. Then she rushed to her door, anxious to join whomever was on the other side, and flung it open. She was greeted by—or rather, *attacked* by—Adelaide and Cassie.

"HAPPY BIRTHDAY!" they screamed. They threw their arms around Brie in an enthusiastic hug. Their fervor knocked Brie off balance, and the three of them fell backward, crashing to the floor. All the air was forced out of Brie's lungs, but once she recovered, she couldn't stop laughing. She loved that they didn't treat her like she was breakable, even though she was still grieving over her family. Eventually, they untangled themselves and stood, then proceeded downstairs to the most important room of the house: the kitchen.

As usual, Milly's domain did not disappoint. It smelled heavenly. Milly, Ava, and Nina bustled around, chopping berries, cooking bacon, and flipping pancakes. Emilee was setting the table. They each greeted Brie with warm birthday wishes.

When Flinton entered the room, he engulfed Brie in a huge hug. He spun her around until she was dizzy, bellowing, "Happy birthday!" over and over.

When breakfast was ready, they all settled themselves around the table. Right on cue, Taeo and Kove burst through the front door. Brie's heart warmed when she saw them, especially when Kove made his way around the table to her. He pulled Brie out of her seat by her hand, spun her around in a circle, and bent over, placing a kiss on the back of her hand.

"Happy birthday, Your Highness," Kove said with a twinkle in his eyes. He examined the heavily laden table and announced, "Everything looks fabulous, but it's missing one final touch." Displaying his "flair" for the dramatic, he waved his hand, and a large vase of yellow roses appeared as a centerpiece in the middle of the table. Then he flicked his fingers in Brie's direction, and rose petals showered down from the ceiling around her, landing on her head and shoulders.

Kove's ridiculous gesture made Brie smile so wide, her face hurt. "Thanks, Kove," she said with a laugh.

Taeo plopped into a seat and said with a shrug, "There's no way I can compete with that. Happy birthday, Your Roseness."

After a luxurious breakfast, Milly shooed Brie out of the house with a bag of coins.

"You'll be in the way of your party preparations if you stay at home!" Milly said. "Have fun and spend your money on something special."

Cassie and Taeo accompanied Brie into Mount Elrad. The small village was beginning to feel like home to the princess. It was an enchanting place, a haven of goodness. As the stronghold of so many selfless people, it held an atmosphere Brie had never experienced anywhere else. She loved her home in Aldestone, but amidst the many loyal subjects, it had its fair share of irritated, foul-mouthed, and self-important citizens. The folks of Mount Elrad stood out as patient, trustworthy, and jolly people.

One morning, Brie and Cassie had been making their way to the arena, chatting with their heads bent together, not looking where they were going. They marched straight into the owner of the bakery, knocking his delivery basket out of his hands, and spilling bread all over the street. Brie had expected a scolding, but the man had merely said, "No worries.

Accidents happen." As they helped him gather the ruined rolls, which were covered in dirt from the street, he'd urged them to take a few. "I can't sell them, but if you break them open, the inside will still taste fabulous." Brie had insisted on giving him a few coins to pay for their mistake, and they'd continued on their way, happily eating the rolls' warm, yeasty centers.

The cozy village was home to a few hundred residents, but it had everything a village might need. The bakery, Kneads and Reads, had a modest-sized collection of books on one side of the store, and delicious baked goods on the other. In addition to the bakery and the Guiltless Pleasure, there was a blacksmith, a butcher, a healer, a general store, an inn that housed the visiting Blameless, and of course, the Council Hall.

When Brie first arrived in Mount Elrad, she had assumed that mostly Blameless lived in the little town, but her experts, Taeo and Cassie, had informed her otherwise. Mount Elrad was the training center for the Blameless, and consequently, most of its members came and went throughout the year. They stayed for a time, and after receiving instruction and training, they were given a task and sent away. The buildings and shops were run by non-magical citizens, many of them family members of the Blameless.

According to Taeo, all the townspeople had sworn an oath to keep Mount Elrad and the Blameless a secret. By taking the oath, the villagers pledged to remain there for the rest of their lives, because should people regularly leave, the risk that the Blameless would be exposed would be too great. If any of them broke the law and left, they would be hunted down and sentenced to death by Lord Renolt's decree.

Brie had been outraged when she'd heard about the rule. She had been ready to march into the Council Hall and demand a change, when Cassie had given Taeo's lie away by her snicker. Brie had sent him a death glare. "If you keep trying to trick me, I won't believe you when a miracle happens and you actually tell the truth."

Walking through the village together on Brie's birthday, the trio filled the air with comfortable chatter. A thin layer of snow covered the ground, and smoke billowed out of the chimneys of the homes as they passed.

They made their way into the store and began to browse the shelves. Brie was grateful for the Blackwoods, who had welcomed her into their home. She was so fed up with herself and every form of self-pampering, she didn't want to spend the money on herself. She preferred to get something the entire family could enjoy. Eventually, she settled on a tea set, thinking it would be fun to have tea parties with Milly and the girls. She'd watched the family drink coffee by the gallons, but she hadn't had one cup of tea since her arrival. She asked for it to be delivered to the Blackwoods' home, then left the store with Cassie and Taeo.

They ended up at what was quickly becoming one of Brie's favorite places in the village: the Guiltless Pleasure. Brie, Cassie, and Taeo ordered hot chocolates with warm apple pie, then settled themselves comfortably at a table near the fire.

As they took their first sips, Derek slipped into the tavern quietly. His tall, lean, muscular frame moved gracefully across the room, and Brie noticed the surrounding conversation die and the gazes of everyone in the room follow him.

The bartender's eyes widened, and he said in a high-pitched voice, "Can I get you a drink, Derek?"

Derek waved him off and continued toward Brie and her friends.

"Why is everyone acting weird?" Brie whispered, thinking Derek was garnering more attention than she had.

"Because Derek is a legend," Taeo answered, his eyes shining with admiration at Derek.

"Why?" Brie asked, noticing a few women sitting up taller in their seats.

"He's the only living Blameless with fire power," Cassie said, "which makes him a pretty big deal."

"Huh," Brie muttered. She'd been so absorbed with adjusting to her new life, she hadn't noticed.

"Kove and Flinton are a pretty big deal too," Taeo added, but before they could discuss it further, Derek arrived at their table.

Unfazed by the attention, Derek greeted them, ruffling the tops of their heads, which Brie secretly loved.

"Taeo," Derek said, "after the three of you have finished eating, please bring the girls to my place." Barely waiting for a nod of acknowledgement from Taeo, he turned to leave. Almost as an afterthought, he threw out, "Enjoy your lunch," over his shoulder as he exited.

Brie took her last bite of pie, trying not to be offended that Derek hadn't acknowledged her birthday. It was odd because just the day before, he had confirmed he would join them for her dinner celebration.

Nudging Brie's shoulder with her own, Cassie threw an understanding glance in her direction. "Don't worry. He probably forgot. Now he'll feel extra bad when he remembers."

They followed their dessert with a hearty beef stew and freshly baked rolls, because a birthday gave a person special permission to overlook rules and do things like eat dessert first. The meal was satisfying, and the company was better.

After they'd eaten an embarrassing amount of food, Cassie boldly gathered together all of the workers and customers in the tavern and led them in a very loud and off-tune "Happy Birthday" medley. At the end of the song, while everyone else sang, "Happy birthday, Princess Briana," Taeo belted out an obnoxiously loud, "Happy birthday, Your Rosey Highness!" But Brie refused to let it bother her; she didn't even spare him a glance. Instead, she stood up and thanked everyone with handshakes and hugs.

The people of Mount Elrad had learned about Brie's identity quickly after her arrival. Everyone treated her with respect and kindness, but they didn't appear to be overly captivated by her royal presence, for which Brie was thankful. Cassie assumed they were so accustomed to keeping the secrets of the Blameless that adding one more secret wasn't such a big deal.

Brie, Cassie, and Taeo left the Guiltless Pleasure, and Taeo led them west into the foothills of the surrounding mountains. After following an uneven path, they arrived at a modest-sized stone home with a grass roof. On the property was a large stable surrounded by a fenced-in pasture that was full of a variety of beautiful horses.

"*This* is where Derek lives?" Brie asked in astonishment. "He owns horses? Why have I lived here for over a moon and never visited?" Brie felt cheated.

"You've been busy, and Derek is a private man." Taeo shrugged. "Actually, both Kove and Derek live here, but Derek owns it. He purchased several horses from my oldest brother—the horse breeder in southern Predonia—but he's grown the herd on his own. Whenever they leave on a mission, I get to take care of the horses," Taeo said with pride.

"Our family boards our horses in his stable," Cassie said. "Ava comes here every day to look after them. I should have thought to bring you sooner."

"I've always loved horses." Brie sighed with longing.

Derek came out of the stable with a large smile on his normally serious face. "Welcome to my humble abode! Thank you for bringing them, Taeo."

"You're welcome. I have some chores to finish at home, but I'll see you this evening at the party." Taeo waved goodbye, then turned around and jogged back down the winding path.

Derek smirked, meeting Brie's hazel eyes with his piercing black ones, and asked, "Briana Rose, did you think I forgot what day it is?"

"You already know the answer to that," Brie said with a sheepish grin.

"I didn't forget. Happy fourteenth birthday, Princess." Derek fondly ruffled her hair again. "I thought you might enjoy spending the afternoon with my horses. Come on; you can help me feed them."

Smiling with delight, Brie grabbed Cassie's hand and followed Derek into the stable. Stall by stall, Derek walked the girls through the barn and introduced them to each of his horses. The girls fed the horses oats out of a bucket, and Derek allowed them to stroke the calmer ones. He taught Brie and Cassie about the horses' colorings and names as they went. There were horses of all different types and sizes: Greys, Blacks, Chestnuts, Palominos, Buckskins, and Appaloosas; mares, stallions, geldings, fillies, and colts.

Brie was in heaven.

Growing up, the only pets Brie'd had were a lazy old Saint Bernard who was always napping, and the bunnies that hopped around in the royal gardens, but they hardly counted. Brie's parents had been overly protective of her, forbidding anything that could possibly cause harm. They had been more cautious with Brie than they had been with Falen, and he was the heir to the throne. Brie had always thought it was because she was younger, but thinking back to it now, she realized it was because of her predicted magical powers. She thought about what Lord Renolt had said during the council meeting—that they had "limited her exposure to situations that could cause extreme emotion." Although Brie didn't understand why that was important, her parents' caution finally made sense. On several occasions, she'd asked them about learning how to ride a horse. They told her it was too risky for a child, saying she could be thrown from the horse and injured, or even bitten. They had promised to reconsider giving her riding lessons when she was older, but that time hadn't come before their deaths.

Derek led Brie and Cassie over to a beautiful yellow dun and a dapple-gray mare. Both were saddled. Brie was immediately drawn to the yellow dun and stroked her forehead. The horse nickered softly and gently bumped her head into Brie's outstretched hand.

"This beauty's name is Ember. How would you like to ride her?" Derek asked.

Brie's eyes widened. "I can't think of a better birthday present than to get to ride this horse."

Derek proceeded to give Brie her first riding lesson. Already experienced, Cassie rode alongside them on Pita, the dapple gray. Derek taught Brie simple commands as he walked beside her. Riding felt as natural to Brie as breathing, and soon she was able to increase Ember's speed to a canter.

Brie whooped in excitement, loving the feeling of the cool wind in her hair and the powerful animal running beneath her. Her chest began to burn, and she got the insane urge to magically fill Derek's pasture with wildflowers, but she refrained. Brie and Cassie spent the afternoon riding together, and it was the happiest Brie had felt in a very long time.

Eventually, Derek signaled for them to return, and the girls rode back to the stable. He helped Brie dismount and showed her how to rub Ember down with straw. As they led the horses back to their stalls, Derek asked, "So, what do you think of her?"

"I think she's the most magnificent creature I have ever seen," Brie said reverently.

"That's what I was hoping." Derek's eyes twinkled as he turned to face Brie. He cleared his throat and said with a small smile, "Happy birthday, Briana Rose. She's my gift to you."

Brie stopped walking and stared at Derek in shock. "What?" She figured she must have heard him incorrectly.

"*What?*" she shouted again.

"Ember is yours. Happy birthday," Derek said with a laugh.

Brie recovered from her shock and jumped up and down, screaming in excitement. Cassie joined her, and together they jumped and hugged and screamed. Shaking his head, Derek watched their enthusiastic response with a smile.

Brie broke away from Cassie and flung her arms around Derek, giving him a kiss on his cheek. "Thank you, Derek!" Then she dropped her voice to a whisper and added for his ears only, "I think you might be my favorite uncle."

Derek laughed, then grabbed her face and held it between his hands. His eyes scanned hers, and his expression grew serious. "I'm going to teach you to be one of the best riders in all of Predonia. I'll show you how to use your bow as you ride. You'll become a warrior princess whose name will strike fear into the hearts of your enemies." He spoke fiercely, his eyes flashing almost angrily, and he lifted his chin, jutting it out, as though daring Brie to contradict him.

Brie took in Derek's words, and goosebumps broke out on her arms. He spoke with such conviction that she believed him. "And then we're going to defeat Vaylec and take back my kingdom," she added.

"That's exactly what we're going to do," Derek agreed.

After Brie and Cassie arrived at home, Ava immediately swept them upstairs to the second floor. She waved them into her bedroom and followed, shutting the door behind them.

"A princess should never, ever, spend her birthday dinner in trousers," Ava said, looking pointedly at Brie's clothing. "It just isn't appropriate. We can't have you turning into a heathen while you're here in Mount Elrad," she joked. "I've been working on something all week, and I just finished it today. I want you to try it on."

Ava pulled an elegant forest green gown out of her wardrobe. It was crafted out of satin with layers of contrasting lace covering the skirt and arms, creating both a delicate and playful appearance.

Brie's jaw dropped open as she looked at the beautiful gown. "You made this?"

"Yes, my mother taught me to sew before she died," Ava answered matter-of-factly. "Someone had to keep the family clothed, and it certainly wasn't going to be Flinton," she scoffed. "Although I'm sure he would've been delighted to knit us all dresses, but it would've taken him years. It takes him forever to manage a pair of mittens. Anyway, I noticed you only have casual clothing, and I wanted to give you something for your birthday. This seemed like the perfect thing."

After a quick bath to wash off the dirt and sweat from riding, Brie tried on the gown with Ava and Cassie's help. It fit perfectly, and Brie wondered if Kove had anything to do with it. The shoulders of the dress were puffy, the corset was snug around her waist, and the skirt billowed out from her hips to the floor.

"It's amazing, Ava. Thank you," Brie said, looking down at the forest green satin. "I've enjoyed wearing my leggings and tunics. I never thought I would say this, but it's nice to be back in a gown. It reminds me of who I am."

"It was my pleasure." Ava smiled. "It looks lovely on you, and it brings out the green in your hazel eyes. Now we just need to do something with your hair."

Ava opened her bedroom door and yelled down the hall, "Emilee, it's your turn!"

After a few moments, Emilee—who, according to Taeo, "no longer knew how to have fun"—entered the room. For once, she seemed excited and not bored. Brie made a mental note to tell Taeo that he had been wrong.

"Sit down right here," Emilee ordered, pointing at the chair at Ava's desk.

Brie obeyed, noticing a theme among Flinton's sisters. All of them were headstrong and bossy, but not necessarily in a bad way. They knew what they wanted, and they found a way to get it. Memories of sneaking into the council meeting with Cassie filled Brie's head, and she smiled.

Emilee's fingers gently brushed the tangles out of Brie's long golden hair. Then she deftly went to work, creating a masterpiece. She wove four intricate braids down the length of Brie's head from temple to nape, then gathered them together, forming one long braid that twisted into a bun at her neck. Emilee left out a few strands of loose curls to frame Brie's face. When she finally finished and stepped back, Brie took a look in the mirror. The hairstyle was elegant, but fun and unique. It had a practicality and beauty that befitted a warrior princess, Brie thought, shivering as she remembered Derek's solemn words. Brie loved it.

"Emilee, this is fantastic," Brie said as she gazed into the mirror. "It's better than anything I ever had done in Aldestone. When I return to the castle, I'm taking you with me," she joked.

"Don't tempt me, Brie, because that would be a dream come true." Emilee sighed with longing.

Together, the three sisters examined Brie.

"You're only missing one thing," Cassie said. "Your crown! Please, please, will you wear it tonight? I've never seen a princess in action before." She clasped her hands together under her chin, begging. "Can I fetch it from your room?"

Brie couldn't help wondering if Cassie even knew what it meant to see a princess in action. Until recently, Brie's life had been full of rigorous education, boring routines, and keeping up appearances at balls and formal functions. It wasn't just about appearing glamorous. It entailed a lot of hard work, even when she wasn't in the mood for it. But Brie didn't want to disappoint Cassie. "Why not? It *is* my birthday." She smiled and shrugged.

With a squeal of delight, Cassie dashed out of Ava's room and ran across the hallway to Brie's. She returned, carrying the crown balanced on a pillow, walking in slow, exaggerated steps. She placed the crown on Brie's head like she was performing a sacred ritual, then stepped back and curtsied so low, Brie worried she would have trouble rising.

Ava rolled her eyes and gave Cassie's bottom a hard smack, causing her sister to lurch forward. Cassie made the best of it and somersaulted, landing at Brie's feet. Her staticky hair stuck out in every direction as she looked up at Brie. "Your humble servant is at your service, Your Royal Highness," she said, her voice quivering an octave above usual. Then she and Brie burst into laughter.

They eventually regained their composure, and everyone stood back to look at Brie. The Blackwood girls *ooh*ed and *ah-h*ed, looking extremely pleased with the result of their efforts.

"Wait for my signal before you come downstairs, Brie," Ava instructed. They pulled Brie to the top of the stairs, then descended without her.

From the top of stairwell, Brie heard Ava announce in a clear, loud voice. "Dear citizens of Predonia: Blackwoods, LeBlancs, and Hawke. May I present to you on this very special day, the day of her fourteenth birthday, your future queen, Princess Briana Rose Eyrhill."

"Goodness, all we need is a trumpet," Taeo muttered. Brie could just barely hear him, but even he couldn't squash her good spirits.

Brie descended one step at a time, slowly and purposefully, as she had been taught by her mother. If they wanted to make a big deal out of her birthday, then she would do her part. The stairs ended in the Blackwood's living room. As Brie's foot came off the last step, everyone stood. Taeo and Kove were present, along with their parents. Derek was there, looking at her with a fiercely proud expression on his face. And of course, Flinton, Milly, and the girls. Flinton had watery red eyes, and the girls were beaming.

Brie looked around the room at her friends, surprised to see that every one of their expressions held respect. Even Taeo was looking at her with something that looked like awe. In unison, the men bowed and the women curtsied.

"Thank you. Please rise, subjects," Brie said, but then ruined it with a giggle. "Oh, this is ridiculous. I'm honored by your respect, but I'm still Brie. And I am very, very hungry. Can we get the party started?"

"As you wish, Your Highness." Milly came forward and pecked her on the cheek. "You look breathtaking tonight, my dear."

Milly served another phenomenal meal of lamb chops, roasted parsnips, and carrots with herbed garlic bread. They finished with a mouth-watering chocolate cake, fresh strawberries and cream, and tea served from Brie's new tea set. It was a perfect end to the meal.

As Brie bit into an exceptionally sweet strawberry, she asked, "Where in Predonia did you find strawberries at this time of year?"

Milly smiled and winked. "My flair is with food. I created them."

"Wow," Brie said in awe. "That makes so much sense. Your food is amazing. I can't believe I've been here this long and never thought to ask you what your gift was," she added, feeling guilty yet again, and making a birthday resolution to be less self-absorbed.

"You should try playing Flair Ball with her," Kove laughed. "It's impossible to win. One time she turned the ball into a peach pie, and I just opened my mouth and let it hit me in the face."

Brie laughed at the mental image of Kove's face covered in pie.

"It's true," Derek confirmed. "No one can concentrate

when Milly's in the Web. We usually end the game early, and everyone goes in search of food. Flinton is a lucky man."

Milly smiled, and her cheeks turned rosy. "I like to think Flinton married me for reasons other than my unmatched skills in the kitchen."

Everyone laughed as Flinton grabbed Milly and pulled her into his lap. "I would eat dirt every day if it meant I could keep you as my wife. Never doubt it," he said, nuzzling her hair.

"They are so gross," Cassie complained, rolling her eyes.

Although Brie had already received several gifts, a few more were presented to her. Nina gave her a book, explaining with a large smile that it was her absolute favorite, and she hoped Brie would enjoy it as much as she had. Flinton presented her with the finished product of his handmade scarf and mittens. Brie couldn't resist a glance at Ava, who gave her a knowing grin. The scarf and mittens weren't perfect by any means, but they were a labor of love, which made Brie's eyes water.

Brie thanked Flinton with a hug and whispered, "You might be my favorite uncle."

Flinton chuckled and gave her a wink. "It will be our little secret," he said.

The LeBlanc family presented Brie with a stunning pair of new shoes that matched her dress perfectly. It was clear that a lot of thought had gone into making sure Brie looked the part of a princess tonight. It wasn't until Kove bent down to help her into the new shoes that Brie realized she had spent her birthday dinner barefoot. Her mother would have been horrified.

The party carried on late into the night and ended with Cassie joining Brie in her room for a sleepover. They lay close together, their heads sharing the same pillow, talking and laughing until the early hours of the morning. As their talking died down, Brie heaved a contented sigh.

It had been a wonderful day. Far better than Brie could have imagined a birthday without her family would be. She sniffed. The ache in her heart was still there, but somehow it had become more bearable because of the family and friends that surrounded her.

"Thank you, Cassie," Brie said.

"I know I'm awesome," Cassie said, deadpan, "but what part of my awesomeness are you thanking?"

"Do you know who you sound like right now?" Brie asked.

Cassie sighed. "Yes, I know: Taeo. How awful of me."

"Thank you for being my friend," Brie said seriously. Then she playfully added, "And for being so awesome."

Cassie smiled, but she became serious too when she said, "I needed a best friend, and so did you. We needed each other."

They lay in contented silence, and Brie noticed Cassie staring at her crown. Brie kept it on her dressing table in front of the mirror. Recently, she'd developed a habit of placing it on her head every morning and looking at herself in the mirror. It reminded her of what had been taken away, and why she was training. Cassie's eyes left the crown, and she looked at Brie. Her brow furrowed. Nudging Brie's foot, she whispered gently, "Tell me about them."

Brie swallowed. She knew Cassie was referring to her family. They'd never spoken at length about them before. "Alright," Brie whispered back. "What do you want to know?"

Cassie rolled onto her side and faced Brie. Tucking her hands under her cheek, she answered, "I don't care what. Just tell me something happy."

Brie stared at the ceiling and thought about some of her favorite memories. For some reason, she didn't want to share Falen tonight. It felt too difficult, perhaps because of the lavender slippers she was wearing at that moment.

Instead, Brie thought about her mom and dad. There were plenty of good memories to choose from. Her parents had been respected and well-loved by the citizens of Predonia, but as their daughter, Brie had seen the very best parts of them. Finally, she selected one that felt safe to talk about.

"We had lots of important visitors in the castle," Brie started slowly. "Other kings and royal diplomats. They would hold private dinners to discuss secret information, and Falen and I weren't allowed to attend. It didn't bother Falen, and he always found something else to do, but I hated being left out. I didn't care what was being discussed; I just wanted to be close to my mom and dad. When I was little, probably around four or five years old, I started sneaking into the dining room early and hiding under the table so I could spend the meal with them in secret." Brie's eyes started to burn a little, but she smiled and continued. "Partway through the meal, I would eventually get hungry or tired and curl up by my mom's feet, hugging her legs and blowing my cover. They must have had a secret means of communication, because my dad would slip pieces of food to me under the table, and as long as I was quiet, they let me stay. I would fall asleep, and my dad would carry me to bed late at night after the guests left the room. It became so common that my mother started to leave a pillow for me under the table. When they tucked me into bed at night, they would tell me I shouldn't be sneaking around, but I think they liked me being there just as much as I did."

Cassie was quiet for a moment. "They sound wonderful, Brie. I wish I could have met them."

"They were the best, Cassie. The absolute best. I wish you could have met them too. They would have loved you." Brie was certain of it. Now that she had started to talk about them, she didn't want to quit. "I look like my mother. I have her same golden hair and hazel eyes. But my mother always said I had my father's zest for life, whatever that means."

Cassie laughed quietly but didn't say anything.

They were silent for long enough that the tiring day caught up with Brie, and she began to doze off. But she was jolted awake again by Cassie.

"So, am I correct in assuming you've been filled with all sorts of kingdom secrets, and if I tortured you long enough, those secrets would be mine?" Cassie cackled an evil laugh, shattering the quiet night.

Brie giggled. "Go to sleep before I decide to have you thrown in prison."

# Game Playing

Brie awoke full of excitement. She wasn't going to the arena to train today. She was staying home, and she, Flinton, and his family had plans to play the game Flinton had created while on their journey from Aldestone to Mount Elrad, which they had since named "Find the Blameless." Similar to hide-and-seek, the object of the game was for Brie to find the Blameless in the room using only her magical abilities. Although it was technically a form of training, including Cassie and the others made it feel more like fun.

However, after Brie dressed and walked down to the kitchen, she found her three uncles eating breakfast, deep in a discussion, with serious looks on their faces. When Flinton saw Brie, his face broke into a smile.

"Sit down, Brie," he said. "We've been talking about you."

"Uh-oh," Brie said, sliding into a chair beside Flinton. "Should I be worried?"

Kove smirked but shook his head. "We were just discussing how, when you're passionate enough about something, your powers should work, just like they did during Flair Ball. Let's talk about the times when you successfully performed magic."

"Okay," Brie said slowly, her brows furrowed in confusion.

"What were you feeling when you summoned your crown?" Kove asked.

"I wanted revenge," Brie answered without hesitation. "Plus, I'd just made the connection that I was Blameless, and I wanted to prove it."

"Your emotions were definitely high," Derek agreed. "What about when you summoned the bow during our first archery lesson?"

Brie tilted her head to the side and smiled. "I was excited! I just knew I *really* wanted to learn how to use a bow."

"You were passionate about it. I should know," Derek said with a grin and a shake of his head.

"And what were you feeling when you created the locket for Adelaide?" Flinton prompted her next.

"Grateful. I wanted her to know I was thankful for her kind words."

"Briana," Derek began quietly, "we haven't talked about this yet, but can you tell us about the night you escaped from the castle? How were you not seen?"

Brie knew Derek well enough by now to know he wouldn't have asked out of morbid curiosity, or to upset her. There was a purpose in everything he said or did. Because of that, Brie shared some of the details of that night with them.

"Vaylec's men burst into my bedroom with swords." Brie gulped, remembering how terrified she'd been. "Bloody swords. We heard my brother's scream cut off down the hall, and my mother yelled at me to run, but I was frozen, and I couldn't move at first. I saw the soldiers kill my parents, and then I turned and fled. I went through my bedroom and into my dressing room. Inside my closet is a hidden passageway that leads down to my maids' quarters. I ran through that passageway to the servants' exit and out into the street." Brie's voice trembled with emotion. "The streets were full of soldiers and citizens. I don't know how they didn't notice me, but I ran through them, down into the city until I came to the smithy."

"Come here, short stuff." Flinton pulled her chair closer to his and put his arm around her shoulder. "And we know the rest of the story."

Derek, however, pressed on. "You were terrified and likely didn't know what you were doing, but Briana, I believe the power of invisibility saved you that night. It's the only thing that makes sense. Once again, it was at a time when your emotions were high. You wanted nothing more than to get to safety in that moment."

Brie nodded. "That's true," she whispered, the terrible memories clogging her throat and making it difficult to speak louder.

There was a long silence, and then Flinton drained his mug and smiled, but for once it didn't reach his eyes. "Let's get this game started." He stood and took his breakfast dishes to the sink. "Girls!" he shouted off into the house. "Who's ready for Find the Blameless?"

His cry was met with whoops and cheers. Derek and Kove slipped out the front door as the family gathered in the living room, scattering themselves across the furniture and floor. "Remember," Flinton said gently, making eye contact with each of his sisters one by one. "Be totally silent so Brie can focus."

Flinton covered Brie's eyes with a blindfold and spun her around in a circle three times. From behind her, Flinton gave instructions. "Milly is the only Blameless in the room other than me. Derek put a shield around me earlier to block my signal, so you can focus completely on Milly. I want you to find her. Place your right hand over your heart; it will help you connect better with your powers."

Lifting her hand, Brie placed it over her heart and closed her eyes, even though she was blindfolded.

"Pay attention to the air around you," Flinton instructed. "Concentrate, listen, and feel. You should begin to sense a vibration, like a humming. Only a Blameless puts off this vibration."

Brie did as she'd been instructed and concentrated on her surroundings. She knew the random hums and buzzes she'd been hearing since she'd met her uncles belonged to a Blameless, but she'd never been able to successfully connect them to their owner. As she focused now, she didn't hear anything other than the occasional scuff of a shoe across the floor. Because of Flinton's warning to his sisters, it was surprisingly quiet in their home for once.

Brie continued to concentrate, trying to hear something other than the surrounding silence. She could feel her heart pounding beneath her hand, so she decided to focus on its beat. She was desperate to learn how to use her magic in a controlled manner; otherwise, she would never be able to defeat Vaylec. Her anger toward him had grown into a living and breathing thing that demanded revenge. She let this motivate her now.

With the beat of her heart as her guide, Brie discovered she could hear a quiet humming behind her. At first, she thought it was Flinton, humming in her ear. But she realized it couldn't be him. Kove was the joker, not Flinton. She listened more intently and decided there was definitely a noise coming from behind her, so she turned around.

"Good girl," Flinton said quietly, turning with her.

Slowly and hesitantly, Brie took two steps in the direction of the noise. There was no difference in the sound, so she took a couple more steps forward. The humming grew a little bit louder. She placed one foot forward and to the left, but the vibrations seemed to slow down. She reversed her footing and took two steps to the right. The pitch of the humming got higher and faster. Milly had to be in this direction.

Brie took another step to the right. And another. She followed the vibrations in the air as they increased in frequency, signaling she was getting closer. Now that she was in tune to the ever-so-small shifts in the signal, she understood why she'd never been able to track it before. It was difficult to notice without intense concentration.

"Now reach out your hand," Flinton instructed.

Brie lifted her left arm and felt fingers wrap around her palm. She knew it was Milly because a warm jolt ran up her hand and into her chest. It was surprising, but not unpleasant or painful.

The room erupted in cheers. Brie had done it! She yanked off her blindfold and opened her eyes to see Milly beaming at her.

"That's our girl," Milly said proudly.

Laughing jovially, Flinton clapped Brie on the back with a

little too much enthusiasm, propelling Brie forward into Milly's lap. Brie smiled sheepishly, but Milly simply laughed and embraced her warmly. There was never a dull moment in their home, and Brie loved it.

Taking Brie's hand and pulling her out of Milly's lap, Flinton declared, "Let's do it again. Brie, put your blindfold back on, and everyone change places."

Winter had settled firmly over Mount Elrad. A blizzard had blown in with terrific fury, leaving the town covered in a thick, beautiful white blanket. In the weeks since her birthday, Brie had continued her training with her uncles, but part of her day now included horseback riding with Ember and Derek.

The morning after the blizzard, Brie was shocked to find Derek at the Blackwoods' house, expecting to take her riding. She merely rolled her eyes.

"How am I supposed to ride through all of this snow?" she asked incredulously, sweeping her hand in the direction of the door. "Have you looked outside? The snow comes up to the windows!" She paused and tilted her head to the side as she realized something. "Wait, how did you get here?"

Derek simply winked and said, "Follow me, and you'll see."

Brie bundled up in her warmest clothes, donning her scarf and mittens from Flinton, and followed Derek outside. She was shocked to discover a perfectly clear, snow-free path—or perhaps tunnel was a better description—leaving the Blackwoods' home.

"How did you manage that?" She pointed at the path.

"Watch." Derek lifted his hands, fingers up and palms out, and directed them toward a large snowbank. The air rippled in waves, moving from his palms to the snow. In a few moments, the pile of snow was gone, leaving nothing but wet grass in its place.

"It's one of my gifts from the sun," Derek explained with a shrug. "Now, how about that ride? I've already cleared the pasture."

"You have a solution for everything," Brie said.

"I'm not sure if that is a compliment or a complaint," Derek said with a ghost of a grin on his fierce face.

"Neither am I," Brie answered with a raised eyebrow. "It's frustrating, and it's wonderful. But today, I've decided it's wonderful because I'll admit I can't wait to see Ember."

Together they ventured down the cleared path, which led them around the edge of Mount Elrad to Derek's place. As they trekked over the hills, Derek brought up Brie's training plan for the holidays. "With the Gifting just around the corner, we'll take a break until after the New Year, but you can come to my place to ride Ember as much as you wish."

"Then you'll see me every day," Brie said, "as long as the path stays clear. You might even get sick of me."

"Try me, warrior princess," Derek responded with a raised brow.

"You know, that has a nice ring to it." Brie beamed.

True to her word, Brie continued to ride every day. She loved every minute she spent with Ember. Sometimes she would ride alone, but more often than not, Cassie accompanied her.

Derek set up various targets for Brie in the pasture and the surrounding trees. With her headband in place, Brie spent hours practicing with her bow while she rode Ember. She found that hitting the target from a horse was much more challenging than it was on her feet. Nevertheless, Brie's arrows occasionally met their mark. Some days, Derek would ride with her and give her tips. He sank every arrow into the bullseye every single time. He certainly provided an example to follow.

On the odd day, Brie and Cassie were blessed with Taeo's presence. Taeo rode with the same confidence with which he walked, talked, and bragged. He took immediately to the challenge of target practice, but instead of using a bow, Taeo preferred knives, just like his brother. Much to Brie's dismay, he was a natural.

With free time on her hands, Brie not only rode, but she played. Like she was making up for lost time, she played to her heart's content. Flinton's sisters and Taeo often took part in the fun. They went sledding, built snowmen, made snow forts, and drank plenty of warm cider, hot chocolate, and tea.

One evening, as they waited on Flinton, Derek, and Kove for dinner, the Blackwood girls plus Brie and Taeo hid behind a wall of snow with a heaping pile of snowballs. As the men came into view, Milly stood up and shouted, "Attack!"

The next few moments were complete chaos as snowballs rained down on the men. Using their quick reflexes and expertise in battle, within seconds, the men were retaliating with snowballs of their own.

Cassie yelled into the frenzy, "Don't you dare think about using your gifts right now, you Blameless machos!"

"I don't need my gifts to do this," Kove teased as he ran at them and jumped over their wall of snow. He tackled Taeo and began to rub snow in his face. Taeo kicked, hit, and pushed his brother, but he couldn't escape. He yelled for help, but his cry was muffled by the snow packed in his mouth.

Brie and Cassie looked at each other, then launched themselves onto Kove's back. Trying to save Taeo, they pummeled Kove with snow. Cassie shoved snow down the neck of his tunic while Brie removed his hat and heaped snow on top of his head.

Flinton appeared to have taken personal offense to the fact that Milly had sounded the attack and was seeking revenge on her by dumping her headfirst into a snowdrift.

Derek was left to fend for himself against Ava, Emilee, Nina, and Adelaide. The fierce Blameless warrior was lying on his back, buried in snow, when Brie finally looked up from her mission of saving Taeo.

Eventually, a truce was called, and everyone trooped inside to enjoy hot tea and coffee with a side of homemade cinnamon bread.

As they warmed themselves with drinks and sweets, Derek spoke up.

"We were returning from a meeting with Lord Renolt before that very special surprise attack."

Everyone laughed.

Derek grew sober and continued, "Unfortunately, he didn't have good news to share with us. Renolt's scouts have returned with reports that two Blameless have gone missing in Predonia."

The room grew quiet. Brie asked, "Does he know what happened to them?"

"We don't know any details yet, but we think Vaylec took them," Kove answered.

Derek explained further, "One of the missing Blameless is gifted with the power of invisibility. He may have been specifically targeted because of his gift."

Brie gasped. "What does that mean?"

Flinton answered, "It's downright concerning and suspicious, and until we know more about what has happened, you are no longer allowed to go anywhere by yourself, Brie. You know we suspect Vaylec has found a way to control the Blameless, and he's just taken the only Blameless in Predonia with the gift of invisibility other than you. It can't be a coincidence. We believe you are his main target. So from now on, you will be accompanied by either a Blameless, or Cassie and Taeo, wherever you go."

The Eve of the Gifting was approaching. The rest of Predonia was likely immersed in holiday preparations, but not Vaylec. He had far too much work to do, though he had no doubts that his time for celebrating would eventually come. He sat on his throne and watched as four of his guards filed in, escorting two men. With Violet's powers of persuasion now transferred to him, Vaylec was confident his men would hold their tongues and keep silent.

One of the captives was middle-aged and stocky, with brown hair that was graying at the temples. The other was younger and thinner, perhaps in his early thirties, with shortly cropped blond hair. Coming to a stop before his throne, the guards bowed deeply, and Vaylec couldn't stop the smile of satisfaction from spreading across his face. After feeling inferior for so much of his life, he loved how it felt to be in control.

The two captives failed to bow, which didn't go unnoticed by the guards. Vaylec looked on in approval as one guard kicked the backs of the prisoners' legs sharply with his boot, causing them to collapse forward onto their knees.

"Show respect for Lord Vaylec," the guard snarled.

Wisely, the captives stayed on their knees with their heads bent.

"Look at me," Vaylec demanded.

Raising their heads, the captives made eye contact with him.

"State your names," he commanded with a lift of his chin.

The middle-aged man answered in a strong, clear voice, "I am Jarvis, my lord."

"And I am Torin, my lord," the younger one said in a higher-pitched cadence.

Vaylec straightened on his throne in excitement. It seemed they had finally found the correct men, but he had to be certain. He turned to Adira, who was standing beside him, and questioned her.

"Are these the men I've been searching for?"

"Yes, Your Grace. It is them," Adira answered in an emotionless voice.

Vaylec examined the men who were still on their knees in front of him, then stood up. "I know you both are Blameless, and I've summoned you for a specific reason. I have a special task for you." He descended the steps of his throne and commanded, "Stand up."

The captives rose from their knees. Vaylec stepped close, no more than an arm's reach from them, and paused, first in front of Jarvis and then Torin. He felt the now-familiar tug around his heart, and he watched with satisfaction as their eyes widened and they clutched at their chests in apparent pain.

"It worked yet again," he said with a triumphant smile. His smile faded and he continued. "All of you Blameless are the same. You assume you're untouchable, but that is no longer true. You're about to experience a new reality." His head swung to the older of the two men. "I've done my research. Jarvis, I know you have the power of invisibility. Isn't that so?" He didn't wait for a response. "Show it to me," he demanded. "Disappear now."

Jarvis was breathing heavily, and the look on his face was one of shock and confusion. Regardless, he vanished.

Vaylec's eyebrows raised, and a triumphant gleam lit his eyes. "Show yourself," he commanded.

In an instant, Jarvis reappeared.

"Extraordinary," Vaylec mused.

He then turned his attention to Torin. "You have a very useful gift as well, which you will perform for me momentarily, but I have some rules to establish first."

Vaylec began to pace slowly in front of the men. "In case you had any doubts about what just transpired, let me clarify it for you. I am your new master. I now have control over your ability to use your powers. You must do exactly as I say and use your powers exactly as I command. If you try to resist, you will find you won't have the ability to disobey. I command you not to speak of this to anyone: not family, nor friends, neighbors, or other Blameless. Your Blameless consciences may not like some of the things you will be ordered to do, but I forbid you from harming yourselves or another Blameless as a means of avoiding my orders. If you somehow find a way around my instructions, there will be very grave consequences."

Vaylec stopped pacing and looked each of the men in the eyes as he addressed them. "Jarvis, I know you have been married for twenty years and have four children. Torin, you are newly married with a baby on the way. Isn't that correct?"

Vaylec could see the fear in their eyes as they nodded. Satisfied, he continued, "Like I said, I've done my research. I imagine you both love your families very much. It would be a tragedy if something were to happen to them."

Vaylec stepped closer, so close that his breath fanned across their faces. "I have eyes and ears everywhere, and you can be sure I will find out. One false move, and your families will pay!"

# Gifts and Shadows

Brie was on pins and needles after Flinton announced his new rule. She jumped at loud noises and imagined something sinister in every shadow. She was worried Vaylec's army of evil men would appear out of the foggy mountain mist at any moment to capture her. When she confessed her fears, Flinton reassured her it would be impossible for an army to navigate the narrow mountain paths that led to Mount Elrad. Yet, despite his claim, two guards were newly stationed at the opening of the tunnel.

Ever since receiving the report of the two missing Blameless, Brie's uncles had been holed up in the Council Hall from sunup to sundown. To make matters worse, Brie, Cassie, and Taeo were prohibited from spying. Flinton warned the three of them that if they were seen or sensed within a stone's throw of the Council Hall, they would forfeit their Gifting presents. They grumbled about it but obeyed. None of them wanted to risk the possibility of no gifts, but in Brie's opinion, Flinton's threat was just further proof there was reason to be concerned.

Brie no longer spent time alone except in the confines of her own room. Being a princess, she was already used to the lack of privacy, so the Blackwoods' constant supervision didn't really bother her.

It didn't seem to bother Taeo, either. In fact, he acted as if he had finally found his life's purpose. Fuel had been added to the healthy fire of his already inflated self-worth, and he now considered himself to be Brie's personal bodyguard.

As Brie got ready for the town's festival on the Eve of the Gifting, Taeo periodically knocked on her door.

"Is everything alright, Your Princess-ship? Are you safe? Should I come in?"

"I'm almost ready," Brie yelled toward the door. She thought Taeo was finished after one jab, but she wasn't that lucky. He kept going. "You're taking forever. We're going to be late for the gathering."

For a moment, Brie debated climbing out her second story window just to give Taeo a panic attack, but she grudgingly admitted that a broken leg would certainly make them late. Instead, she took one last look at her braided hair, another creation of Emilee's, and opened her door. "I realize I take a lot longer to get ready than you do," she said, trying to look down her nose at him. This was pretty much impossible, since he was a head taller than her. "But for the love of the Blameless, have some patience. My hair hangs clear down to my Blameless Highness and yours doesn't." She rolled her eyes, trying not to grin, and brushed past Taeo, making her way downstairs. Her ears caught the sound of his snicker coming from behind her, and she grinned. He was fun to tease when he wasn't driving her crazy. They joined Cassie, who had been stuffing her mouth with cookies while waiting for them in the kitchen, and together the trio left the house and made their way into the village.

"Brie, we are going to have a good time tonight!" Cassie commanded, brushing crumbs off her hands as she finished her last bite. "We are *not* going to worry about the evils of the world until tomorrow." She paused. "No, I take that back. Tomorrow is the Gifting. We'll worry about evil the day after the Gifting, or maybe a week after the Gifting . . ."

"Okay, I understand. You can stop now." Brie elbowed Cassie playfully.

"Actually . . ." Cassie gave Brie her most mischievous smile. "I could keep this up for a really, really long time."

"What would I do without you, Cassie?" Brie sighed, asking herself as much as her friend.

"Let's never find out," Cassie said happily.

"Tell me what to expect tonight," Brie said, changing the topic. "I've never been to anything like this before."

"It's tradition that on the Eve of every Gifting, the entire village gathers in the center of town for an enormous bonfire, delicious food, and music," Taeo said. "There's dancing and singing, and we even have a retelling of the original Gifting, when the Blameless were first gifted with magic." He sighed happily. "It's the best night of the year."

"Wow," Brie said. "I can't believe that for my entire life, I just thought of the Gifting as an excuse to exchange presents. Now, here I am at the Blameless headquarters, celebrating the anniversary of the first Gifting with actual Blameless!"

"And you're like . . . the queen of the Blameless." Cassie grinned.

"Ooh, good one, Cassie," Taeo said. "You just gave me more possibilities for names."

"Tonight is going to be so much fun!" Cassie shouted, ignoring him. She tipped her face toward the sky and spun around in a circle with her arms out to the sides. "Hurry up," she said after finishing her spin. "I'm starving!" She grabbed Brie's hand and skipped forward. Cassie reached back for Taeo's, but he yanked his hand out of the way.

"I am *not* holding hands or skipping with you," he said. His face paled, and his eyes widened in horror.

The three friends arrived in the center of the village to find it already packed with people. The Council Hall was directly across from Kneads and Reads, the bakery. The general store and the blacksmith stood to either side, creating a large square in the middle. An impressive fire blazed in the center of the square, and whole hogs roasted over the flames. Torches had been placed around the buildings, providing ample light for the festivities, while the mountains beyond remained shrouded in darkness.

The villagers congregated in small groups with drinks in their hands, talking and laughing, while musicians played a jolly tune. The trio made their way over to a stand operated by the owners of the Guiltless Pleasure, which was offering free drinks. Brie got a hot chocolate, Cassie got a warm apple cider, and Taeo ordered a warm whiskey, which Kove snatched out of his hands before he had a chance to bring it to his lips.

"Hey, that's mine!" Taeo tried to snatch it back, but Kove ducked away.

"It most certainly is not," Kove said as he took a large sip of the whiskey. "You're too young."

"But it's freezing!" Taeo complained. "It would warm me up. Plus, *you* were the one who told me last Gifting Eve that I could try some this year."

"Don't trust what I said a year ago," Kove said. "I have three hundred and sixty-five opportunities to change my mind. But try again next year," he added with a wink. Then he leaned a little closer to Taeo and muttered, "You're on duty. It could addle your brain, and you need to stay sharp."

Taeo's attitude changed when he heard this. He threw his shoulders back importantly and said, "Yes, I suppose you're right. It's a sacrifice for the greater good."

Kove smacked him on the back. "That's the spirit!" He winked and drained the rest of the whiskey.

Soon, the hogs were removed from the fire, and the meat was shredded and served with bread and potatoes. The delectable aroma of smoked meat and herbed potatoes filled the air. Kove, together with a few other Blameless, conjured benches around the fire for eating and visiting. Brie sat close to the flames with her friends and enjoyed the mouth-watering meal. She glanced around the square and smiled as she watched the happy villagers enjoy the magical evening.

As Brie's gaze swept past the blacksmith, the trees at the edge of the square rustled. Brie peered intently into the shadowy darkness and saw that two men were creeping through the woods. Her heart rate sped up. Why would they be lurking in the forest and not enjoying the meal with the rest of the villagers?

Brie turned her head and whispered in Cassie's ear, "Look past the blacksmith and into the trees. Do you see two men?"

Cassie followed her gaze, but the men had disappeared. The corners of her mouth turned down, her eyebrows furrowed, and she shook her head. "Brie, what did I say? No worrying tonight. Worrying and celebrating should never be mixed together. Remember, it's safe in Mount Elrad. Nothing bad ever happens here. It's boring. At least, it was before you came along," she added with an enormous grin. "If you saw two men in the woods, they probably just had to sneak off to relieve themselves. Give them some privacy, for goodness' sake. Don't ruin your night—or more importantly, their night—by falsely worrying." Then she snickered. "Can you imagine if we sent Derek, Flinton, and Kove charging after them with swords, only to find them with their pants down? It would scare the crap right out of them, if they hadn't already gone."

Brie nearly fell off the back of her bench laughing.

The fiddlers and musicians began to play a lively tune, and couples got up and began to dance around the open space in the square. Kove came over to Brie and grabbed her hand, pulling her to her feet.

"Come on, sunshine; let's dance," he said, spinning her in place.

The next few hours were a whirlwind of fun, and Brie quickly forgot about the men in the shadows. She experienced dancing like she had never seen in the castle. People jumped, twisted, spun, and kicked. She was taught to lift her knees and tap her feet and twirl to the music. Partners swung each other around high into the air. It was exhausting and exhilarating. Flinton danced with Milly, each of his sisters, and Brie. Cassie somehow managed to partner with every man in the village, young and old. Kove spent extra time dancing with Ava, whose radiant smile could have lit up the entire village square. Derek had a never-ending line of admirers who awaited their turn in his arms. Brie danced with almost as many people as Cassie and got to know more villagers as the evening progressed into night.

At the conclusion of one of the band's many moving melodies, a sudden hush fell over the crowd as Lord Renolt climbed the steps of the Council Hall. He made his way across the spacious landing, which functioned as a stage between two of the marble pillars. Elevated above the crowd, he announced, "Villagers and Blameless, settle in and relax for this year's retelling of the first Gifting."

The crowd gathered around the portico on stools, logs, and chairs as they prepared for the story. Having received their cue, six villagers ascended the steps and took their places around Renolt. The women wore flowing, shimmery white gowns, and the men wore loose, billowing white tunics and pants.

Musicians began to play, providing a slow background medley, and the six villagers on the stage started to sway to the sound.

Lord Renolt began his tale.

"Over fifteen hundred years ago, the Three sibling gods created our world. Terren, the oldest, shaped the earth and everything that grows in it. Cael, the youngest, formed the air, the winds, and the atmosphere. And Solis, their sister, forged the sun, moon, and stars. Together, the Three created the human race. Then they returned to their homes in the heavens.

"For the first several hundred years, there was peace in the kingdoms of Predonia, Westlor, Estelon, and Alderia. People lived and thrived together in harmony." As Lord Renolt spoke, the dancers broke off into three pairs. They looped their arms together and shook hands with the other couples, smiling, and reenacting the story as Renolt told it.

"As time passed and the population grew, people settled together and created towns. They farmed the land, tended their animals, and created businesses. Yet while some families thrived, others didn't prosper." The dancers mimed plowing in fields, building houses, and working with their hands, all as they twirled to the background melody.

"As towns grew larger, social classes were formed, and ripples of dissatisfaction broke out. The poor became envious of families who lived in luxury. The wealthy judged those who were less fortunate as lazy. When accidents happened, fingers were pointed, and accusations were made." The drumbeat picked up, and the six dancers formed a straight line. They lifted their knees high and brought their feet down with aggressive stomps.

"Families and villages divided, people fought, and the world plunged into a time of great oppression. Powerful and unjust men became leaders. Not only were the poor and rich divided, the weak or sick, the deformed, women, children, foreigners, and even elderly were treated with cruelty." One pair of dancers stood tall, raising their arms high into the air, while the four other villagers dropped to their knees and covered their heads, writhing and moaning in time to the music.

"Eventually, the oppressed became filled with anger. Hatred simmered in their hearts until it boiled over. Not wishing to seek a peaceful solution, they formed an army and revolted. In the Horde's Mutiny, they attacked and fought against their persecutors until the streets were bathed in blood, and they had secured their freedom." The six villagers slashed at one another with invisible swords, and some fell to the ground as Renolt continued. His voice dropped in volume, and yet it could still be magically heard in every corner of the town square. "But with their newfound freedom, those who had been oppressed didn't learn from history. They didn't rule with the kindness they had so desperately craved. No—they eagerly switched roles and became the oppressors, plunging the world into even more chaos. Dark years followed that were filled with prejudice, persecution, and more fighting." The white garments of the dancers magically stained red as they swayed, clutching their middles in agony.

"Our gods, Terren, Solis, and Cael, saw the condition of the world they had created and were grieved by the evil that had filled it. When there was no end in sight to the warfare, the Three left the heavens again and intervened. Terren caused a mighty earthquake to shake the ground, which split the land with wide crevices." Brie jerked in surprise as the log she was sitting on trembled violently. "Cael ordered the wind to blow with such ferocity that funnel clouds were formed." The wind picked up and whipped Brie's hair around her face. "And Solis made the sun blaze with such intensity that it turned blue with nearly unbearable heat." The bonfire momentarily doubled in size, blazing high and hot, then returned to normal. "And people throughout the four kingdoms cowered in fear at the open wrath of the gods.

"Then the Three searched every corner of their creation and found a collection of noble people who had resisted the evil around them, risking their own lives; yet they had been powerless to make a change. The Three declared them without fault, or Blameless. Then the gods opened their palms and touched the hearts of those who most pleased them, giving them gifts of magic. Some were touched by Terren, some by Solis or Cael, and others by a combination of the Three. After bestowing the magic, the Three warned the Blameless that their powers would only work when not used selfishly. Before their departure, the Three tasked them with the responsibility of being peacekeepers and protectors of humankind. Then Terren, Solis, and Cael returned to the heavens.

"Heeding their instructions, the Blameless harnessed the powers of the earth, air, and sun, and went to work. They removed tyrants from thrones and doled out justice. They appointed new rulers who could be trusted to lead with fairness, and they assigned each a Blameless advisor. Working tirelessly, they restored the earth that had been ravaged by fighting. With their gifts, they grew crops, trees, grass, and flowers. They rebuilt businesses and homes. They bred livestock, set up fair trade, and enabled towns and cities to flourish once again."

In their blood-red garments, the dancers mimed working and rebuilding.

"After many years of labor, peace was solidly restored once again. And even though the kingdoms of Predonia, Westlor, Estelon, and Alderia believe the Blameless disappeared after their work was complete, they didn't. After all had been made right, they went into hiding. Generation after generation, through the ages, the Blameless have continued to fulfill their duty and worked tirelessly to maintain harmony in our world, which has now enjoyed peace for over one thousand years. It is for this monumental reason that we celebrate the Gifting!" Renolt's story ended with a shout. The music came to a crescendo, and the garments of the dancers morphed from red back to white.

Silence descended over the crowd as the dancers linked hands and performed a graceful bow in unison.

Villagers and Blameless leapt from their seats and erupted into thunderous applause, whistling, cheering, and stomping their feet. Brie joined them, wholeheartedly clapping, in awe of the performance. Through books, Brie had learned of the Horde's Mutiny, the first Gifting, and the Blameless restoring peace, but she had never heard it quite like this before, nor seen such a moving reenactment.

Once the crowd in the square quieted, a fiddler made an announcement. "We are fortunate to have a very special guest with us this Gifting Eve. Princess Briana, we dedicate our last song to you. To your sorrows of the past, to your happiness today, and to a brighter tomorrow for you and all of Predonia."

Flinton lifted Brie onto his shoulders as the musicians played their hauntingly beautiful tune, and Brie swayed to the music from her perch above the crowd. The song progressed into a beautiful rolling melody and finished loudly in what Brie imagined sounded like a victorious battle cry.

When the music ended, Lord Renolt stood before the villagers and spoke again in a thunderous voice, full of authority. "Friends, we have entered turbulent, dark times, and war has touched our world once again. Princess Briana, you are the true heir and ruler of Predonia! Together as Blameless, we unite and stand behind you!"

An ear-splitting shout of approval rose up among the people. Lord Renolt bowed to Brie. The villagers, Blameless and commoners alike, followed his example.

Later that night, when Brie finally lay her head on her pillow, she realized Cassie had been right. The night's festivities had helped her forget about the evils of this world, and it felt wonderful. There would be plenty of opportunities for worry later, but Brie simply felt gratitude as she drifted off to sleep.

# *Now You See Me*

Gifting morning with the Blackwoods was unlike anything Brie had ever experienced before. There was no fancy breakfast served on fine dishes, and no well-organized exchanging of gifts. In fact, there was no breakfast at all. Cassie pulled Brie from her bed while the sky was still dark.

"Earth, air, and sun! Why are you awake?" Brie grumbled as she shuffled out of her room. "I feel like I just closed my eyes."

"Don't be silly, Brie. It's already morning, and you're the last one up. I wanted to wake you ages ago, but Flinton made me wait."

Brie blinked and struggled to comprehend her friend's behavior. Cassie was a little nutty, but her problems went much deeper if she thought *this* was sleeping in.

Nevertheless, Brie stumbled downstairs with her eyes half-shut, following Cassie's exuberant, bouncing steps. The moment she entered the family room, however, her grogginess evaporated. The room had been transformed overnight.

The pine tree in the corner had been decorated with red berries, strings of popcorn, shimmering gold bows, and magically crafted twinkling candles for the entire twelfth moon. Gifts now surrounded the tree on all sides. There were so many packages that it was hard to find the floor space to walk. Milly and Flinton were sifting through the presents, creating stacks for each person, and the excitement in the air was contagious.

Once everyone found a spot to sit amidst the clutter, the fun began.

The opening of presents was unorganized and loud. It was filled with shrieks of excitement, laughter, tears of joy, and Flinton's deep bellows. Halfway through the gift exchange, Derek walked in, followed by a stack of floating presents. The presents proceeded to pass themselves out as Derek walked straight to the freshly brewed coffee. He joined the ruckus after pouring himself a mug and found a small spot on the couch to watch. Adelaide snatched her floating package out of the air and jumped onto Derek's lap to unwrap it. Afterward, she gave him a kiss on the cheek as a means of thanks, wishing him a merry Gifting.

"And *that* is why I get up at this insane hour to join you." Derek smiled warmly at Adelaide, his dark eyes twinkling.

Adelaide squeezed his cheeks together with her little hands, then got off his lap and went back to her mound of unopened gifts.

As Brie unwrapped her presents, she grew overwhelmed. Each gift was extremely personal and had clearly come from her new family's hearts. Despite her wealthy childhood, Brie valued everyone's thoughtfulness more than all the riches in the world. She received another book from Nina, a brush and comb set from Emilee, and an exquisite lavender gown hand-crafted by Ava. Flinton gave her a matching hat to go with her scarf and mitten set. He must have made it in secret, because Brie hadn't seen him work on it. A warm, fuzzy feeling spread through Brie at the thought of Flinton sneaking around to surprise her. Together, Adelaide and Milly had built Brie a chess set. Adelaide had painted uneven squares on the board, and Milly had carved the wooden chess pieces. Derek gifted Brie a quiver of arrows for her bow, and her fingers started itching to use them as soon as she opened them.

Lastly, Cassie gave Brie a pocket-sized notebook and quill. The notebook, titled *Blameless Facts,* was filled with several pages of handwritten facts, followed by blank entries for Brie to use. Brie glanced through the book and read one of the first entries to herself.

> There are five Elders who either live at Mount Elrad or come here to act as advisors to Lord Renolt. They vote on important decisions, but Lord Renolt has the power to overturn them if he wants, because he's more important and powerful.

Brie turned the page and grinned when her eyes landed on another fact. The gift made much more sense as she read:

> Never fart in front of Derek and deny it. He will know you're lying. I write this from personal experience.

Brie looked up and met Cassie's gaze, and the two of them burst into laughter. Brie put the notebook on the end table next to the couch. She couldn't wait to read more of the entries later.

After everyone finished opening their presents, Brie ran to her room to get her creations. In all the chaos, she had forgotten to bring her own gifts to share! Although she could have used money to purchase gifts for the others, Brie had decided to magically create something for everyone. Alone in her room at night, she had focused and worked. It had taken several weeks. Some items had been easy, requiring little effort, while others had taken a lot of time and practice.

Arms full, Brie teetered down the stairs and passed out the gifts with excited butterflies in her belly. She'd made Adelaide a horse charm to add to her heart locket. She gave Emilee a collection of hair ribbons and clips. Nina got bookends, each crafted to look like half of one mountain; this had been one of Brie's more time-consuming inventions. Brie presented Ava with a pair of matching red slippers. "Matching" was an important word, because her first few tries had been a disaster. The slippers kept appearing as different sizes, or slightly different shades of red. Milly got a set of cinnamon colored kitchen towels, Flinton a colorful roll of yarn, and Derek a new headband with a flame crafted on the front.

Last but not least, Brie gave Cassie her very own crown. She hoped Kove approved of her use of Predonia's mines, because she had created a silver crown, covered in rubies to match the red highlights in Cassie's dark hair.

In true Cassie fashion, she let out an ear-piercing shriek of delight and promptly placed the crown on her head, declaring she would never take it off. She issued commands like "Pass the salt!" and "Shut the door!" with such enthusiasm that Brie's stomach cramped from laughing so hard. By late morning, however, Flinton and Milly looked like they wanted to grab the crown off Cassie's head and throw it into the fire.

Milly served brunch, and of course, they were joined by Kove and Taeo. More gifts were exchanged. Because of their shared love of coffee, Brie had crafted matching mugs for the brothers. Taeo gave Brie a lock-picking set, and Kove had made her a golden necklace. The necklace was a large amulet featuring the same design as Derek's headband and the Council Hall: the symbol of the Blameless. Woven over the Blameless symbol was an intricate vine of roses in the shape of a numeral ten.

"This is beautiful, Kove. What does the ten represent?"

"Look around you, and count," Kove said.

Brie was confused at first. Count what? Then she glanced around the table at all the smiling faces and knew. Her eyes widened in understanding. It was them, the ten people who surrounded her.

Kove saw that Brie understood, and he nodded in confirmation. "It's for the ten of us who represent your new family. When you wear it, the Blameless symbol will remind you of your future and who you are. The roses represent your heritage and your past, and the ten will be a reminder that each of us will always be close to your heart."

Cassie sighed loudly and said in a dreamy voice, "That's beautiful. I wish I would have thought of that."

Happy tears leaked out of Brie's eyes and down her cheeks. Kove stood up and fastened the necklace behind her. Brie hugged him and whispered, "You know, you just might be my favorite."

"I never had a doubt," he answered with his signature wink and a rare, tender smile.

After brunch, Brie, Cassie, and Taeo went to Brie's room to take stock of their gifts. Holding up her present from Taeo, Brie asked, "Taeo, what in the name of the Blameless am I going to do with a lock pick? I don't want to be a criminal."

Taeo directed a very serious look her way. "Your Brajesty, picking a lock does not make you a criminal. What if you were locked inside a burning building and needed to get out? What if a bear was charging after you, and your only means of escape was to get inside of a locked fishing hut?"

"Is the bear inside of the burning building or outside of it?" Brie asked.

Taeo didn't catch that she was joking. "Pay attention; those were two different scenarios. You never know when you might need to open a locked door. Just promise you will always keep it with you."

"Okay, fine. If it means that much to you, I promise. But I have no idea how to use it."

"Ooh, let's practice now!" Cassie's eyes lighted with mischief. "We can try to open Nina's door! I don't know why, but she always keeps it locked. It makes no sense to me, because the only thing inside is a bed and hundreds of books."

"That's a marvelous idea." Taeo jumped up, grabbed Brie's hand, and pulled her to her feet. "Come on, Your Roseful Blamelessness."

Cassie snickered. "Okay, that was a good one."

"Why can't you just call me Brie?" Brie grumbled.

"Because that would be boring," Taeo said, as though it

was a perfectly reasonable explanation.

They left Brie's room, and Cassie led them to the third floor of the Blackwood home. They gathered quietly outside Nina's bedroom door.

Brie looked down at the lock-picking set in her hand. A variety of pointy-shaped instruments hung on a metal ring. Some were straight, others jagged, and a few curved.

Taeo pointed to Nina's door and explained. "This is a simple lock. One of the straight ones will work. You just have to find the right size. Insert it into the door and move it around until you feel it catch." He moved his hands around dramatically, miming the action. "Start with this one." He pointed.

Against her better judgement, but envisioning herself trapped in a burning building, Brie inserted the metal tool into Nina's lock. She moved the instrument around blindly without a clue what she was doing.

Taeo watched with exaggerated patience, then expelled a long, drawn-out sigh as Brie continued to unsuccessfully "feel it catch."

"Step aside," he eventually said.

Taeo took the ring of tools and quickly inserted the same one Brie had tried. In a matter of seconds, a satisfied smile graced his face, and he motioned with his head toward his hands. "Feel this."

Brie wrapped her hand around the tool as Taeo slipped his hand out from under hers. It was no longer loose. Instead, it was fit snugly up against an unseen surface inside the lock.

"Now, twist your wrist, and turn it."

Brie did as instructed and was rewarded with a loud click.

Her eyes widened, and she looked at Taeo in shock. It had worked!

Taeo beamed down at her, a huge grin overtaking his entire face.

The door swung open from within, and Brie found herself face-to-face with Nina. Brie had only ever seen Nina with a sweet smile, but this Nina was no longer smiling. Her cheeks were flushed, and her narrowed eyes flashed past Brie and blazed into Cassie and Taeo.

"You little scoundrels! How dare you defile Brie by teaching her your conniving ways! Don't ever pick my lock again, or I will think up the worst revenge possible and carry it out on your skinny arses!"

Then she slammed the door shut and followed it by the distinct click of the lock.

Brie, Cassie, and Taeo took off running. Brie wasn't exactly sure why, since the threat had just locked herself away, but it seemed like the right thing to do after being caught red-handed. Brie's legs felt weak from the whole experience, and as they ran, she noticed Cassie's shoulders were shaking. Compassion filled Brie, and she assumed her friend was crying, perhaps feeling guilty over suggesting the break-in.

They thundered their way down two flights of stairs into the kitchen and collapsed into the chairs at the table. As soon as their bottoms hit their seats, Taeo and Cassie burst into peals of laughter. Brie realized Cassie's shaking shoulders had been from laughing, not crying.

"That was *priceless*," Cassie gasped. "She likes her books much more than I realized."

Taeo snickered. "She's scary when she's mad. Who would have known? I'm going to have to watch my skinny arse whenever I'm around her."

Brie couldn't believe they were laughing. She wasn't used to this type of excitement. She was out of breath and felt like she was going to have heart failure. Nevertheless, she added, "You saw all of the books in her room. Who knows what kind of evil revenge could be lurking in their pages?"

The three of them stared wide-eyed at one another for a moment and then dissolved into more laughter.

Milly was standing in the kitchen, cooking like always. She placed her hands on the counter and closed her eyes. Brie's laughter faltered, and she tilted her head to the side, noticing dark circles under Milly's eyes. She looked exhausted.

"Flinton!" Milly yelled.

Flinton slowly ambled into the kitchen with a contented smile on his face, looking like he didn't have a care in the world. He had several days' worth of scruff on his face, and the beard suited him well. To Brie, it made him look even more endearing, like a big, snugly grizzly bear, and she snickered at the thought.

"Yes, dear?" Flinton asked, in his deep, gentle voice. Brie could practically see the love oozing out of his eyes as he looked at Milly. Cassie made a face that mimicked Flinton's expression perfectly, and a fresh wave of laughter erupted out of the three of them.

"Why don't you take these children out of this house before I mess up your favorite meal?" she said slowly, sagging against the counter. "Please?"

Flinton took one look at his wife's face, and his dove eyes flew out the window. He speared the kids with his sharp gaze, now resembling an eagle swooping in for the kill. "Come on, hellions. Let's go."

Derek and Kove walked into the kitchen from the living room, with empty coffee mugs.

"Where are we going?" Derek asked.

"Outside," Flinton barked.

Kove bounced up and down on his toes. "Sounds good. Too much sitting around drives me crazy."

Cassie *harrumph*ed as they bundled up in cloaks, hats, and scarves and were quickly ushered outside, regardless of their wishes.

"What should we do now?" Taeo grumbled while kicking at the snow with his leather boots.

Kove began jogging in place, Derek twisted from side to side, stretching his back, and Flinton stood a few feet away, twirling a metal chain through the air, making a figure eight with it. It seemed everyone was feeling restless. Brie suddenly had the urge to do something useful after having a week of free time.

"Can we play Find the Blameless?" she asked.

"That's a great idea," Kove agreed. "Flinton, Derek, and I will split up and hide. The three of you can stay together and try to find us."

Everyone readily agreed, and Brie began counting loudly, giving her uncles time to hide. After reaching one hundred, Brie took off in pursuit, accompanied by Taeo and Cassie. She wasn't blindfolded this time, so every few steps she would stop, close her eyes, and place her hand over her heart in concentration. She could feel small twinges of vibrations, and, assuming these represented the many other Blameless members inside of their homes, she would shake her head, and together the trio would move on. They walked a full lap around the village before Brie finally became aware of more specific humming. It was coming from the trees near the Blackwood home.

"I feel vibrations!" Brie said excitedly. "I think they're coming from over there," she whispered, pointing.

"Someone was lazy and didn't hide very far away," Taeo smirked.

"It's probably Flinton sleeping off his lunch," Cassie snickered.

They crept slowly into the woods, and, sure enough, the vibrations began to quicken into a steady hum. Brie looked around expectantly in every direction but couldn't see her uncles anywhere.

Brie grinned. She was close. She could feel whoever it was, and their vibrations were strong. She looked at Cassie and Taeo and pointed up, signaling for them to search the trees. They nodded and spread out. Together they began to examine the branches of the pines. Maybe it was Kove. Knowing him, he had probably climbed to the very top of a tree.

From far away, Brie heard heavy crashing and the sounds of snapping twigs, like someone was running through the woods toward them, heedless of the noise they were making. She frowned.

"Briana, shield yourself!" Derek's remote voice cut

through the silence in a panic.

*Shield myself?* Brie's frown deepened. That wasn't part of the game. Besides, she had never been successful at creating a shield before.

Standing frozen in confusion, Brie was grabbed from behind and caged tightly in a strong set of arms. She looked down, expecting to find herself in Kove's familiar hold, but she couldn't see the solid arms that held her. They were invisible. A sick, nauseous feeling rose up in Brie's gut. She was in trouble.

Brie decided she wouldn't be taken without a fight. She kicked, bit, and thrashed, trying to free herself from the arms. She tried to remember Derek's self-defense training, but it was impossible to aim for the weak spots on an invisible man, especially while wearing mittens. Before Brie could break away, another set of invisible hands grabbed her feet, lifting her horizontally into the air.

A quiet voice spoke in her ear. "Be still. We won't hurt you."

But Brie pinched, kicked, screamed, arched her back, and fought even harder. In a panic, she searched the trees for someone to help and met Taeo's gaze across the forest. The look on his face was one of complete bewilderment. Amid her fear, Brie realized how bizarre she must look. She was suspended in midair, awkwardly thrashing around like a maniac. A hysterical laugh flew out of her mouth.

Her laughter must have snapped Taeo into action, because he started sprinting in her direction.

But darkness was pushing in on her vision, and Brie could

no longer fill her lungs with air. The last thing she remembered was hearing Taeo scream, "BRIE!"

The frustrating boy had finally called her by her name.

Then the woods around her vanished, and her world went black.

# *No Longer Home*

Blackness began to recede into the corners of Brie's mind. Her chest burned like it had been set on fire, and her lungs gulped for the air that had been squeezed from them. Brie gasped, desperate for breath, as the arms that had been holding her upright released her, and she fell weakly onto her hands and knees.

Dizzy and disoriented, Brie slowly lifted her head and took in her surroundings.

Much to her surprise, she was on a hill overlooking the city of Aldestone. The forest loomed behind her, and Predonia's capital city sprawled out in front of her. Familiar cobblestone streets were bustling with life, lined with businesses, markets, and well-kept homes. Elevated in the distance above it all was the castle, Brie's home, proudly displayed in the mountains. The flags that flew from the ramparts and turrets no longer displayed her family's banner. New flags featured Vaylec's green crest.

Brie sank down and sat back on her heels. *I must be dreaming. Nothing else can explain how I can possibly be back home in Aldestone.*

As Brie tried to make sense of what was happening, two men materialized out of thin air in front of her. She blinked slowly at the strangers, more certain than before that it was all a dream. One of the men was middle-aged with graying hair, and the other was younger and blond. Brie felt a vague buzzing in the air around them, but she was too confused to focus on it. The strangers knelt in front of her with concern in their eyes, and the buzzing grew louder. Brie swatted the air in front of her, hoping to scare away the bees.

"Princess, we don't have much time," the older man said. "We've taken a huge risk by stopping and speaking with you, and we are prohibited from saying certain things, but we wanted a moment to explain what little we could. I'm Jarvis, and this is Torin. We are Blameless, and we've teleported you back home to Aldestone. We're sorry, Your Highness, but we had no choice in the matter. Our hearts are loyal to you, and although we don't know how, we promise to do everything within our power to try and help you."

Torin held Brie's gaze and said urgently, "We can sense you're Blameless. Shield yourself when we arrive at the castle."

"But I don't know how," Brie whispered in confusion. Her brain was desperately trying to process their words, but it was still functioning in slow motion. She was just now coming to the conclusion that there were no bees, and the buzzing sounds came from the Blameless in front of her.

"If you wish for it strongly enough, it will happen," Jarvis instructed. "We have to go now."

The men vanished from before her, and Brie's heart rate

sped up as she felt their hands grasp hold of her again. Then the air left her lungs, and her world went black.

Brie felt herself being carried. Her chest continued to painfully burn, and her mind remained in a dreamlike state.

A cold voice spoke. "You were successful. Bring her to me."

More voices.

A cool hand touched Brie's forehead.

"My lord, she needs rest. Look at her."

"Teleportation can be very taxing on the body, especially in the beginning. She will be unconscious for some time, Your Grace."

"Very well," the same cold voice said. "Take her to her chambers to sleep, but I want triple the usual guards to be stationed outside her rooms."

Brie woke up in the most unexpected place. She was back home in the castle, in her old bedroom. Initially, a feeling of safety washed over her as she lay between the familiar sheets. But soon, Brie's memories came rushing back, and panic seized her. A cold sweat broke out all over her body, and she ran into her bathroom and vomited. It was true—she was back in the castle—but it was being controlled by a madman.

She was no longer safe, and this was no longer home.

After emptying her stomach, Brie wiped her face with a shaky hand and returned to her room. She began to pace the floor, wondering how long she had been asleep and how she had miraculously returned to the capital city of Aldestone so quickly. It had taken over two weeks to travel to Mount Elrad on horseback, and there was no way she had been asleep for that long. Her eyebrows furrowed, and she stopped pacing. *At least, I hope I haven't been asleep that long.*

Brie looked down and examined her clothing. She was still wearing the tunic and leggings from Gifting day, and she discovered with relief that her necklace from Kove was still around her neck. Reaching into her pockets, Brie's fingers wrapped around the lock-picking set from Taeo. She doubted she would need to be saved from wild animals or burning buildings in the near future, but for some reason it gave her a small measure of comfort.

Next, her eyes scrutinized her bedroom thoroughly. Everything looked exactly as it had moons ago—before her entire world had been turned upside down—except lying on her bedside table were her scarf, hat, and mittens from Flinton. Someone must have taken them off while she slept. Brie rushed to them and picked them up. Burying her nose in the soft yarn, she sniffed deeply. They smelled like Milly's kitchen, like cinnamon. After another deep sniff, she placed them back on her nightstand and swallowed the thick lump in her throat, forbidding herself to cry. If she was going to make it out of this situation, she needed to keep her wits about her.

Brie resumed her pacing and tried to think of something she could do to help her predicament. For the time being she was alone, but in her gut, she knew it wouldn't be long before she was summoned. Her fingers absentmindedly played with her necklace as she tried to recall everything she knew about Vaylec.

Vaylec was gathering Blameless, and, according to Derek, he was somehow controlling them. Since Brie's escape, Vaylec had also been searching for her. On the night when he murdered her family, when she fled the castle, Brie had assumed he wanted her dead. But after learning about Vaylec's visit when she was a baby and her predicted powers, it no longer seemed likely that he wanted to harm her. It seemed even less likely after Brie had woken up in the comforts of her own bed. But if Vaylec didn't plan to hurt her, what then could he possibly want? It was all so confusing. Regardless, Brie knew she needed to be on-guard against Vaylec, even if she didn't understand his schemes.

The last thing Derek had yelled to Brie was, "Shield yourself!"

A hazy memory came to her of a dream she'd had during her travels. In the dream, she'd been instructed to shield herself, too, and she wondered if it was important or just a strange coincidence. She couldn't be sure. She'd also teleported in the dream, which until she'd done it herself, she hadn't even known was possible—but it could possibly explain how she had arrived so quickly to Aldestone.

A knock sounded on the door of the room, halting Brie in her tracks.

Brie wished more than anything she could teleport right back to Mount Elrad and her friends and ignore whatever was waiting for her, but unfortunately that wasn't an option.

Instead, she slowly walked toward the doorway and paused. She sensed familiar vibrations in the air and understood that a Blameless was on the other side of the door. Her heart rate picked up in anticipation and dread. Taking a deep breath, Brie reached for the handle and swung it open.

Adira stood in the hallway, clothed in a regal, floor-length burgundy gown. Her long auburn hair, streaked with silver, was neatly braided and draped over her right shoulder. She was accompanied by six guards. Brie tensed, not knowing what to expect as Adira's eyes swept over her face with apparent concern.

Adira sighed. "It's so good to see you alive and well, Princess Briana."

Anger, confusion, and hurt rose up in Brie, and she raised her eyebrows. "It is?" she asked boldly. Brie would have been overjoyed to see the old Adira, the one she had grown up with—but the last time they had seen each other, Adira had been attacking Brie and her friends.

A look of guilt, or perhaps regret, came over Adira. Ignoring Brie's question, she asked one of her own. "I'm here to give you some instructions. May I come in?"

Brie hesitated. "Do I have a choice?" she asked.

"No, I'm afraid not."

Sighing, Brie stepped aside and let Adira in, quickly shutting the door behind them before the guards tried to follow.

As soon as they were alone, Adira turned to Brie, her eyes pinched in concern, and said in a very quiet voice. "Princess Briana, I need to apologize and beg your forgiveness for the ambush. Please believe me when I say that I had no choice in the matter, but Vay . . ." Adira's eyes widened, a strangled sound came from her throat, and her words cut off.

"What about Vaylec?" Brie whispered back. She hadn't

expected Adira to bring up the ambush, but having known Adira her whole life, Brie recognized genuine regret in her eyes. "What did he do?"

Adira shook her head. "I . . . I can't tell you."

"He's forcing everyone to do what he wants, isn't he?" Brie asked.

Adira's eyes widened in surprise. "How could you possibly know that?"

"Derek," was all Brie said.

Adira looked heavenward. "Thank the Three. There's hope, then." She released a long, deep sigh, like she had been holding the weight of the world on her shoulders, and she wiped one hand over her forehead. Nodding in satisfaction, her expression grew even more serious. "Listen to me, Briana. Keep this information to yourself. I'm not sure how Vaylec would respond if he knew you were aware of this, but my guess is he wouldn't react well. And it wouldn't be wise for you to confide in your servants or guards, either. The old staff is gone, and he's brought in new people, and all of them are loyal to him." Adira paused before continuing, "Be especially careful how you conduct yourself around me. It would be best if you treated me like we are no more than acquaintances. If he knew our history, that we're friends, I suspect he would keep us apart."

Brie nodded her head, the seriousness of Adira's words sinking in. She couldn't afford to get comfortable, even here in her own home. "I'll be careful. I promise."

Adira looked over her shoulder at the door and winced, like she was expecting it to open. "The real reason I'm here is that Vaylec sent me to summon you for dinner. You've been asleep for several hours, and he's becoming impatient. You are to dress in one of your finest gowns, which he has selected, and then I will escort you to the dining hall. Please dress as quickly as possible."

Hearing that she was being summoned by Vaylec caused Brie to instantaneously feel sick again.

Adira placed a comforting hand on Brie's shoulder and squeezed it. "Be strong and do not lose heart, Princess Briana. If Derek, Renolt, and the Elders know Vaylec is up to no good, then I'm sure they're working on finding a solution even as we speak." She turned to leave.

As Adira reached the door, Brie blurted out a question: "Adira, did I really teleport?"

Adira raised her eyebrows. "Yes, Princess, you did."

"It actually happened," Brie said in awe. "What exactly is teleporting?"

"It's instantaneous travel between two locations. A very rare flair among the Blameless."

Brie nodded thoughtfully. "Well, that explains it. I was sure it had been a dream. I suppose Jorin and Tarvis are real too?"

Adira's lips twitched. "You must mean Jarvis and Torin, Princess. But to answer your question: Yes, they are very real. As real as you and I."

Adira left the room, and an unfamiliar maid entered. Her brown hair was pulled back in a severe bun, and she carried a gown in her arms. She laid the gown on Brie's bed and curtsied, then quietly assisted Brie out of her garments and into a horribly stiff, cream-colored lace creation, with a collar that was so high, it poked uncomfortably into Brie's ears. The dress was folded into multiple layers, causing it to poof out ridiculously. Brie sighed, already missing her soft leggings and tunic.

After styling Brie's hair, the maid curtsied again and dismissed herself, leaving Brie alone in her room. Brie quickly took the lock-picking set out of her tunic and placed it in a pocket in the folds of her dress. Finally ready, but feeling completely unprepared, she opened her door to face the unknown.

Adira was in the hall waiting, and she stepped forward, offering Brie her arm. "I'm to escort you to dinner, Your Highness."

Grateful for the support, though being careful not to show it, Brie looped her arm in Adira's, and together they walked through the familiar hallways of the castle, followed by a host of guards.

"You look lovely, Your Highness," Adira said.

"I do not," Brie snapped, her nerves getting the best of her. "I look and feel like a stuffed chicken."

They made their way through several corridors, toward the royal family's private dining hall. The path was familiar—Brie could have walked it in her sleep—but there were subtle changes all around her. The Eyrhill family portraits were no longer hanging on the walls, and banners with her family's crest, a shield bearing a yellow rose, were gone. In their place hung banners displaying Vaylec's crest. Up close, Brie saw the hunter green background featured a large silver V; a silver fox, mid-jump, covered the letter. Pain knifed through her, followed by moons' worth of anger.

"Whether you look like a stuffed chicken or not, it will be a breath of fresh air to have you in the castle again," Adira said quietly.

Too soon, the dining hall loomed in front of them. Brie's hold on Adira's arm grew so tight, she knew she was probably leaving bruises.

"Take courage," Adira whispered, then stoically led Brie into the room.

They entered, and Brie came to a halt, her legs unable to carry her further. At her family's dining table—the table where they had shared countless meals and happy memories—sat four strangers: an elderly couple with graying hair, a very thin and frail looking young woman, and an impressive looking man with perfectly parted dark hair and a goatee. The man sat in Brie's father's seat at the head of the table, and he wore a crown on his head.

It was Vaylec, the man responsible for murdering her family.

Sorrow, fear, and rage filled Brie as Vaylec raised his head and locked his eyes with hers. Slowly, very slowly, he pushed himself out of his chair and rose to his feet. He looked at Brie, his eyes narrowing slightly as they scanned her entire length. They focused on her face, and his eyes widened, his nostrils flared, and he rubbed his hands together. A sickeningly sweet smile spread over Vaylec's face.

"Welcome, my dear Briana. At last, you are home with me, where you belong."

# *Dinner with a Lunatic*

Brie watched helplessly as Vaylec analyzed her with an intensity that made her shudder. With a calculating look, Vaylec left the table and made his way toward her. Panic crawled up Brie's throat as he drew closer, and she realized she was almost out of time. She loathed the idea of being under his control; if that happened, her family would never be avenged. Being back in the castle had also sparked another desire. Since her family's death, Brie had almost rebelled against the idea of being queen. But seeing the castle under the control of the wrong man, she realized she wanted her kingdom to have its rightful leader.

Brie's body began to tremble, and she cursed herself for never mastering how to create a shield.

Jarvis's words returned to her. *If you wish for it strongly enough, it will happen.*

Brie had nothing to lose. She closed her eyes and wished harder than she had ever wished for anything in her life. *Protect me!* she commanded silently in her mind.

Nothing happened.

*Protect me!* she repeated urgently.

Feeling no different, Brie opened her eyes as Vaylec closed the distance between them.

A sharp ache suddenly struck Brie's chest, and she lifted her hand to rub the area over her heart as Vaylec's feet slowed to a stop.

Risking one last attempt, Brie pleaded, *By the Three, SHIELD ME!*

A small rush of wind, like a subtle breeze, blew over her skin, followed by a burst of heat. Brie wasn't sure what just happened, but she hoped Terren, Solis, and Cael had just answered her prayer and she was successfully shielded.

Adira jerked her arm away from Brie with a quiet hiss, like she'd been shocked. Recovering quickly, she performed a deep curtsy and announced, "Your Grace, I present to you Princess Briana."

Vaylec flicked an irritated look in Adira's direction. "Yes, I can see that for myself."

Then Vaylec returned his gaze to Brie, his eyes roaming everywhere, intently taking in every inch of her. He stepped closer, intruding into her personal space, and Brie barely suppressed the overwhelming urge to back away from him. He cocked his head to the side, scanning Brie as if he was searching for something. Eventually, he stopped perusing and reached out his hand, bringing it to her cheek. Brie flinched slightly as Vaylec brushed her skin softly with his thumb and asked, "Do you know who I am?"

Brie cleared her throat. "Yes. You're Vaylec Spaur," she said, the strength in her voice surprising her.

Vaylec smiled in satisfaction. "Good. You've been told

about me. It makes me wonder what your kidnappers had to say, but we'll save that conversation for another time." His eyes flashed angrily for a moment, but they grew softer as he continued, "You look well. I hope you've recovered from your travels."

Brie was confused and disgusted by his kindness, and she longed to tell him exactly how much she loathed his very existence—but rebellion probably wasn't a smart move. At least not yet.

"No, I'm tired, and I don't feel well. Maybe I should return to my bed," she suggested hopefully.

Vaylec's smile grew wider, and he chuckled. "I don't think so. It's the Gifting, and I want you to sit and have dinner together with me and my family. We have reason to celebrate, and the food will replenish your strength."

Taking Brie by the elbow, he nodded dismissively toward Adira and his guards. Adira met Brie's eyes briefly before she dropped into another curtsey, then left the room.

Guards took their places on either side of the door. Keeping hold of Brie's elbow, Vaylec put his other hand on her back as he led her to the open seat next to his at the head of the table. He released her and pulled out her chair, placing her between himself and the sickly young woman.

"Briana, these are my parents, Eldon and Cecily Spaur," Vaylec began his introductions. "Mother, Father, you remember Princess Briana."

Brie smiled hesitantly at the gray-haired couple sitting across from her as she inspected them. They looked exactly how she imagined a loving set of grandparents should be, with wrinkle lines around their eyes and mouths from years of happiness and laughter. But as she looked closer, she could see their eyes were no longer laughing. Instead, they looked terribly sad. Brie decided she wouldn't hold it against them that they had a lunatic for a son.

"It's a pleasure to meet you," Brie said with sincerity.

Eldon smiled sorrowfully at her. "The pleasure is ours, my dear child."

Cecily held a hand to her mouth, cleared her throat, and said in a wobbly voice, "You have grown into a very beautiful young woman, Princess Briana."

"That's very kind of you to say." Brie smiled at the woman, deciding she definitely wouldn't hold their son against them. Maybe she could somehow make life a little less miserable for them while she was here.

Brie glanced at Vaylec to find him watching their exchange like a hawk. His narrowed eyes relaxed, and he smiled. He motioned to his sister next. His voice filled with pride, he said, "This is my twin sister, Violet. I hope the two of you will become friends."

Brie turned in her chair to greet Violet and almost gasped in shock. From a distance, Violet looked frail, but up close she looked positively dreadful. Her skin was thin and ghostly white, like it hadn't seen the sun in years. The top half of her dull black hair was pulled away from her face with a clip. Wispy strands had escaped from the clip and framed her cheeks, which were sunken and hollow. The dark circles under her eyes didn't make her look sad. No, they made her look much worse. Her blue eyes were haunted.

Violet opened her mouth and spoke. "Welcome back to your home, which you never should have been forced to leave. No one else seems to want to acknowledge it, but I'm sorry for the upheaval you've experienced. It does my heart good to see you looking so well."

The Spaur parents gasped.

Vaylec lowered his voice and said sharply, "Violet, watch yourself!"

Violet hissed back, "How can you act like everything's okay?"

"Enough!" Vaylec shouted. "I will not discuss this over Gifting dinner. Do not push me, or you will be sent back to your room."

Violet's very pale face flushed pink, but she nodded her head and kept quiet.

After watching their argument with wide eyes, Brie decided that she liked Violet.

"Thank you," Brie risked saying into the awkward silence. "For being happy that I look well," she clarified with a small smile.

Violet smiled back at her and quietly said, "You're welcome."

Vaylec eyed Violet warily for a few moments until he seemed convinced that she was done speaking. Then he clapped his hands as though nothing unusual had happened, and servants entered the room, their arms laden with platters of food. A feast much larger than what five people could consume was set before them. There was turkey, roast beef, leg of lamb, and freshly caught fish. Potatoes, vegetables, cheeses, and breads of every kind were served as sides. Puddings, pies, and sweets were stacked on trays all around them. It was outlandish and wasteful. As a princess, Brie was used to being served plenty of delicious food, but even to her, this abundance was ridiculous.

Vaylec showed no evidence of his previous anger. He was smiling again as he piled his own plate high with food, passing the dishes to Brie and making sure she did too. But he was the only person who seemed to have an interest in the meal. Eldon, Cecily, and Violet just picked at the feast before them, and Brie couldn't eat a bite. She pushed her food around on her plate to make it look like she was eating, but the truth was, sitting at the table with a murderer had taken away her appetite.

Vaylec began to speak. "Briana, did you know I held you in my arms fourteen years ago when you were a baby?"

"No, I don't remember that," Brie answered quietly.

Vaylec acted like he found this immensely funny, laughing while shaking his head. "Of course, you wouldn't remember it. Mother and Father, what about you? Do you remember that day?"

Brie froze in her seat. She'd already heard about it while spying in the Council Hall, but she was very much interested in hearing their side of the story.

"Yes, of course we remember it, dear," Cecily said. "It was a monumental day for us all when we met the princess."

"Violet, you were there. Do you recall it?" Vaylec didn't wait for her to answer. "Perhaps you were too preoccupied with the arrival of your new powers for it to have registered as important." Bitterness had crept into his voice.

Violet looked pointedly at her brother. "Nothing was more

important than serving the royal family on that day. Not even my powers."

Vaylec narrowed his eyes at her, but he turned to Brie and continued. "You were a beautiful baby. When I held you in my arms all those years ago, a plan began to form in my mind. A plan to take over Predonia and assist you in your rule."

Brie was stunned by the words that had just casually left Vaylec's mouth. As nonchalantly as one would speak about the weather, he'd revealed that fourteen years ago he'd begun to cold-heartedly plan the disposal of her parents and her older brother.

Brie's voice shook with barely suppressed rage. "Your plan was flawed if you thought that after killing my family, I would somehow want to have anything to do with you."

Vaylec put down his fork. Perhaps he had finally lost his appetite like the rest of them.

"Your parents' and brother's deaths were an unfortunate side effect of my plan."

Brie gasped at his callous dismissal of their murders.

"It wasn't me who killed them, you know," Vaylec continued. "My orders were merely to overthrow them. I had a problem with the laws your father enforced, and I needed to remove him from the throne in order to carry out my plan. But think about it. Would they have been happier rotting away in a prison cell? I highly doubt it. Perhaps death was a kinder choice, Briana."

White-hot rage boiled inside of Brie like she had never known before. For the first time in her life, she felt hatred.

Vaylec studied Brie openly for a moment, while she took in

shallow, uneven breaths, trying to control her fury.

Finally, he said, "But there is an element of truth to what you said; therefore, the soldiers who killed your family should be punished for the grief they've caused you. Tomorrow morning at dawn, they will be executed in your presence. I hope you will eventually understand my side of the story, once you've worked your way past your grief."

Vaylec turned his attention back to his plate, picked up his fork, and began to eat again.

Brie, who had been sitting stiffly in her seat, slouched weakly, resting her back against her chair as she drew in a shaky breath. She blinked and willed herself not to cry. Underneath the table, she felt a soft hand reach over and pat her leg. Brie grasped hold of Violet's hand with her own and held onto the small offer of comfort with all her might.

Brie somehow made it through the rest of the meal and was eventually dismissed to her room. An escort of no less than a dozen guards accompanied her; they were instructed to remain outside of her door.

After being helped out of her gown by the same maid, Brie was finally left in peace. She collapsed in her bed and wept.

Vaylec was a madman. He was going to execute the soldiers who had carried out *his* orders. The fact that Vaylec hadn't held the sword himself was a minor detail, in Brie's opinion. He was going to have the soldiers slain, all in the name of trying to please her, which was absurd. Brie shuddered as she thought about his words from dinner and the calculated plan he had begun to develop when she was a baby. Which of her father's laws were so terrible that Vaylec had to overthrow him?

Brie was trapped with no idea what to do. She wished she could escape from the castle again, but it seemed impossible with so many soldiers surrounding her.

Thinking back to her first escape from the castle all those weeks ago, Brie's heart started pounding, and she sat up in bed. Teleporting must have addled her brain, or she would have remembered sooner. The secret passageway! How could she have forgotten?

Brie jumped out of bed and sprinted through her dressing room to the closet, which contained her hundreds of gowns. She raced to the wall where the secret passageway was, with no plan other than to get as far away from Vaylec's evil clutches as possible. Brie separated the dresses where the door should have been, but all she found was a bare wall. She pushed the dresses aside further and groped along the length of wall, certain the door would appear if she kept reaching. But eventually, she ran out of wall to search, and her heart sank.

The passage had been sealed.

Brie slowly made her way back to her bed and flopped down, staring blankly up at the ceiling. Fresh tears coursed down her cheeks and fell into her golden hair. Her only hope was that Flinton, Derek, and Kove would find a way to rescue her.

She reached over and took her scarf, hat, and mittens off her nightstand. Needing the comfort, she hugged them tightly, letting more tears fall. She pulled the lock pick out of her pocket and ran her hands over it, thinking about Taeo and Cassie. She missed them terribly, and she'd only been away from them for less than a day. Brie clasped Kove's necklace and remembered his words: it was a reminder that her family and friends would always be close to her heart. She cried some more, holding onto her trinkets, the separation from them feeling unbearable. She hadn't even had the chance to read through Cassie's book of facts. The thought made her angry, and she punched the bed. What good was her magic if she couldn't even—

An amazing possibility suddenly occurred to Brie. She could summon Cassie's book! She knew exactly where she'd left it: on the end table next to the couch in the Blackwoods' living room.

Without wasting another second, Brie closed her eyes and felt the rush of magic pull at her heart. Something small landed in her lap, and she opened her eyes to see the only thing in the entire world that could possibly have brought her joy at that bleak moment: Cassie's gift of *Blameless Facts.*

After the horrible events of the day, Brie's ability to summon the book seemed too good to be true. She opened it, tempted to devour every entry in one setting; but at the same time, she wanted to savor it so it would never end.

Brie flipped to the beginning and read the very first entry.

*Princess Briana Rose Eyrhill,*

*You once thanked me for our friendship, and I recently realized I never returned the thanks. If I'm being honest, you're the very best thing that has ever happened to me. The sky is bluer, the grass is greener, and my laughs are deeper when you're around. I hope you never leave Mount Elrad, but if you do, please take me with you. Thank you, Brie, for being my very best friend.*

*-Cassie*

Brie sighed and wiped away another tear. The passage contained more serious emotion than she had ever heard Cassie express in person.

Staring at her little treasure, Brie realized she would have to be very careful with it. She would have to hide the book when it wasn't in her possession. It hadn't been with her when she'd arrived, and if someone were to see it now, it would raise suspicions of her magic. Plus, it was probably filled with all sorts of evidence against Brie, proving she was Blameless. She couldn't risk her maid or Vaylec finding it and reading it. She thought about tucking it under her mattress, but it would be safer to just return it and summon it again later.

Brie gasped as another idea formed in her mind. "Terren, Solis, and Cael!" she prayed. She rushed to her desk and sat down. "Please, let this work." Brie grabbed a quill, dipped it in ink, and turned to the back of the book, to the blank entries Cassie had left for her to fill.

Dear Cassie,

I've been taken back to Aldestone. I'm in the castle with Vaylec, but he hasn't harmed me. I've learned how to create a shield, so I'm okay and my powers are intact. Please tell Flinton, Derek, and Kove to come as soon as possible. I miss you.

—Brie

Brie closed her eyes and placed her hand over her heart. The book disappeared and returned to its place in the Blackwood living room. She only hoped someone would think to open it.

# *The Execution*

The next morning, true to his word, Vaylec summoned Brie at dawn. A different maid helped her into another fancy gown that was just slightly less restricting than what she'd worn the night before. Brie tried to think of a way she could avoid witnessing the execution, but no solid excuse came to mind. She could feign an illness, but she was certain Vaylec would be too shrewd for that. He would likely just postpone the killings, since they were being done for her supposed benefit.

A part of Brie was glad that the men who took her family's lives were going to pay for their actions, but she had no desire to watch it. And worst of all, the man ultimately responsible for their deaths would continue to walk free. Brie shuddered in disgust. Not only would Vaylec stay free, but he would remain a self-appointed ruler.

After the maid left, Brie fastened her necklace and made sure her lock pick was safely tucked within the folds of her dress. Then she concentrated for a moment and raised a shield around herself. She was relieved to discover that making the shield was much easier to do the second time.

With a heavy and confused heart, Brie finally left her room. Once again, a dozen guards led her through the corridors of the castle, marching in front of, beside, and behind her.

Vaylec was waiting for Brie outside of the throne room, and he stepped forward as she approached.

"Good morning, Princess Briana. I hope you slept well," he said kindly, confusing Brie again with his courtesy.

"I did," Brie answered stiffly, which was a lie. She had tossed and turned all night long, and when she finally did get to sleep, it was filled with horrible dreams—but she wasn't going to admit that.

Vaylec held out his arm for Brie to take, but she didn't accept it. His eyes narrowed at her subtle act of rebellion. He grasped her arm and latched it around his, holding on firmly so she couldn't pull away.

Suppressing the urge to stab him with her lock pick, Brie obediently accompanied Vaylec outside to one of the castle's many courtyards. Outside, Adira stood among a host of guards, and her eyes briefly met Brie's. If Brie hadn't talked to Adira the night before, she would have wondered where the woman's loyalties lay; Adira's face remained expressionless, and she didn't acknowledge Brie in any way.

Vaylec led Brie toward the only two seats in the courtyard, which were two cushioned thrones. He held Brie's arm as she turned and sat in one chair, then he took the larger chair for himself, and loudly commanded, "Bring the prisoners forward!"

Brie tensed in her seat and watched as guards dragged

two men toward them. Their hands were tied behind their backs, and their ankles were chained loosely together. They were still dressed in their uniforms, looking no different than the other guards. Their chins were held high; yet, by their confused expressions, Brie guessed they hadn't been informed about today's plan.

As they got closer, Brie focused intently on their faces. As recognition dawned, she inhaled quietly and began to tremble.

It *was* them.

Brie's vision swam as she was transported back to the only other time she had seen these men. She'd watched in horror as they laughed and drove their swords through her parents. Brie jerked her head away, no longer wanting to watch, and her eyes met Vaylec's.

Vaylec was watching her reaction, focused and intense. Brie knew he must see that she was trembling, but his face remained devoid of emotion. Eventually, he turned back toward the men who now stood before them.

"Finn and Clay, you have been some of my most loyal followers, and you have served me well." The soldiers' faces looked hopeful at Vaylec's praise. "But you have fulfilled your purpose. You are my past, and Princess Briana is my future. The two of you wielded the swords that brought about the death of her family; therefore, you must pay for the pain it has caused her."

The hope vanished from the men's eyes, and panic took its place.

One man dropped to his knees and began to beg. "My

lord, please! I can make it up to you. I'll do whatever service you request!"

Vaylec merely stared at the other man, then finally said, "I'm sorry, but there's nothing you could say that would change my mind. Pull him to his feet," he ordered.

Brie felt sick. If this was how Vaylec treated his most loyal followers, how did he treat his enemies? She swallowed the bile that rose in her throat, realizing she had seen firsthand the way Vaylec treated his enemies.

"Adira!" Vaylec barked. "I believe you're best suited for the task. Come here."

Lifting her eyes, Brie couldn't help but watch again as Adira walked toward the chairs and curtsied to Vaylec. A pleased smile formed on Vaylec's face.

Vaylec rose as Adira approached. Stooping down, Vaylec placed his mouth beside Adira's ear, and his lips moved. Adira's eyes widened with regret and flashed toward Brie, then looked away just as swiftly.

"Your Grace," Adira said, quietly but loud enough for Brie to hear. "I don't see how that could possibly help the princess."

"I did not ask for your opinion," Vaylec said. He returned to his seat and commanded, "Do it now!"

Adira's eyes glazed over, and her face took on the same distant expression Brie had seen her wear during the ambush. She raised her arms into the air and snapped her fingers. Seemingly in response, the surrounding guards froze in place. They were unable to move or intervene, but their eyes were open and focused. Every gaze was homed in on Adira, watching her every move. Goosebumps ran down Brie's arms as she realized Adira was going to use magic in front of everyone. That would be considered exposing the Blameless, which was forbidden. An uneasy feeling came over Brie as she watched Adira drop her arms to her sides. Then, she began to slowly raise them with her palms facing toward the sky.

As Adira lifted her arms, Brie noticed other movements. The swords of the six closest guards rose out of their scabbards. The soldiers watched in disbelief, paralyzed and unable to move. The higher Adira lifted her arms, the higher the swords rose, until they broke free from their scabbards. Suspended in the air, they hovered as though waiting for direction. Then Adira pointed one hand at Finn and the other at Clay. The prisoners watched in horror as the swords sped toward them. In a series of sickening *thump*s, three swords embedded into each of their chests. Then the prisoners collapsed.

Brie squeezed her eyes shut and took a deep breath, trying to hold her composure, refusing to show weakness in front of Vaylec. A myriad of emotions ran through her, but mostly she was equal parts confused and disgusted. She knew Vaylec was somehow forcing Adira to fulfill his wishes, but it was hard to watch Adira carry out the execution without putting some blame on her as well.

When Brie opened her eyes, Adira snapped her fingers again, releasing the invisible bonds on the guards, allowing them to freely move again. Some shuffled uncertainly in place while six moved forward to reclaim their swords from the bodies of their fallen comrades. They returned to their positions in the courtyard, and fear filled their eyes.

Vaylec stood. "The Blameless have lived and practiced

their magic in secret for too long. As my castle guards, you have witnessed their magic, but I order you to keep quiet about it until the appropriate time of my choosing. One day very soon, Predonia will witness it too." He motioned to a few of his guards. "Clear the courtyard. Give Finn and Clay a proper burial."

After a dismissive nod, Vaylec took Brie by the hand, pulling her gently out of her chair, and together they left the courtyard. As they walked through the massive doors into the castle, Brie could feel Vaylec's eyes on her the entire way.

Finally, he spoke. "Tell me. Do you feel any measure of relief?"

Brie hesitated before answering. "No words could possibly describe how I feel," she said carefully.

Vaylec must have interpreted her answer as positive, because he smiled in satisfaction. "You may go anywhere you wish within the castle, except for my rooms and the north tower. But for your own safety, your guards must always accompany you."

Brie nodded. "I'm feeling very emotional right now, so I'd like to go back to my room," she said, which wasn't a lie. But more importantly, she wanted to summon Cassie's little notebook of Blameless facts to see if there was an answer.

"Of course. You are dismissed," Vaylec said with a tip of his head.

Brie turned and proceeded down the hall, feeling Vaylec's eyes boring into her as she went. Once she was out of his sight, she sprinted the rest of the way to her room. She slammed her door shut, summoned the journal, and flipped to the back of it. She quickly found her own entry, and then her heart sank. There was no response.

"Cassandra, if you cannot stop crying, you'll have to leave the room!" Flinton spoke firmly, yet somehow still infused care into his command.

"It's been two days. SHE'S GONE!" Cassie wailed loudly and pitifully, glaring at Flinton with puffy, bloodshot eyes. Her black hair was a mess, and the crown Brie had given her sat crookedly on the top of her head.

Taeo sat next to Cassie, trying to provide comfort by patting her back, but he looked like he was wallowing in the depths of despair himself. "It's okay, Cassie. We'll find her," he said in a very unconvincing tone.

Everyone sat around the table in the Blackwood kitchen: Flinton and Milly, who were holding hands; all of Flinton's sisters; and Derek, Taeo, and Kove. Each one of them looked exhausted and worried.

"Listen to me," Flinton continued. "I understand you're upset. All of us are, but we need to eliminate distractions so we can focus. Let's pull ourselves together."

Flinton looked around at the rest of his sisters. "All of us love Brie and want to find her, but we need to put our emotions aside and review our plan."

"Technically, this is Blameless business," Derek said, "and it shouldn't be discussed in front of the children, but . . ."

"I'm not leaving!" Cassie shouted.

"Neither am I!" Nina said, slamming her book onto the table.

"You couldn't drag me away with a herd of your wild horses," Taeo said, his eyes flashing.

"We have the right to be here," Emilee added, crossing her arms.

"Yeah!" Adelaide yelled.

"For the love of the Blameless, relax! I wasn't finished yet," Derek said with a shake of his head. "Although we wouldn't normally hash out our plans in front of children or non-Blameless, I think we can make an exception to the rules."

The children heaved audible sighs of relief around the table.

Flinton's stomach suddenly growled so loudly that Adelaide dropped her glass of water, which shattered. Cassie jumped, sending her already crooked crown off her head and into her lap.

Kove looked at Flinton with his eyebrows raised. "What were you saying about distractions?"

Derek smiled, and with a sweep of his hand, he magically cleaned up the water and the shattered glass.

Flinton ran his hands over his face and through his unruly brown hair.

"Serves me right," he said. "Milly, love, I haven't eaten anything since yesterday. Can you please make us something to eat?"

Milly clapped her hands, and the table filled magically with platters of bread, meat, cheese, and grapes, and a pitcher of water.

It was a simple meal by Milly's standards. She shrugged and said, "I'm not leaving the table, either."

Nobody objected. They simply helped themselves to the food.

"I can't believe I was so stupid," Cassie said mournfully as she shredded a piece of bread with her fingers. It wasn't the first time she'd said something self-deprecating since Brie's disappearance. "I was so busy climbing that tree, looking for you guys, that I didn't see a thing. I didn't even know anything was wrong until I heard Taeo yell." She sniffed loudly.

Taeo shook his head sharply, like he was trying to dislodge something. "She just rose up into the air like she was floating. She was struggling and kicking at something I couldn't see. I should have realized sooner that something was wrong. I should have run to her faster. Actually, I never should have left her side in the first place." Taeo released a long sigh. "When I finally came to my senses, it was too late. *POOF!*" He smacked his hands together, causing everyone to jump. "She vanished into thin air," he finished, dropping his head into his hands. "Turns out, I'm a horrible protector."

"Cassie, Taeo," Derek said, "you know it wasn't your fault. None of us anticipated an attack on Gifting Day. Our guards were down."

Taeo swallowed thickly and nodded, but he didn't look convinced. Cassie shrugged and moved on to decimating her meat and cheese.

"I just don't understand how something like this could happen in Mount Elrad," Flinton said. "There's no trace of Brie anywhere. Her trail stops in the woods, right where she vanished."

"What does that mean?" Ava asked.

"Her trail vanished, and apparently so did she," Flinton explained.

"According to the registry," Derek jumped in, "the two Blameless who recently went missing have very unique gifts. One has the gift of invisibility, and the other can teleport. They must have been linked together, and by touching Brie, they transferred their gifts to her."

"In other words, all three of them teleported out of here," Kove clarified.

Milly's eyes flashed angrily. "So, they slipped in right under our noses, took Brie, and vanished."

"That's what it looks like," Flinton said. "There was no way to foresee it or stop it."

"Rotten Vaylec puppets," Taeo muttered.

"Where do you think they took her?" Nina asked.

"We don't have proof, but we believe she's back in Aldestone," Derek said grimly.

"*What?*" Cassie yelled. "Vaylec will hurt her, or control her, or maybe even kill her!" She dissolved into tears again.

No one seemed to have the heart to kick Cassie out of the room. Rather, Flinton opened his arms, and Cassie collapsed into his lap, sobbing.

"There, there, Cassandra Elane. He won't kill her," Flinton said, his deep voice quieting, taking on a soft, soothing tone as he patted her back. "She's far too valuable to him. We don't think he wants to harm her."

"But will he control her?" Cassie asked in horror.

"He might," Flinton said, nodding.

"But even if he does, we can't lose hope. We're working on a plan to rescue her, and we're brainstorming on how we can stop his control," Kove added.

Derek spoke up. "We plan to leave first thing tomorrow morning, but we aren't traveling straight to Aldestone. We had a brief meeting with the Elders this morning. After speaking with them, we've decided that all the Blameless in Predonia need to be warned. They need to shield themselves or go into hiding to prevent Vaylec from finding them and gaining control over their powers."

"Until we figure out how he's executing his control, no one is safe," Kove said.

"Girls," Flinton began seriously, "all of the Blameless in Mount Elrad are needed for this mission, even Milly."

Adelaide sighed and very maturely declared, "I knew it."

None of the other girls objected. Instead, they nodded like it was something they had been expecting.

"Ava, you'll be in charge again," Flinton continued. "All of you must listen to her and be on your best behavior."

"We'll be fine. Don't worry about us," Ava reassured him.

"I won't be gone long," Milly said with a small smile, her voice unwavering and calm. She pulled Adelaide onto her lap. "I'm being paired up with Elder LeBlanc. We're traveling east to Glenfer. We'll be back within a moon."

"And what about you guys?" Ava asked. She turned to the uncles, but her eyes remained on Kove. "Who are you traveling with, and how long will you be gone?"

"The three of us are sticking together," Kove answered. "We plan to travel south through the middle of Predonia and reach as many Blameless as we can before continuing on to Aldestone. I'm afraid we don't know how long it will take, but a couple moons is likely."

Ava swallowed hard and nodded.

"As we travel south," Derek explained, "we'll appoint some of the Blameless we meet to spread the word further, so it won't lie entirely on our shoulders. Then we'll proceed to Brie as soon as possible."

"Why can't you rescue her first?" Cassie asked, her voice rising an octave with worry.

Derek continued, "We think Vaylec currently has control over his parents; his sister, Violet; Adira; and the two most recent Blameless, Torin and Jarvis. He already has a small army on his side. If he gains anyone else, it will become nearly impossible to get Brie out of his clutches. As it is, we're going to need a foolproof plan."

"It's going to take time," said Flinton, fisting his hands on the table, "but we'll bring her home."

# *The Best and Worst Discoveries*

One week passed. One long, torturous week. Seven days of uncomfortable dresses, awkward dinners, lingering guards, and unfamiliar faces. Brie missed her friends. Every day, Brie summoned Cassie's notebook, but so far no one had noticed Brie's message in the back of it. If someone had found it, she was certain there would have been a reply.

Trailed by her guards, Brie spent most of each day as far away from Vaylec as possible, reading through tidbits of information in Cassie's notebook while sitting in the castle library, or hiding in the nook under the second-floor stairs, where she used to play with her friend Delia. She'd even wandered down to the kitchens in search of Delia's grandmother, the cook who used to spoil her with sweets, but everything in the castle was different. It looked the same, but the people she loved had been replaced. It was painful to be back in Aldestone, a city she had once cherished, when it had changed so much. She found herself longing for Mount Elrad.

Even though Brie escaped Vaylec's presence during the day, every evening he expected her to eat dinner with him. She was grateful that his parents, Eldon and Cecily, always joined them. They eased the awkwardness around the table by chatting with Brie about safe things like the weather, favorite foods, places they'd traveled to, and so on. Vaylec watched their exchanges with a pleased expression, but he rarely joined them. His sister, Violet, was noticeably absent from meals. Brie wondered where she was, though she wasn't brave enough to ask.

During one dinner conversation, Brie innocently asked what Eldon's and Cecily's magical abilities were. They answered, but not without casting hesitant glances in Vaylec's direction. Eldon's powers came from the air, allowing him to manipulate the weather. Cecily's powers came from the earth, and she had a gift with animals. Even though Vaylec didn't speak up, the atmosphere at the table grew uncomfortable. Brie took the hint and changed the subject, but she stored the information about them in the back of her mind in case she would need it later.

On the first day of the new year, Brie was informed that a celebratory dinner would take place. They would eat in the formal dining hall and ballroom, which was much larger and grander, allowing for the added guests. The room had been redecorated in recent years by Brie's mother, and it hurt Brie to think about celebrating in it without her. The walls were now cream and lined with royal blue curtains trimmed in gold accents. Huge golden chandeliers hung from the ceiling, providing not only lighting but breathtaking beauty, and plush blue chairs surrounded the largest dining table Brie had ever seen. Her fourteenth birthday party was supposed to have been held in the hall; but of course, that had never happened.

Brie entered the beautiful ballroom feeling a painful stab

to her heart, and she distracted herself by focusing on its occupants. She noted several grim-faced looking men seated around the table—presumably Vaylec's friends, if such a thing were possible. Some had companions at their sides, and some were alone.

Members of the castle guard were present, standing strategically around the room, wearing uniforms that looked freshly cleaned and pressed. Brie recognized a few of them, as they were often assigned to watch over her. One of them caught her gaze as she looked around the hall. He was young with a thick neck and big, beefy arms, beautiful caramel skin, and tightly curled brown hair. He tilted his head and gave a barely perceptible nod of greeting to Brie. Surprised, Brie nodded back and then made her way to her predicted assigned seat next to Vaylec.

After sitting, Brie continued her perusal of the room and noticed Adira seated at the far end of the table with two familiar-looking men. She recognized them as the Blameless who had captured her and brought her back to the castle on Vaylec's orders.

Brie carefully examined Torin and Jarvis clearly for the first time, now that her brain was free of the teleportation fog. She wasn't sure what she had expected to feel, but she had mixed emotions upon seeing them. They'd stolen her away from the safety of her new family, which made her terribly sad and angry. On the other hand, they'd claimed to be her friends and taken a risk by warning her to shield herself. If it hadn't been for their warning, she would likely be under Vaylec's control right now.

Jarvis looked in her direction and gave her a hesitant smile. After a moment of internal struggle, Brie offered a small smile in return. A look of relief washed over Jarvis's face.

Brie's gaze next went to Adira, whom she hadn't seen since the execution. Adira looked regal in a shimmery white gown, with white flowers woven into the braid that was piled on top of her head. She conversed quietly with the people around her, and yet Brie could tell by her familiar mannerisms that she was worried. Adira fiddled with the thick gold bracelet at her wrist, and her pinched brows covered eyes that repeatedly strayed to Brie. Brie had to remind herself that, despite what Adira had done, she was still a Blameless in her heart. She wasn't evil.

Suddenly, something occurred to Brie. Adira could communicate telepathically, just like Derek. If Brie tried, maybe she could send Adira a message or get information out of her without Vaylec knowing. Brie had no idea if she herself could speak telepathically or not, but it seemed she possessed an unlimited range of gifts that she had yet to master. Instead of discouraging her, that thought boosted her resolve. It certainly couldn't hurt to try.

Brie glanced at Vaylec, making sure he wasn't silently watching her, a creepy habit he had developed. Luck was on her side, and Vaylec was engrossed in a conversation with one of his grim-faced friends. Brie overheard the tail end: "Come to my study before you leave. I may share my secret." Her interest was piqued, and for a moment she wondered what secret Vaylec was referring to. But she pushed curiosity aside. Her desire to communicate with Adira was more pressing.

With no clue what she was doing, Brie held her right hand

over her heart, then focused on Adira. She thought, *Adira, can you hear me?*

Seemingly, nothing happened. Adira remained fully engaged in her conversation with Torin.

Brie tried again, staring at Adira so intensely that her eyes began to water. *Adira, can you hear me?*

"Briana, is everything alright?"

Brie jerked in surprise and cleared her throat. "Yes, Vaylec. I was just wondering about the men seated with Adira. They look familiar, but I can't remember where I've seen them." Cassie would be proud of how quickly Brie had invented a convincing lie.

Vaylec leaned toward her and quietly said, "They are the ones who brought you home to me. You don't remember them?"

"No, not really. It felt like a dream," Brie answered him.

Vaylec eyed her suspiciously but said, "You'll be properly introduced to them soon enough."

Brie nodded while Vaylec continued to watch her. She spooned small bites of potato into her mouth until he eventually turned aside and resumed his conversation with the man next to him.

Sighing in relief, Brie refocused on her task. She thought again about Derek. He'd told her once that telepathy was simply "sending thoughts through the air to one another." The only thing Brie could think of that she had sent through the air was an arrow. She closed her eyes and willed her thought to be like an arrow speeding toward its target. With her hand over her heart, she opened her eyes and hurled her question at

Adira: *CAN YOU HEAR ME, ADIRA?*

Adira's eyes widened, and she choked on a sip of wine. She cast a quick but meaningful look in Brie's direction as she continued to cough. Torin thumped her on the back until her coughing fit subsided.

Brie's heart fluttered in her chest. She'd done it! She tried her best not to show her excitement. She fiddled with her hair, twirling the ends of it around her finger. Then, after ensuring Vaylec's focus was somewhere else, she asked, *Can we speak together this way? Are you able to answer me?*

Adira didn't look at her, but Brie watched her shake her head. It looked like she was merely responding to Torin's concern over her choking fit, but Brie knew better. The shake of Adira's head combined with her silence was answer enough for Brie to understand.

Brie's heart sank in disappointment. It seemed that Vaylec had control over Adira's telepathy, too. Then a very scary possibility entered Brie's mind, and she tensed in her seat. Not daring to look in the direction of her captor, she asked, *Can Vaylec hear me, too?*

Adira took a bite of her steak, closed her eyes, and gave another small shake of her head. To anyone else, it looked like she was simply enjoying a tasty morsel of food.

Brie sagged in relief. That felt like a close call. At least she could send Adira messages, even if Adira couldn't respond. Brie was certain it would somehow come in handy. She decided to send Adira one final thought.

*I know you didn't have a choice at the execution. I didn't like it, but I understand.*

Adira swallowed her meat and met Brie's gaze. She fisted her hand over her heart and nodded.

It was a frustrating way of communicating, but Brie took it to mean she had been correct with her conclusions. Adira didn't have a choice. She was simply carrying out Vaylec's orders.

Brie was completely distracted from all thoughts of Adira when Violet entered the dining hall. Brie hadn't seen Violet since Gifting Day, and she was thrilled to see Vaylec's sister join them again. Violet looked just as sickly as she had then, which sparked Brie's curiosity and concern.

Violet took the empty seat beside Brie and immediately reached under the table to pat Brie's knee in a form of silent greeting.

Warmth filled Brie's chest at the gesture. Despite the health condition Violet was obviously suffering from, she wanted to reassure Brie. Brie smiled at Violet as brightly as she could through her worry, but she just couldn't help herself. She blurted out, "You look like you're not feeling well. Are you sick?"

Violet glanced at Brie and gave her head an infinitely small shake. Was she warning Brie to keep silent, or was she answering the question?

Brie didn't have to wonder for long, because Vaylec answered. Apparently, he was paying attention again. "Violet is merely frail. She is not sick." His eyes, however, shifted to the side as he spoke, which made Brie question his honesty. Did monsters feel guilty when they lied?

"Is that why you haven't been eating dinner together with us?" Brie pushed, directing her question at Violet instead of Vaylec.

"Yes," Violet said. "I don't get out much."

"Well, if you aren't strong enough to come out of your room," Brie said, "perhaps I can visit you sometime. Where is your room?"

Conversation continued to swirl around in different parts of the room, but by the sudden tension at her end of the table, Brie could tell she had hit on a touchy subject.

"The north tower," Violet answered quietly.

Brie froze in her seat. The north tower. Red flags went up in her mind. Vaylec had told her a week ago, "You may go anywhere you wish within the castle except for my rooms and the north tower." Why was Violet's room way up in the north tower, and why couldn't Brie go there? Something very strange was going on, and Brie was determined to figure out what it was.

Brie turned in her chair to look at Vaylec. She had to get into that tower. She put on her most dazzling smile and asked, "Vaylec, could I please visit Violet in her room? I promise to be especially careful and not tire her out. It would make me so happy to have another girl to talk to. No offense, Cecily," Brie added in a rush, throwing a sympathetic smile in Cecily's direction, "but I miss being with someone younger. I know Violet isn't quite my age, but it would mean the world to me. I need a friend." She was rambling, she knew, but there was a mystery to Violet that Brie needed to solve.

Vaylec examined Brie intensely, as though measuring her motives. Unsure of what else to do, Brie smiled even wider at him. Her face hurt, she was grinning so hugely, and she worried she looked crazy rather than hopeful.

Miraculously, Vaylec agreed. "I suppose occasional small visits wouldn't hurt, but you cannot go alone. You must be accompanied by your guards or myself."

"Thank you, Vaylec. You won't regret it. I want to get to know your family better." Brie was going over the top, she realized, but if she was going to play the part, she might as well do it soundly.

Two positive things had been accomplished during dinner, and Brie was feeling very pleased about it.

After the first course of the meal was complete, Vaylec stood up.

"I have an announcement to make," he said. "Today is the first day of the new year, which is in itself a cause for celebration. But we have a greater cause for festivity today. As some of you already know, it grieved my heart terribly that during our overthrow of the city, Princess Briana was lost."

People murmured in acknowledgement around the table.

Brie stopped eating.

"Not everyone here has heard the wonderful news, but it pleases me greatly to tell you that after searching the kingdom, we found the princess unharmed and brought her back home!"

Cheers and clapping resounded through the hall, and a few people looked in Brie's direction with interest and newfound understanding.

Vaylec turned to her. "Princess Briana, please join me."

He held out his hand to Brie. After hesitating briefly, Brie took it and stood up next to him. He placed his arm firmly around her shoulder. Perhaps she had gone a little overboard with her performance, Brie thought fleetingly.

"It gives me great pleasure to announce that Princess Briana is royalty and will remain as such. She is to be treated with respect and dignity by each of you. But due to her young age, she is not yet ready to rule. I have been acting as regent in her absence, and I'll continue to do so until she reaches the age of eighteen and can assume her role as queen. At that time, with her full support, I will continue to advise her in making decisions for the good of the kingdom." Vaylec's arm clenched painfully around Brie's shoulder as though daring her to contradict him. He'd said his plans came with her full support, but Brie was certain she didn't have a choice in the matter.

More clapping followed this awful news, as well as a few loud shouts of approval from Vaylec's friends.

Not fully understanding what was happening, Brie used all the acting skills she possessed and stood by Vaylec's side with a fake, wide-eyed smile. She peered around the room at the reactions of the other guests. Eldon and Cecily met each other's eyes and shook their heads in dismay. Violet's eyes widened, and she covered her mouth with her hand. Her already pale skin lost more of its color, making her appear more haunted than ever. Vaylec's friends continued to smile and cheer, and the remaining Blameless seemed furious. Jarvis's face turned red; Torin fisted his hands on either side of his plate. Adira's eyes flashed, her lips formed a straight line, and she began to heatedly whisper to the others.

After being released to her seat, Brie didn't eat another bite of food for the rest of the meal.

As the night progressed, most of the guests departed. Finally, Vaylec excused Brie and Violet, and together they stood to leave.

A servant approached the table, carrying a tray laden with tea, coffee, cream, and sugar. Distracted by her load, she didn't see Violet, and they collided. Violet tumbled to the floor as hot tea spilled on her garments.

Vaylec jumped out of his seat, his face a mask of panic. Rushing to Violet's side, he helped her to her feet. He patted her arms, scanned her body with bulging eyes, and whispered in her ear. Violet nodded and pointed at her clothing, and her wet garments immediately dried. Some of the panic left Vaylec's face after watching her perform magic, but once he was certain she was fine, his tender demeanor transformed.

Vaylec grabbed the tray out of the servant's hands and threw it against the wall, shattering the remaining crystal vessels. He kicked a chair out of the way, then another as he screamed, "If you cannot watch where you are going, you are not fit to serve in this castle!"

Then he pulled on the servant's arm, twisting it behind her back, yanking her toward him.

"Vaylec, I'm *fine*. Calm down!" Violet urged.

Vaylec didn't acknowledge his sister's words. After glaring down at the servant, he twisted her arm again and began to drag her from the room as she sobbed and apologized.

When Vaylec reached the hall, he shouted, "Take her to the dungeons!"

"Please, sir," the woman begged. "Who will care for my son?"

"SILENCE!" Vaylec bellowed. "Or I'll have you killed instead!"

The servant whimpered but fell quiet.

Trembling, Brie fled to her room before she could witness anything else. She had bottled up so much emotion during the evening, she couldn't contain it any longer. Angry tears dripped down her cheeks as she ran ahead of her guards.

Slamming the door shut, Brie fell onto her bed and punched her pillow. Despair filled her. Vivid memories flashed through her mind: Vaylec's treatment of the servant, her own kidnapping, and the entire awful predicament she was in. She wanted to rage and pace and scream, but she knew none of those things would change her situation. She wished her uncles would hurry up and rescue her, so together they could devise a plan and overthrow Vaylec.

Feeling terribly alone and needing a distraction, she summoned Cassie's notebook and madly flipped to the back of the book.

There, written with an abundance of capital letters, was a message from Cassie.

BRIE!!!!! BRIANA!!!! IT'S CASSIE! (Of course, it's me. You already know that.) I'VE BEEN CRYING FOR AN ENTIRE WEEK AND MISSING YOU IN THE WORST POSSIBLE WAY. When I saw my gift on the table, IT MADE ME EVEN MORE SAD (and a little bit jealous because Taeo thinks his gift was in your pocket). But two days ago, THE BOOK WAS SUDDENLY GONE! I'm sorry to admit that for an entire day, I yelled at everyone in the house and accused them of taking it. They denied it, of course, and when I pointed *at the table to prove it had disappeared, IT WAS BACK AGAIN. The next day, THE EXACT SAME THING HAPPENED: IT WAS GONE, I YELLED, THEN IT REAPPEARED. I took it to my room to protect it from my nosy family members and decided I might as well add more Blameless facts. AND GUESS WHAT??? (You already know the answer to this.) I FOUND YOUR MESSAGE! You've probably wanted to magically strangle me for taking so long. Please write again soon! I've told everyone still at home that you're okay and all of us are anxiously waiting for more news from you!*

*Love,*
*Cassie*

Brie was beaming by the time she'd finished reading the entry. She rushed to her desk and immediately wrote a response. She wanted to tell Cassie everything that had happened, but she was worried it would take up too many of the book's precious blank pages. Instead, using a tiny scrawl, she filled four entire pages, highlighting the main points since her capture: being teleported, the execution, and the evening's dreadful dinner. She ended the note with a question.

You said you told everyone still at home. Who's still at home, who has left, and where did they go?

—Brie

P.S. I hate to admit it, but Taeo was right. I have his gift.

# *Under Lock and Key*

Over the next several days, Brie and Cassie developed a routine for communicating. Every evening, Brie would summon the notebook and write a summary of her day, and then she would return it to the safety of the Blackwoods' home. Every morning, she would summon the book again to read Cassie's response.

Brie learned that Flinton, Derek, Kove, and Milly had left Mount Elrad three days after her disappearance, before Cassie had discovered Brie's message. Unfortunately, they had been sent on a Blameless mission, and according to Cassie, it would be a while before her uncles came to rescue her. Brie was devastated when she heard the news, and she couldn't help but question why she wasn't their first priority. Doubt crept in, telling her she wasn't as important to them as they were to her. Brie could hardly stand the thought of remaining Vaylec's prisoner and she tried her hardest to devise a plan of escape. But sadly, Brie couldn't figure a way out on her own. Starting each day with a note from Cassie helped to keep Brie's spirits from plummeting in despair.

One morning, the message was especially heart-warming.

*The house is too quiet with you, Flinton, and Milly all gone. We try to act like everything is okay, but really, we're all worried and grumpier than usual. However, you'll be happy to hear I haven't accused anyone of stealing lately. Adelaide's been sleeping in bed with me, and she refuses to take off the locket you gave her. None of us are great cooks (it's a hazard of living with a Blameless chef), so we're barely surviving on burned bread, dry meat, and watery soups. I'm losing so much weight, you may not recognize me when we see each other again.*

*Taeo hasn't been himself since you were taken. I think he feels as guilty as me that he wasn't able to save you. He's quiet, and I haven't heard him brag once. (See? Something is seriously wrong with him.) We miss you.*

*Love,*

*Cassie*

In very tiny print written under Cassie's entry was another note.

*Cassie made me write ridiculously small because she's afraid I'm going to use up all her space. I'm glad you're alive, but I'm still worried you aren't safe. Don't trust anyone, and keep practicing your magic. Mount Elrad is terribly dull without you.*

*-Taeo*

Since Brie had first arrived back in Aldestone, she'd maintained her shield continuously except for when she slept at night. However, after a few days, she discovered that keeping it in place wore her out. Similar to a simmering pot of soup, maintaining a shield required a bit of concentration and effort. Like soup, the setup was the hardest part, but once it was put together, it still needed a watchful eye—or an occasional stir, so to speak. Brie found the mental stimulation exhausting. After giving it some thought, she'd decided that she only needed her shield in place when she was with another Blameless—or when Vaylec was near.

One afternoon, Brie was summoned to Vaylec's study. She ensured her shield was in place, then made her way to his rooms. One of the guards accompanying her was the beefy young man who had been present during dinner on New Year's Day. She had since learned his name was Odin. Over the past few days, Brie had begun to chat with her guards rather than ignore them. Not only did it help pass the time, but it wouldn't hurt to try and gain as many allies as possible. So far, Odin had been surprisingly kind to her; he was by far her favorite.

Brie hesitantly entered Vaylec's study while her guards lined up in the hallway outside his door. Vaylec sat behind his desk with his fingers steepled beneath his chin. He appeared to be deep in thought. He looked up as Brie entered and motioned for her to sit across from him. As she cautiously lowered herself into a chair, Brie was startled to see Adira standing like a statue, stone-faced, in the corner of the study.

Once Brie was seated, Vaylec wasted no time with small talk. "What have you been told about your gifts?"

Brie hadn't expected this question, but she knew she needed to be very cautious about what she disclosed.

Before she was able to respond, however, Vaylec turned his head toward Adira and said, "You will use your magic to discern if she is being truthful."

Brie swallowed, even more nervous than before. She was going to have to tell as much of the truth as possible. "I was told that when I was a baby, I was touched by the gods and became invisible," she provided. This was safe to say, even though it wasn't revealing anything he didn't already know.

"Yes, I was there to witness it," Vaylec said matter-of-factly. "Did your parents ever explain what happened to you or provide you with education or training?"

"No," Brie said quietly, "they never spoke about it." Vaylec had hit a nerve. It bothered Brie more than she cared to admit that her parents had never mentioned the possibility of her being Blameless and possessing magical abilities.

Vaylec shook his head, but he softened his tone. "Doesn't it bother you that they didn't trust you with such important information? Information you had the right to know?"

Brie shrugged. "Maybe a little bit."

"More than a little bit, Your Grace," Adira interrupted in a monotone. Her eyes had a distant look.

Vaylec's brows furrowed. "What about the Blameless who kidnapped you? Did they provide you with details or any sort of tutelage?"

It took Brie a moment to realize he was talking about Flinton, Kove, and Derek. She had to bite the inside of her cheek to keep from defending them. They weren't her kidnappers; they had been her saviors. Her mind raced as she tried to think of a truthful answer that wouldn't reveal that her magic had surfaced. "They told me a Blameless can harness power from the earth, air, or sun. Since I became invisible as a baby, that means my powers will come from the sun."

"Hmm." Vaylec stroked his chin. "So they taught you a bit of theory. I suppose that's something. What about training?"

Brie's throat felt dry as she swallowed again. "They tried to get me to do all sorts of things, but I failed at all of them," she answered. This was also true. At least in the beginning.

"They should have been more persistent," Vaylec shook his head, his lip curling in disgust. "Briana, I believe most of your life, you have been stifled by your parents."

These words sunk slowly into Brie's mind. Even though she hated to admit it, a small part of her agreed with Vaylec: she *had* been stifled during her childhood. She was never made aware of her potential. She'd never received training. She'd floated through her childhood, completely ignorant of her calling as a Blameless. Her parents had not just withheld information from her, but by forbidding her from doing anything dangerous, unusual, or exhilarating—even something as wonderful as riding a horse—they'd actively tried to prevent her magic from ever surfacing.

"We are going to remedy their failure." Vaylec put his hands down on the desk and shuffled through some papers. Eventually he extracted a piece of parchment that appeared to be an outline and handed it to her.

"Adira and the Blameless who rescued you, Jarvis and Torin, have been instructed to begin your training. Jarvis and Adira have powers from the sun, like you. Torin's are from the air, but it won't hurt to have him along as well. You will train with them a minimum of three days a week. Here is your schedule."

Brie focused on the paper, a storm of emotions crashing around inside of her. She was excited to learn more about magic, but she was also worried that Vaylec would discover that her powers were alive and growing. How would he react if he found out she had been deceiving him this whole time?

"I've put a lot of thought into this, Briana," said Vaylec. "I believe it will do you a world of good to focus on your magical training. But never underestimate me." He gave her a stern look. "I grew up in a family of Blameless and learned all of their secrets. My parents constantly practiced magic in our home and freely spoke about their community. I know what a special child you were, and I understand your enormous potential for power. I have no doubt your magic will appear, likely sooner rather than later. Adira, Torin, and Jarvis will report to me every day regarding any progress you make."

Brie suddenly realized how foolish she'd been to use her magic in front of Adira. If Vaylec asked the right questions, Adira would have no choice but to reveal her secret. Unsure of what else to say, Brie gave a simple, "Thank you."

Vaylec nodded, then turned to Adira, motioning with his hand. "Come here, Adira."

Adira did as she was instructed and stepped forward, closing the distance and stopping beside Brie.

"Perform a scan and tell me if you sense any signs of magic within Brie," Vaylec ordered. "I want to know if there are any indicators before she begins her training."

Brie gulped. Even though her shield was protecting her, she was nervous. Adira turned and faced Brie, and Brie saw a flicker of some unnamed emotion in her eyes before they blanked and closed. A blast of heat covered Brie, and she closed her own eyes, focusing on maintaining her shield, hoping it held.

The heatwave passed, and Brie looked up. Adira was staring down into Brie's hazel eyes as she spoke to Vaylec. "I sense no magic within her, Your Grace."

Brie slowly released her breath, trying not to show her relief.

Vaylec pursed his lips and nodded in disappointment. "You're dismissed, Adira." As Adira exited, Vaylec stood up and spoke to Brie. "I thought today would be perfect for visiting Violet. Shall we?"

"Uh, yes. That would be lovely," Brie stuttered, surprised by the abrupt offer. The idea of visiting Violet excited Brie, but she was disappointed that Vaylec would be accompanying her.

They left his study and strode through the many corridors of the castle. For once Brie was without her entourage of guards. She almost missed them, and she felt on-edge as she walked alone with Vaylec. His pace was quick and purposeful, and there was little conversation, which made Brie feel uncomfortable.

They finally arrived at the base of the north tower, and together they climbed to the very top of the spiral staircase.

The stairs opened to a small landing, where two soldiers were guarding a large wooden door that was probably also locked. Brie looked around, wondering if the door could possibly lead to Violet's room. *Is this some kind of joke?*

She watched in confusion as Vaylec pulled a key out of his pocket. He inserted it into the lock, twisted, and released it.

Brie swallowed thickly. Vaylec kept his sister under lock and key? Surely not.

But Vaylec opened the door and motioned for Brie to follow him into the room.

Brie's confusion turned to outrage. She followed Vaylec through the open door, anger sizzling in her veins, to find Violet sitting in a cushioned chair, looking surprised. Eyes wide, Violet jumped to her feet and ran toward them. She gave Vaylec a kiss on the cheek and threw her arms around Brie. In a daze, Brie returned the hug as she tried to absorb her shock over Violet's living arrangement. Brie couldn't imagine a single reason good enough for keeping a family member locked away in a tower; yet Vaylec, the guards, and even Violet acted as though it were normal.

"Oh, Vaylec," Violet said, "thank you for bringing Brie! This is wonderful!"

Vaylec smiled at his sister. "I was due for a visit, anyway."

Violet grabbed Brie's hand and led her to a second cozy armchair next to her own. She had a giddy smile on her face as she began to ramble in excitement. "I was just about to open my book, but it can wait. I would much rather talk with you." She paused for a heartbeat. "This morning, I spent some time painting on a new canvas . . ."

As Violet carried on about her day, Brie examined the room. Several books littered the table between them. An easel with a partial painting had been cast off to one side. A beautiful four-poster bed with bright yellow bedding dominated the curved stone wall on the right, and a rich rose- and gold-trimmed rug decorated the floor. Dried flowers hung from the walls around the inside of the circular tower, and the fireplace blazed with warm, welcoming flames. On the floor in front of the fire, a small brown bunny slept in a basket.

For a prison, it was lovely.

Brie's eyes landed on Vaylec. She was surprised to find him smiling at Violet with a soft look of genuine care on his face.

Brie brought her gaze back to Violet, who had finished describing her day up until the present and was now grinning expectantly.

"How are you feeling today?" Brie asked, scanning Violet's face with concern.

Violet waved her hand dismissively. "Oh, I'm feeling just fine."

Violet looked just as pale and sickly as ever, but happiness shone in her eyes. Whatever mystery surrounded her, it was clear this visit meant a great deal to her.

"And how are you?" Violet asked.

"I'm adjusting," Brie answered vaguely, giving Violet what she hoped was a convincing smile. Brie didn't want to talk about herself. She wanted to learn as much as she could about Violet. "Do you like to read?" Brie motioned toward the books on the table.

"Yes, I do!" Violet pounced on the subject and proceeded to tell Brie all about the book she was currently enjoying.

With Vaylec standing in the room like a guard dog, Brie knew she wouldn't be able to ask any of the important questions bouncing around inside of her head, so she decided to relax and enjoy the visit for Violet's sake.

Something twitched in the corner of her eye, and Brie turned her head toward the fireplace. The rabbit had awoken and was sniffing around in its basket. It had floppy ears and large blue eyes, and it was one of the cutest little creatures Brie had ever seen.

Violet followed Brie's gaze and smiled. "Would you like to hold him?"

"Yes, I would love to." Brie smiled. She adored most animals—not just horses.

Violet knelt down in front of the fire and picked up the bunny. She patted the floor beside her, and Brie sank down to join them. Violet gently deposited the bunny into Brie's lap. The furry little guy rose up on its hind legs and sniffed around in the folds of her dress.

Brie couldn't help but giggle. "I'm sorry, but there's no food for you here." She ran her hands through his soft fur, and eventually he stopped his search and settled into her lap. "What's his name?"

"It's not very original, but I've named him Nibbles."

Violet grinned as Brie laughed. "I like it."

"My mother found him outside in one of the courtyards. Because of her gift, animals love her. This little bunny hopped up to her and wouldn't leave her alone. He followed her around the courtyard until she finally picked him up and brought him inside." Violet smiled fondly at the little animal.

"It was Vaylec's idea to give him to me."

The girls became instantly preoccupied with petting and cooing over Nibbles.

Too soon, Vaylec announced it was time to leave. Violet's shoulders drooped, and the corners of her mouth turned down, but she quickly covered her disappointment with a smile. She gave Brie one final hug and said, "Come again soon."

As Violet hugged Vaylec goodbye, Brie overheard her whisper, "Thank you, Vaylec. There is good inside of you, and despite everything, I love you. Please, reconsider your plans. Your intentions are good, but it will end in disaster. You can still stop it."

"It's too late for that, Violet," Vaylec responded in a low grumble. "You can't change my mind." He kissed Violet on the cheek, then turned his back on her and left her room, locking her up in the tower once again.

The next day, Brie found herself at her first training session with Adira, Jarvis, and Torin. According to her schedule, it would be held in the indoor training room, which contained a myriad of weapons, coats of armor, and a large open area for sparring.

Adira smiled encouragingly as Brie entered.

"Good afternoon, Princess!" She declared warmly, seeming more like the Adira Brie had known before. As Brie stepped closer, Adira dropped her voice and asked Brie quietly, "How are you holding up?"

"It hasn't been easy, but I'm trying to be positive," Brie admitted with a shrug. "I'm looking forward to my training." She smiled.

"Good. It's helps to keep the mind busy." Adira nodded. "Allow me to formally introduce Torin and Jarvis," she said, signaling to them as she said their names.

The two men stepped forward and bowed deeply.

"Your Highness, it is an honor," Torin said.

"We are pleased to see you safe and well," Jarvis added.

"Thank you." Brie nodded to each in turn. "I have to admit, I'm rather excited to be taught by the only person I know of with the power of invisibility."

Jarvis' eyes twinkled. "A rare gift," he said. "One that takes time to master, although I heard it happened rather instantaneously for you as an infant."

Brie sighed. "Yes. Unfortunately, I have no recollection of how it happened."

She had given today's training a lot of thought. As she'd tossed and turned in bed the previous night, she'd decided on a course of action. She would listen intently to their advice during training, but she wouldn't allow herself to practice in front of them. That way, Vaylec wouldn't know about her progress. However, when she was alone in her room, she would put her training to the test.

Even though the three Blameless had previously been exposed to her powers, Brie made sure her shield was in place, and she carried on with her plan. "You can teach me, and I'll try my best to practice, but don't get your hopes up. I'm afraid my magic is buried deep within me and hasn't found its way out yet."

Adira snorted at the lie.

Jarvis and Torin grinned.

"An excellent plan, Princess," Jarvis agreed happily.

"Before we start, can you please answer a question I've had?" Brie asked Jarvis. As she roamed the castle each day, many mysteries plagued her. Perhaps she could start to gather some answers.

"Yes, of course, Your Highness," Jarvis replied with a tip of his head.

"If only you have the gift of invisibility, how is it possible that both of you were invisible when you captured me?" Brie looked between the two of them.

"We were linked together with a simple rope," Jarvis explained. "Invisibility can extend to whatever or whomever I touch, if that's what I choose."

"It's the same with teleportation," Torin added.

Brie nodded, storing away everything she learned. She was brave enough to ask another question. "If Vaylec has control over your powers, how can you train me today?"

The men glanced at one another, their eyebrows raised in surprise. Jarvis opened his mouth to speak, but no words came out. He snapped his mouth shut and groaned in frustration.

Adira shrugged. "He ordered us to help you," she said. "But you already know that we've been instructed to train you." She dropped her voice again and glanced at the door, as though looking for eavesdroppers. "And we've already discussed that we are limited with what we can speak about."

Brie nodded, trying to dissect Adira's answer. Vaylec

didn't have to be in the room for them to carry out his orders. Brie had already witnessed this undeniable fact during Adira's ambush and Jarvis's and Torin's capture. But she was frustrated with the mystery of it all, and she wanted to learn more.

Brie whispered back: "You keep telling me you're limited with what you can say, and I'm trying to figure out why. Can't you refuse his orders?" she asked.

They merely stared at her and didn't offer a response.

"You can't speak about it, but can you signal or nod your heads?" Brie pressed.

The men looked at one another in bewilderment, and eventually Torin shrugged, then grinned and nodded.

"So you *can* signal!" Brie whispered excitedly. "Well, can you refuse Vaylec's orders?"

The three of them shook their heads.

"Can you use your magic without him commanding you to?"

Torin readily shook his head again, but Adira cleared her throat, and her eyes shifted to the side.

A familiar voice came from the doorway. "How is the training coming along?" Goosebumps spread up Brie's arms as she whipped around. Vaylec was leaning against the doorway. How long had he been standing there?

"I've introduced the others, and we're just getting started, Your Grace," Adira responded, dropping into a curtsey.

"Very good. Report to my office when you're finished," Vaylec commanded. His footsteps echoed down the hall as he left.

"That was too close," Adira murmured, wiping her brow. "Jarvis, you take the lead on the lesson today."

Jarvis nodded and began by explaining why the power of the sun gave the gift of invisibility. Brie had heard it before from Derek, but she listened anyway. She was anxious to hear more about *how* it was done, not *why*. Finally, the time came for Jarvis to demonstrate.

"Close your eyes, and place your hand over your heart," Jarvis instructed.

"Why does placing your hand over your heart matter?" Brie interrupted. She was pretty sure her uncles had mentioned it allowed one to better connect with one's powers, but they hadn't ever sufficiently explained why that was. "I've seen the Blameless perform magic many times without doing this." She thought back to the extravagant waving of Kove's arms and Derek's quick snaps.

"It's not necessary for executing magic," Adira confirmed. "But it allows for us to put aside all distraction and connect with the very core of our power, which lies in our hearts. Blameless often do this when we first learn how to use our gifts, or when we perform important magic."

Brie thought of Flinton placing his hand over his heart as he broke them out of the smithy. Kove had done the same thing when he created her bow. Brie's eyes began to burn. It felt like a confirmation that she was important to them. Her heart ached. She missed her uncles terribly. It had been two weeks since her capture, and despite Cassie's warning that it would take time, Brie was counting the days and clinging to the hope that her uncles would arrive soon to rescue her.

"Let's try again. Place your hand over your heart," Jarvis repeated.

Brie did as she was told without further questions.

"I want you to imagine the warmth of the sun on a very hot summer day," Jarvis continued. "Bring to mind the way it feels as it shines down on you, warming your skin. Focus on the sun, and pretend it's beaming into you. Imagine how terribly hot and thirsty you are, as it's heating up your insides, straight through to your bones."

Brie listened with rapt attention, recalling a memory of when she was younger. She had gotten such an awful sunburn, her skin had blistered. She could still clearly remember what it felt like. For a week, it had been so painful, the touch of her clothes or sheets was torture.

"Now look around you," Jarvis continued. "Observe your surroundings. Imagine the rays of the sun traveling straight through your body to the items in the room."

Brie watched in amazement as Jarvis disappeared before her very eyes. Her jaw dropped, and she began to clap.

"*That* is amazing!" she whooped. "I can hardly believe it's happened to me before." If Brie could master the power of invisibility, there were endless possibilities to what she could do. Investigating why Violet was locked away in the north tower was at the top of her list.

"Now you try," Adira ordered in an unexpectedly sharp tone. Brie could tell by Adira's expression that it was an act. Her gaze was still soft and kind, but her eyes flicked toward the door as she spoke.

Brie followed Adira's gaze. Two guards had stepped into

the room to check on them. Vaylec was keeping a close eye on their training.

Looking back at Adira, Brie called on her newfound acting skills, and arranged her face into the picture of innocence. "As you wish," she said dramatically, then closed her eyes, put her hand over her heart, and made absolutely no effort to connect with her powers. After counting to thirty, she opened one eye and asked, "Well, can you still see me?"

Despite their somber acts, everyone laughed.

"It was a dismal failure," Torin confirmed.

After several more failed attempts, Adira ended the session.

Brie could hardly wait to get through the remainder of the day. She planned to practice the moment she was behind the closed door of her room.

When evening finally arrived, Brie sat excitedly in the middle of her bed and recounted Jarvis's instructions. She closed her eyes, placed her hand over her heart, and tried her very hardest to imagine the sun shining down on her. She focused on the memory of her sunburn, and how overheated her skin had felt. She tried to empty her mind of all else and lose herself in that feeling. After nearly a half hour of concentration, Brie's body started to warm up. It felt exactly like she was sunbathing on a cloudless summer day. Brie relished in the feel of it, and envisioned the heat searing through her, all the way to her bones.

She opened her eyes and looked down at herself. She could still see her dress, but she felt different somehow.

Jumping off her bed, Brie ran to the mirror and shrieked in astonishment. A headless reflection stared back at her. The shock caused Brie to lose her focus. Thirty minutes of concentration flew out the window, and her head appeared suddenly on her neck. She gave a blood-curdling scream at her head's absurdly sudden reappearance.

The door to her bedroom burst open, and two guards rushed in. One was Odin. He scanned her room, looking for the threat as he pulled out his sword and stood protectively in front of Brie.

"Princess, are you alright?" he asked as he searched the room, his posture tense. The other guard rushed past to survey her bathroom and closet.

"Yes, I'm perfectly fine, but I . . . I saw a mouse," Brie stuttered, feeling foolish for reacting so loudly. She shuddered to think of what would have happened if they had walked in after her first scream, when her head had still been invisible.

Odin's posture relaxed, and he let out a low laugh. "We'll set some traps, Your Highness."

"Thank you. I'm sorry. I was just startled. . ." Brie cleared her throat and blushed.

The two guards shut the door, shaking their heads as they left.

Brie flopped backward onto her bed and breathed a sigh of relief. She would have to be much more careful during her evening practice sessions. Regardless of the close call, she grinned and summoned her notebook. She couldn't wait to tell Cassie all about it.

# A Successful Plan

For the next moon, Brie's spirits were high. She was filled with nervous energy, half expecting her uncles to barge into the castle and save her at any moment. She wasn't worried about the details of their rescue, because her confidence in them was absolute. The anticipation, however, was making her jumpy. Brie found herself pacing through the familiar halls of her old home, unable to relax. She would stop and gaze out every window she passed, grasping Kove's necklace and looking over the hills and valleys surrounding Aldestone, searching for signs of them.

Even Vaylec seemed to notice Brie's uplifted mood. He caught her smiling brightly during dinner one evening and commented on it.

"Briana, you seem to be adjusting at last. You've been acting happier. I'm pleased."

Brie shrugged. "I am happier, Vaylec. Things are looking brighter."

Vaylec smiled, looking smug. "Shall we visit Violet tomorrow morning?"

Vaylec gave Brie permission to visit Violet twice a week.

Unfortunately, he usually accompanied her. The visits were frustrating, leaving Brie with more questions than answers every time she left the dreaded north tower. Her curiosity continued to build until she thought she would explode, yet she didn't dare ask Violet anything useful in front of her twin.

Brie had to find a way to speak with Violet alone. With that in mind, she threw herself into practicing invisibility with even more determination. Brie devoted all of her free time to it. During the late hours of the night, she was able to push herself without being disturbed. Unfortunately, she still couldn't make her entire body disappear. After several evenings with no progress, she finally concluded that she would have to take the risk and ask for help.

Brie waited until her next lesson with her Blameless tutors.

"I have a hypothetical question," she said before they got started.

"And what might that question be?" Adira smirked.

"If a Blameless was trying to turn invisible, but they had only succeeded at getting their head to disappear, what might they be doing wrong?" Brie asked sheepishly. Everyone in the room knew perfectly well she was referring to herself.

Jarvis threw his head back and exploded in laughter. Adira and Torin joined him, though not quite as enthusiastically.

Brie put her hands on her hips and glared at them. "This is not a humorous hypothetical situation."

Wiping tears from his eyes, Jarvis answered. "Actually, it's a simple mistake—er, hypothetically. If this person was looking in a mirror, I would first ask him," he coughed, "or *her*, if she had looked at her hands."

Brie cocked her head to the side, then glanced at her hands. She flipped them over. What was she missing?

Jarvis continued. "It is likely that, in this hypothetical situation, the person was only really looking at her face in the mirror. She was—I mean, she *would be* only seeing her head disappear. However, I would bet a bag of gold coins that her entire body had vanished, leaving her clothes behind in full view." He chuckled quietly.

Brie tried to recall if she had looked at her hands, but she couldn't remember. She had been certain her throat was still visible, but thinking back, the collars of her dresses were so high, it was possible her neck had vanished too.

"Remember to look at your surroundings and extend the heat of the sun to them as well. This includes your clothes," Jarvis said quietly.

Brie blushed furiously but nodded in understanding.

During the practice that followed, Brie made sure to fall short once again, failing every test they gave her. Vaylec came in to observe the training, and Brie carefully disappointed him. Eventually he left, still under the delusion that her gifts hadn't manifested themselves.

Later that night, Brie sat before the mirror one more time, placed her hand over her heart, and looked up at her reflection. She went through her routine, like she had every other night, focusing on the sun and heating up her body. She felt a familiar shift inside, and she watched in awe as her head disappeared. This time, however, she looked at her hands. Jarvis had been right; her hands were invisible too. She lifted the hem of her dress to look at her legs, which had also disappeared, making her dress look like it was floating in midair. Brie had indeed managed to make her body invisible—but she had yet to master her clothing.

Another week went by—seven frustrating nights—and on the eighth night, Brie became so angry with herself that she swore she wouldn't sleep until she was entirely invisible, clothes and all. She closed her eyes and focused long and hard. In a few moments, she felt the warmth of the sun in every fiber of her being. But she didn't dare open her eyes. She carefully envisioned the details of her clothing, her pale lavender nightgown and robe, trimmed with embroidered green leaves. Squeezing her fists, she imagined them catching on fire. Ever so slowly, Brie opened her eyes and anxiously looked down at herself. Her heart skipped a beat when she didn't see her robe. She rushed to the mirror in excitement, and sure enough, only her empty bedroom was reflected back at her.

Squealing in delight, Brie spun around in a circle with her arms out wide. If the guards opened the door, they wouldn't see a blessed thing. She leapt onto her bed and jumped up and down in glee, feeling a small twinge of sadness that Cassie wasn't here to celebrate the accomplishment with her. Still invisible, she wrote her nightly summary, giggling as she watched the quill dance across the page seemingly on its own.

She smiled invisibly, feeling like a whole new world of possibilities just opened up for her.

Eventually, Brie flopped backward onto her pillows and began to plan her excursion to the north tower. She wished she could ask for Adira's help, but it would be too risky. Her biggest dilemma was getting past the guards outside Violet's door. She needed a diversion, or perhaps a sleep tonic, but she was at a loss for the time being. Deciding to visit the castle's library in the morning to search for ideas, she slid under her covers for the night.

Sleep didn't come easy, and after tossing and turning, Brie eventually got out of bed and walked to one of her windows. She looked out over the city, which was bathed in moonlight.

Her thoughts went to Kove, Flinton, and Derek yet again. Nearly six weeks had passed, and winter was already ending. Brie had hoped her uncles would have rescued her already. If only she could talk to them and ask what was taking so long! Huffing in frustration, she went back to her bed and summoned Cassie's notebook for the second time.

Brie opened the notebook, and instead of writing an entry, she read one.

*Flinton has the ability to track any living thing, not just a person or a member of the Blameless. Once, he even found my pet hamster in Emily's sock drawer. Whether or not I put it there hoping to scare Emily is irrelevant.*

Smiling, Brie turned the page.

*Derek told me the longest distance he's ever been able to communicate telepathically was 102 miles. He discovered this through some kind of Blameless competition he had with Adira.*

Brie gasped. Bless Cassie's brilliant heart. The next time Brie saw Cassie, she would make her a thousand crowns. It was so obvious, Brie felt like a fool for not realizing it sooner. If she could speak to Adira telepathically, then why couldn't she speak with Derek? If he was anywhere near the city, he would hear her.

Too excited to put it off, Brie ran back to the window, placed her hand over her heart, and sent her thoughts flying. *Derek, it's Brie! Can you hear me?*

She waited in anticipation for several minutes, but no answer came.

*Derek, are you there?* She tried again, hoping for an answer—though she already knew there wouldn't be one. If he was near enough to hear her, he would have answered her first call.

Brie was right. Nothing but silence followed.

Trying her hardest not to be discouraged, Brie returned to bed. She wouldn't lose heart. They would come.

At the end of training the next day, after much internal debating, Brie worked up the nerve to ask a question. She needed to word her questions carefully so the Blameless didn't suspect what she was planning. It would be especially tricky to pull off with Adira and her gift of discernment.

"I've been having trouble sleeping at night, and I'm exhausted," Brie said. This was at least true for some of the nights she had spent traumatized within the castle. "Do you know of a strong medication or tonic that would put me into a deep sleep?"

Adira's eyebrows furrowed immediately in suspicion, and the corners of her mouth turned down. She probably was discerning Brie's partial lies as quickly as Brie spoke them.

Torin was oblivious to her deceit. "My mum used to give me a drop of somnum oil in my tea at night to help me sleep. It works wonders."

"Somnum oil? What's that?" Brie asked.

"It's a sleep aid that comes from the somnum leaf found in the Mountains of Westlor," Torin explained helpfully. "It's difficult to find in Predonia, but my mum's cousin lives in Westlor, and she keeps us well stocked. The leaf releases a potent oil when it's crushed. It doesn't take much; just a drop will do the trick."

"What would happen if I accidently took more than a drop?" Brie asked, looking as wide-eyed and innocent as possible.

Adira's eyes narrowed further, but she kept her mouth shut.

"You'd probably be unconscious for hours," Torin declared, laughing.

A slow smile spread over Brie's face. "Good to know."

Brie now had a way to get past the guards by Violet's door. It didn't look like she would need that trip to the library after all. She just needed to find somnum oil.

Later that week, on Brie's next scheduled visit with Violet, luck was on her side. Vaylec was busy and sent Brie with her guards instead, which suited Brie's plan perfectly. She had developed a delicate relationship of sorts with the guards, and

Odin remained especially friendly with her. Her decision to get to know them seemed to be appreciated, and in return, they chatted with her about their families, homes, jobs, and other things. Brie's efforts had paid off, and the guards were definitely more relaxed in her presence than they had been at the start.

When Brie reached the landing outside of Violet's locked door at the top of the north tower, she smiled at the two guards who stood blocking the entrance.

"Good afternoon!" she said brightly. "It's nearly lunchtime. Are you hungry? I brought muffins for Violet, but I have way more than we could possibly eat. Would you like one?"

The guards faltered, as though they weren't used to receiving small acts of kindness. Finally, the large, burly one on the right muttered in a deep voice, "Yes, that would be very nice. Thank you, Your Highness."

Brie beamed and handed one muffin to him and another to his equally fit female companion. Then Brie turned around and gave one apiece to Odin and the others. The result was a very happy group of munching soldiers.

Brie gave them a moment to enjoy their treat, then innocently asked, "Whenever do you find the time to eat up here?"

"The kitchen staff bring us meals at the same time as Violet," one guard said.

"Don't worry, Your Highness; we're very well fed," another guard added, patting her belly. "They serve us every day at dawn, noon, and dinner, and we even get a midnight snack."

"Well, I'm happy to hear they aren't starving you," Brie said.

A few days later, her plan nearly complete, Brie asked her maid if they kept any somnum oil in the kitchen, but they did not. However, the maid informed her that they carried somnum oil in the castle's infirmary. Brie debated faking an illness to give herself access to the oil, but in the end, she decided to just summon the bottle.

That night, after completing her usual bedtime routine, Brie slipped out of her dress and into a nightgown with the help of her maid.

Following the timeline of her plan, Brie spoke up. "My stomach is feeling queasy tonight." This was true. Her stomach was an anxious ball of nerves. "Could you bring me a cup of tea? It might help."

"Certainly, Your Highness," the maid said, looking pleased to have been given an assignment. She curtsied and hastily left the room.

As soon as the door was shut, Brie leapt up and went to work. She changed out of her nightgown and hastily put on her leggings and tunic. A sigh slipped out of her mouth. They felt so comfortable after weeks of stiff dresses. She rushed back to her bed and rearranged the bedding, stuffing it with extra pillows until it looked like Brie was lying under the covers.

Heart pounding, Brie went to her mirror and connected with her powers, remaining there until she confirmed both her body and clothing had disappeared completely. Satisfied, she walked to her nightstand and grabbed her lock-picking set, the bottle of somnum oil, and a large rock. She extended the warmth of the sun to them as well, until they disappeared, and she placed them into her pockets.

Next, she tucked herself behind her bedroom door and waited.

Her maid eventually returned, carrying a tray of tea, cream and sugar. She entered Brie's darkened room and announced, "I have your tea, Your Highness."

Brie held her breath from behind the door, hoping her plan would work.

The maid glanced at the unmoving form in Brie's bed and whispered, "The poor dear must have fallen asleep."

The maid walked into the room and set the tray down on Brie's nightstand. While her back was turned, Brie slipped out into the hallway. The maid came out after her, quietly shutting the door behind them.

Brie breathed a quiet sigh of relief. Phase one was a success.

She silently made her way through the mostly empty corridors to the base of the north tower, and then she sat down on the cold floor and waited.

An hour passed, and eventually two middle-aged servants approached carrying the anticipated midnight snack for Violet and her guards.

Brie stood and quietly padded after them up the stairs in her bare feet, conscious all the while to keep her breathing under control. She watched them deliver the snack to Violet, pushing it through a slot in the bottom of her door. Then they set a tray down on the floor for the guards.

This part was going to be tricky. Brie pulled the somnum oil out of her pocket and uncorked the bottle as carefully as possible. Unfortunately, it still made a small *pop*. Heads swung in her direction, looking for the source of the sound, but when there was nothing to see, the guards turned away. Sighing in relief, Brie leaned against the wall and waited for an opportunity.

Luckily, the kitchen staff and the guards seemed familiar with one another, and they struck up a casual conversation. When they were engrossed in a discussion about a delicious bread pudding one of the cooks had recently made, Brie slowly got down on her hands and knees. She crawled, inching her way among the four of them, and carefully tipped the open bottle over the first mug of coffee. Her plan had been to put three drops of liquid into each cup, but she hadn't considered the fact that she wouldn't be able to see the bottle of oil or its contents. She wasn't used to carrying out secret missions while invisible.

Brie counted to three while tipping the bottle, and then tipped it once more for good measure, desperately hoping it was enough somnum oil to put them to sleep but not enough to put them in a coma. She did the same to the second cup and then hastily backed away. But as one woman turned to leave, her foot came down on the fingers of Brie's outstretched hand.

Brie bit her lip to keep from crying out in pain. The woman lifted her foot—giving Brie time to hastily withdraw her hand—and examined the floor curiously. Not seeing anything, she left the landing with a slightly confused expression on her face.

Brie moved to sit against the far wall across from the guards, and once again she waited. She watched as the men finally sat down on the floor and began to enjoy their snack.

“Ah, this coffee hits the spot,” one said, sipping deeply.

“Mmm,” the other agreed. “It tastes extra strong tonight.” He took a bite of cookie and washed it down with a large swig of coffee.

“It better be extra strong, because I’m suddenly feeling exhausted.”

Three minutes later, both guards collapsed onto the floor. One of them spilled the remainder of his coffee into his lap, and the other one began to snore loudly.

Brie got to her feet and punched the air in celebration. Phase two was a success.

She reached into her tunic pocket and pulled out her gift from Taeo. Unfortunately, she couldn’t see it because it was invisible. Rolling her eyes, she decided it was safe to lift the invisibility. She reversed the heat of the sun, and in the next instant, she materialized into view.

Brie approached Violet’s door and studied the lock. It looked larger and more complicated than Nina’s had been. Taeo was right. You never know when you might need to open a locked door. If she ever—no, *when* she finally made it back to Mount Elrad, she would make sure to tell Taeo how useful his gift had been.

Brie randomly selected an end that was thin and crooked. She inserted it into the keyhole and moved it around, but nothing happened. She selected another long, thick metal piece that was jagged at the tip, but it was too big to even fit into the lock. She went through two more, sweating at the amount of time she was wasting. The fifth tool finally worked. It slipped right in and fit snugly up against the inside of the lock. As Brie twisted her wrist, the lock turned with a loud *click*. Giving a whimper of relief, Brie grabbed the handle and heaved the heavy door open.

Phase three was a—

Brie shrieked as Violet grabbed her arm and yanked her inside of the room. For such a frail thing, she had a surprising amount of strength.

"What are you doing here?" Violet hissed, looking around in panic. Her eyes widened when she saw the guards, but she slammed the door shut behind them anyway.

"Please don't be mad. I needed to talk to you alone," Brie explained.

"So you snuck out of bed and drugged the guards in order to do it?" Violet asked incredulously.

Brie's eyes brightened. "Yes; can you believe it? And don't forget I picked your lock too."

Violet folded her arms and looked at Brie crossly, and then her disapproving frown slowly turned into a reluctant grin. "It was a horrible idea that could get us both into a lot of trouble, but bravo for you."

"I couldn't think of any other way. Everything is so secret around here," Brie said, throwing her hands into the air. "It's driving me crazy! I need answers! Please tell me something, anything! What in the name of the Terren, Solis, and Cael is wrong with you? And why are you locked away in this tower?"

Violet looked torn as she motioned for Brie to have a seat. When Brie sat, Violet remained on her feet and began to pace the length of the small room.

"Briana, there are some things I can't speak about. Even if I wanted to, I physically am not able."

"Because Vaylec has forbidden it?" Brie asked.

"Yes!" Violet shouted.

"Violet, I know he's controlling you, your parents, and the others, but I don't know how he's doing it."

Violet came to a stop and stared at Brie. "How do you know this?" she asked urgently.

"Derek figured it out, and he told me all about it." Brie didn't think it would do her any favors to admit she had learned this by spying.

Violet collapsed in the chair beside Brie. "He knows. Thank the earth, air, and sun, he knows!"

"That's exactly what Adira said," Brie murmured, scratching her head in confusion. "So, are you forbidden from explaining how he is controlling you?" Brie pushed, hoping to gain as much information as possible.

"Yes!" Violet said again, wringing her hands and thinking. "But there are some things I can tell you."

"Okay," Brie said slowly, thinking. "Are you dying?"

Violet looked at Brie sadly. "I am not dying, but death would be a welcomed relief. I'm tormented by guilt."

"But it's not your fault," Brie said.

"Yes, it is," Violet whispered. "But Vaylec tricked me."

"How did he trick you?"

Violet wrung her hands again, looking frustrated. "I can't."

Brie stared at Violet in wide-eyed horror. "Why are you locked away in this tower? Is this your punishment?"

"No, Briana, I'm not being punished. I'm in this tower because Vaylec is protecting me. He is terrified I'll become sick or injured. You saw what happened to the servant who ran into me. Except for my travel to the castle from home, I haven't been outside in many years."

Brie was stunned. There could only be one reason for Vaylec to go to such extremes to protect Violet. "You're the key, aren't you? His control over them is somehow linked to you."

Violet did not—or rather, *could* not—offer an answer, but the look on her face was confirmation enough.

"But how?" Brie whispered. "Is it because you're his twin?"

"Partly," she whispered back. Violet's eyes grew wide and searched around her room frantically.

"Is there anything else you can tell me?" Brie asked as Violet began to dig through her belongings on the table, clearly on the hunt. Brie felt once again like she had come in here for answers but would leave with more questions.

Violet let out a triumphant shout and turned around, clutching an ornate hand-held mirror.

She grabbed Brie's arm. "What am I holding?"

"A mirror." Brie gave the obvious answer.

"Correct!" Violet yelled feverishly. "And what does it do?"

Brie began to worry about Violet's sanity. Her cheeks were flushed, and she'd begun to sweat. Brie slowly answered her question. "It shows your reflection."

"You're right! That's the answer, Briana!" Violet was nearly weeping by then. "That's the correct answer." She put down the mirror and clutched Brie's shoulders, looking her in the eyes. "When you see Derek again—and you *will* see him—tell him what I've said. He was my instructor. He knows my gifts. He taught me how to use and master shields. Tell him to think about my gifts, tell him about the mirror, and tell him Vaylec was a very jealous child. Promise me, Brie!"

The snoring outside of the room suddenly stopped, jarring them out of their intense discussion. Brie must not have dropped as much somnum oil in the coffee as she had hoped. Her time was up. "I promise!" she whispered.

Brie stood and hastily turned herself invisible. Violet yelped in surprise. Hopefully Vaylec would never question Violet about Brie's gifts. Not looking back, Brie opened the door. The guards were stirring, but their eyes were still closed. Brie shut the door and quickly locked it, wincing at the noise it made. One guard sat up and looked around in blurry-eyed confusion, then slumped over again. Brie didn't wait to see what happened; she fled down the stairs.

Phase four had been a confusing success.

Brie made it to the corridor outside of her room safely. The only remaining challenge was to get back inside of her bedchamber undetected. Luckily, she had thought that through. She reached into her tunic pocket and pulled out the large rock she had taken from the courtyard earlier this week during a rarely granted walk.

Brie carefully took aim and hurled the rock down the corridor past her room. The rock left her hand invisible, but it appeared suddenly as it soared away from her and collided with a large painting. The canvas fell to the ground with a resounding crash.

The company of guards by her door jumped at the noise and took immediate action, rushing down the corridor to investigate. Brie used the distraction to open her door and slip inside. Within the safety of her room, she reversed the invisibility, then stuck her head back out into the hallway.

"What's going on out here? I heard a loud noise," she said in the most innocent voice she could muster.

"All is well, Your Highness. A picture fell from the wall. You may go back to sleep."

Brie shut her door and sagged against it, then she slowly slid down all the way to the floor. She closed her eyes and didn't move until her heart rate recovered from the night's events.

All five phases of her plan had been successful.

Too overwhelmed to get up, she summoned her cup of cold tea and took sips of it as she called out to Derek.

*Derek, it's Brie. Where are you?*

Once again, there was no response.

# *Poor Reactions*

Several weeks passed after Brie's successful break-in to the north tower. Spring arrived, but she saw little of it from inside the castle. Brie no longer felt joyful and optimistic. Instead, she was devastated to the very core of her being.

Not only was Brie plagued by Violet's secret, but her uncles hadn't yet come for her, and she couldn't fathom why. On the night of her family's death, after rescuing her, Flinton had promised they would never leave her. Brie understood that they hadn't actually left her. Rather, she had been *taken* from them. But in her heart, it felt like a betrayal that they hadn't immediately saddled their horses and rushed to save her.

Brie's thoughts ran through a continuous loop of possibilities as to why they had been delayed. Maybe they'd changed their minds and decided she wasn't worth the risk, and they were on their way back to Mount Elrad. Maybe they'd tried to rescue her and had been thwarted or captured. What if they were sitting in prison, or injured—or worse yet, killed? Brie's only consolation was that the Blackwood girls and Milly, who had made it home again, hadn't heard from them either.

Brie and Cassie continued their daily chats in *Blameless*

*Facts*, but even Cassie could no longer keep Brie's spirit's uplifted. In return, Brie sensed an uncharacteristic melancholy tone to Cassie's responses.

Every evening, before Brie went to sleep, she continued to reach out to Derek with her thoughts. And every evening, the only answer she received was silence.

With Kove's necklace still resting in its place over her heart, Brie drifted through her days, forlorn and unfocused. Her appetite vanished, and her desire to solve the many mysteries around her was nearly nonexistent. Even her interest in training sessions with Adira, Jarvis, and Torin, which she usually looked forward to, had waned.

One morning, Torin was explaining how teleportation worked. Somewhere in the back of her mind, Brie understood this should be fascinating and useful information, but she couldn't muster up one bit of enthusiasm. She was staring blankly into space, bemoaning her situation, when Adira must have decided that enough was enough.

Adira slammed her fist down on the table and bellowed, "This has gone on long enough!"

Brie jerked back into reality and looked at Adira with surprise. "What has?"

"All of this moping around, Briana!" Adira said. "Where is the fighter who arrived at the castle three moons ago?"

"I can't seem to find her," she whispered. "Why haven't they come for me, Adira?" Then she added the thought she didn't dare speak out loud: *What if they're dead?*

Adira's face softened, and she gently whispered to Brie, "They are not dead, child. Do not lose heart."

Then she opened her arms and gave Brie a comforting hug.

Adira looked at the other two Blameless and said to them, "She isn't up for this. We're finished for today."

In that precise moment, Vaylec walked through the door into the training room. By the angry look on his face, it was clear he wasn't pleased by what he'd seen or heard.

"Step away from her. You are Briana's trainer, not her comforter," he spat, and he narrowed his eyes. "You have barely begun today's session. It's not up to you to decide when you are finished."

Adira stepped away from Brie and curtsied briefly to Vaylec. "I'm sorry, Your Grace. I didn't mean to overstep my boundaries, but the princess is not feeling well today."

Vaylec's sharp gaze landed on Brie. He took in her appearance and some of the ferocity in his expression vanished. After scanning her face, Vaylec seemed to find something that caused him concern.

"What's wrong, Briana? You haven't seemed yourself lately," he asked in a strained tone.

Brie's chin wobbled. She didn't have it in her to lie today, and she was sick of acting. "I miss my family," she choked out. She began to cry.

Vaylec froze in uncertainty. Emotion flickered across his face, but it was gone before Brie could name it.

"Very well," he conceded. "Training is done for today. Briana, is there something that would make you feel better?"

"I want to see Violet," Brie said through her tears.

"That can be arranged," Vaylec said, nodding. He motioned to the guards and ordered in a gruff tone, "Accompany her to the north tower."

Brie was still crying when she reached Violet's room. After the door was unlocked, she followed the guards inside and rushed straight into Violet's outstretched arms. She began to sob loudly and pitifully as Violet rocked her back and forth, patting her back.

"Briana, whatever is the matter?"

"I miss *everyone*," Brie wailed. "My family, my friends, my horse."

"I know, sweetheart, I know," Violet murmured, running her fingers through Brie's long hair.

Violet turned away from Brie for a moment and spoke to the guards with an authority Brie had never heard her use before. "Have some decency and give us privacy. The princess needs to be comforted, but not in front of an audience. I don't care what protocols you have to break in order to do it!"

Brie glanced up in time to see Odin motioning the others out of the room without a single word of resistance.

After the door was shut, Violet asked, "What is this really about, Briana?"

"My uncles haven't come for me," Brie choked through her tears, "and I don't understand why."

Violet pushed gently on Brie's shoulders, guiding her to sit up straight, so they could look directly into each other's eyes. "Sweet girl, are you afraid they've abandoned you?"

"*Yes!*" Brie sobbed harder, covering her face with her hands.

"Briana, listen to me carefully." Violet waited for the crying to die down. "Maybe you've forgotten, but I also know your friends. I've been to Mount Elrad, and I've trained with them."

This got Brie's attention, and she looked up.

"I've even played Flair Ball." Violet smiled when Brie's jaw dropped. "I came to know the hearts of the very same friends. Hearts that are kind and patient beyond what is deserved. Hearts that beat for others, that sacrifice everything for the greater good. Hearts that are blameless. Hearts that would never, *ever* abandon their friends."

Violet's words washed over Brie, and she knew they were true. She hung her head in shame.

Violet continued quietly, "If they have not come for you, then you must believe it's for a good reason."

"Do you think they've been hurt or captured?" Brie asked.

"If anything had happened to them, Vaylec would've told me, and I haven't heard a thing."

Brie heaved a relieved sigh. "Thank goodness."

A few moments of comfortable silence passed as Brie restored her regular breathing and dried her tear-streaked face.

"What should I do, Violet?" Brie moaned. "I feel like I'm in a prison. I can't go anywhere without being spied on or surrounded by guards. I hate what Vaylec did to my family, but he treats me kindly, and it confuses me."

"Briana, I love my brother, but Vaylec can't be trusted. Jealousy has completely warped his sense of right and wrong, and I'm afraid he's never going to find his way out of it. I want you to watch, listen, and wait, just like you've been doing. And when an opportunity arises for you to take action or escape, you grab it!" She shook Brie's shoulders gently. "Having you here, Briana, has changed my outlook, and I want to thank you for that. Before you arrived, I was overcome with sorrow and guilt, but witnessing your bravery has been contagious. It's reignited my fighting spirit."

Brie hugged Violet tightly, feeling ashamed that her own fighting spirit had temporary taken a vacation. "Thank you for being my friend, Violet."

They ate lunch together, and Brie spent the afternoon lying by the fire, holding Nibbles, while Violet read. It was exactly what she needed.

During the quiet afternoon, Brie had plenty of time to think. After scolding herself soundly for becoming discouraged, she decided on a few things. For starters, she wasn't going to sit around feeling sorry for herself anymore. She was going to devote more time to training, and she was going to actively watch for an opportunity to escape.

Several hours later, Vaylec eventually came to check on them. Brie was still sitting by the fire, and Violet was braiding her hair. When Vaylec entered the room, he smiled.

"You look much better," he said to Brie.

"I feel better, too," Brie answered hesitantly as she rose to leave. "Thank you for your kindness, and for letting me visit with Violet. It was exactly what I needed."

Violet beamed at Brie as they hugged goodbye. Brie looked up in time to see hope flash across Vaylec's face, and her good mood was dampened as she realized her creating a friendship with Violet was exactly what he wanted.

Leading Brie down the spiral staircase, Vaylec mentioned, "It's an unusually warm day for this time of year. My parents and I are taking a late afternoon tea outside. Would you care to join us?"

Brie didn't really want to have tea with Vaylec, but being outside on a warm day sounded too irresistible to pass up. She'd hardly left the castle in moons.

"Yes, I would like that," she agreed.

They made their way outside to the castle gardens, where a table was set for tea. Cecily and Eldon were already there; they stood to greet Vaylec and Brie as they approached.

"It's good to see you smiling again, Briana," Cecily whispered in her ear as they hugged.

Brie smiled sheepishly, feeling embarrassed that her recent emotions had been so transparent.

Tea was served, and thankfully Brie's shame didn't last long. It was swept away by the beautiful spring day, warm and sunny with a perfect breeze. Birds chirped and flew in circles around them. Brie found their proximity odd until she remembered Cecily had a gift with animals.

Brie sighed and closed her eyes, tilting her face upward toward the sun and basking in its warmth. Her chest began to burn in a familiar way as she felt her magic stirring within her, and her whole body felt energized. If she wasn't careful, she might accidentally turn herself invisible. She smiled at the thought.

"Would you care for a cookie, Briana?" Eldon offered.

"Yes, thank you," Brie said as she opened her eyes and accepted the plate of cookies. She took a large bite of a tasty gingersnap and washed it down with a warm sip of tea.

Their peace was abruptly disturbed, however, as a horse

galloped up the garden path and swiftly approached their table. The rider pulled the horse to a stop beside them and quickly dismounted.

He bowed to Vaylec. "Your Grace," the man said, out of breath, "I have urgent news from the city."

Vaylec stood up and motioned for the man to follow him. They walked several paces away and began to speak in heated whispers.

Brie tried to listen, but it was futile. They were too far away for her to hear. Instead, her eyes went to the chestnut horse standing just feet away from her, panting. Seeing another horse so close made her think about Ember and how much she missed riding.

Brie's heart tripled its pace as an idea occurred to her. There, just a few short steps away, was a horse with an empty saddle. It felt like Brie had suddenly developed tunnel vision, and the *only* thing she could see was the horse. It shook its mane and met her gaze, its intelligent eyes beckoning to her, seeming to know exactly what she was thinking.

Hadn't Violet just told her, "If you see an opportunity, take it"?

Did she dare try?

Brie glanced at Vaylec. He was distracted.

She looked at Cecily and Eldon. They were happily eating biscuits, completely oblivious to Brie's internal struggle.

Brie began to sweat. Where had the breeze gone? The heat felt stifling.

Earlier that very day, she had made the decision to escape if an opportunity presented itself, but she hadn't expected one to appear so soon. She wrung her hands in her lap as she weighed the risks in her mind. Something was preventing her uncles from rescuing her. If she escaped, she could search for them. It sounded like a much more appealing plan than wasting away here, surrounded by watchdogs.

Throwing caution to the wind, Brie leapt out of her seat, raced to the horse, and mounted him in the blink of an eye. As she dug her heels into the horse's sides, it rose up on its hind legs, neighing and shaking its mane. Brie couldn't have planned a more dramatic exit if she'd tried. The horse came down on four legs, and together, they galloped away from the castle.

Behind her, Brie heard Vaylec yell in panic, and she drove the horse harder. She tried to focus on the warmth of the sun, knowing if she could manage to disappear, her escape would be guaranteed. Unfortunately, it was much more difficult to concentrate on becoming invisible while bouncing around on the back of a horse. A dark cloud had also covered the sun, which made it even harder to tap into the sun's heat.

The cloud suddenly opened up and began to pour down rain so heavily that Brie could hardly see where she was going. To make matters worse, the horse came to a gradual halt. Ignoring her commands, it turned around and began to lazily trot back toward the table. Brie swung one leg over the saddle and prepared to jump from the horse and run, but she looked up and stopped. A group of guards were sprinting toward her, too close to evade.

With a sinking realization, Brie understood that her plan had failed. Cecily and Eldon had used their powers to stop her.

It was pathetic how easily she had been thwarted. This was likely the worst escape attempt in history.

Before the horse even came to a complete stop, Vaylec grabbed Brie's arm and pulled her roughly from the saddle, his face mottled red and filled with a rage like she had never seen before. He didn't say one word, and his silence scared her. Brie barely managed to land on her feet before Vaylec dragged her by the same arm toward the castle. Still, he kept quiet; the only audible sounds were his angry intakes of air and Brie's occasional whimpers.

As she passed Vaylec's parents, Brie could see the sadness on their faces. Eldon whispered, "Princess, what have you done?"

When Brie and Vaylec entered the castle, guards stepped into place and followed them. Brie could see their disappointment. Was it because she'd attempted to escape, or because she had been thwarted?

Vaylec yanked on Brie's arm once more, and she cried out in pain. It felt like her arm was being ripped from its socket. But Vaylec didn't relax his pull. If anything, he grabbed on more strongly.

"Vaylec, please stop!" Brie eventually blurted. "You're hurting me."

Vaylec came to an abrupt stop in the middle of the corridor, but he continued to hold onto Brie with a vice-like grip. A vein throbbed in his temple as he turned his furious gaze on her.

"I told you when you first returned to the castle," Vaylec said in a deadly quiet voice, "that my plans were to assist your rule over Predonia. I had hoped you would be a willing participant, but it appears that is no longer the case. You have just made a very grave mistake, Princess. Your kind treatment is over."

Anger exploded in Brie like a volcano. Her pretending was over too. She glared at Vaylec and shouted, "I will *never* willingly stand by your side while you rule over *my* kingdom. The kingdom that belonged to my parents—but you took it away from them, and then you took them away from me! I know all about you controlling the others. I can see it with my own eyes, and they hate it. They hate you! You're a selfish, evil monster, and you will never control me or my powers!"

Vaylec's control snapped. He slapped Brie across the face with such force that her head whipped to the side, and she tasted blood in her mouth.

Odin took a step closer.

"You're wrong." Vaylec's voice shook with anger. "Having you on the throne will just be a technicality, because we both know I will be the one ruling. When your powers finally surface, I will control them, and you, and all of Predonia."

Vaylec turned to the guards and ordered, "Take her to the dungeon. Lock her in the deepest cell." Then he turned to Brie. "If I have to keep you in chains for the next four years, so be it."

The guards led Brie outside and across the stone courtyard. As they descended the steps to the dungeons, they handled her gently. Despite their kind treatment, fear filled Brie as she was guided down the dark, narrow corridors. The stench of mildew, body sweat, and waste hit her, and she covered her nose, trying not to gag. She had never been in the dungeons before. Her father had forbidden it. He'd told her it was filled with the worst citizens in the land and it was no place for a princess. Brie glared at the guards through her tears, covering her fear with anger. She challenged them bitterly. "Why do you choose to serve such an evil man?"

It was Odin who answered. "He lured us with promises of riches and greatness, which I'm ashamed to say, I fell for. I no longer follow him willingly, Your Highness. I do it out of fear. He has already killed members of our families, and he's threatened to harm others if we do not follow his orders."

Brie shuddered. Vaylec's depravity seemed to have no limits.

They walked further into the depths of the dungeon, the torches on the walls providing intermittent bursts of light. Their steps echoed loudly, and vacant-eyed prisoners glanced up listlessly as they passed. Brie wondered if Vaylec had released her father's prisoners or simply added to them.

The guards reached the very last cell and opened it. They let Brie walk into the dank space of her own accord. Odin paused before shutting the cell door. He whispered, "I'll come check on you, Your Highness. Be brave." Then the door slammed shut with an eerie *clang*, the lock clicked severely, and she was left alone.

Brie dropped her head into her hands. She couldn't believe she was in prison. She hurt all over, and she regretted her stupid attempt at freedom. She had reacted without a plan, changing her situation from bad to worse. How was she ever going to escape from a dungeon?

Flopping down on the small, thin mattress in her prison

cell, Brie cried tears of embarrassment and despair.

Angry and overwhelmed, she threw her thoughts out in a final attempt to reach her uncles. *Derek, it's Brie. Where in the name of all that is Blameless are you?*

*Briana Rose?* came an instantaneous response. *We're in the city, and we're coming for you.*

# Two Is Better than One

*DEREK! DEREK?* Brie thought frantically as she sprang out of bed, no longer feeling her aches and pains. *Is it really you?* She paced back and forth within her small cell as her heart tried to pound its way outside of her chest.

*Yes, it's really me, Princess,* came Derek's warm, reassuring reply.

Tears of relief began to stream down Brie's face, and her mouth split into an enormous smile. A loud sob worked its way out of her, but it quickly changed into laughter. She shook her head, feeling like an emotional mess. *You have no idea how good it is to hear your voice.*

*Actually, I know exactly how good it is.* Derek's relief mirrored hers. *Briana, please put me out of my misery and tell me how you're doing. We've been worried sick about you. Are you hurt? Have you been treated poorly?*

*Vaylec's treated me kindly.* At least, mostly—but Brie didn't need to share the details of Vaylec's recent anger with Derek yet. *But it hasn't been easy. I've been homesick for Mount Elrad. Are Kove and Flinton with you?*

*Yes, they're right here beside me, and all three of us have missed you too.* Derek's tone abruptly changed into exasperation. *Ouch! If you fools don't stop, I won't be able to focus, and I'll lose our connection. . . . She says she's fine. . . . Yes, I'll tell her.* He addressed Brie again, *Flinton and Kove want you to know they wish their gifts were as awesome as mine so they could speak with you directly.*

Brie smiled, envisioning the three of them bickering. Derek was the most serious one in their group. The fact that he was joking meant he must be feeling as giddy as she was about being reconnected.

*Kove, if you smack me again, you'd better be prepared for a fight. . . . Almighty Three, give me patience,* he muttered mentally. *Fine, I'll tell her!* He continued, *They want me to let you know they can't wait to see you, and they've been miserable wretches without you.*

Brie laughed again as more tears escaped. Earth, air, and sun, she was a wreck. A princess shouldn't cry so much. She would have to work on controlling her emotions better before she became queen.

Shaking her head, Brie refocused. *Where have you been? What took you so long? When are you taking me home?*

*It's a long story, but we'll explain everything when we see you. We just arrived in Aldestone this morning. Originally, we planned on scouting out the castle and working on the details of your rescue over the next few days, but I think we were sighted today by one of Vaylec's men. We're not going to wait around and give them the opportunity to attack. We're coming for you tonight.*

Brie groaned in relief. She could hardly believe it was true. *Thank you.*

Derek added, *You learning telepathy is a game-changer. It's given us a huge advantage. Where in the castle are you?*

*I'm in the dungeon.*

*You've been locked away in a dungeon this whole time?* Derek asked with a steel edge in his voice.

*No, I was just sent here today after I tried to escape.*

*I see. You've been busy, haven't you?*

*I guess you could say that,* Brie muttered. *I have a lot to tell you. But the most important thing is that you need to shield yourself, Flinton, and Kove, when you come into the castle. I've kept myself shielded, and Vaylec hasn't been able to control my powers. He doesn't even realize I have them.*

Derek chuckled. *That was my plan. You're full of surprises tonight. I'm proud of you, Briana.*

They proceeded to discuss the details of her rescue. Derek promised to be inside the walls of the castle by midnight. Brie's job was to break out of her cell and meet them in the courtyard at the top of the dungeon steps.

*What if I can't break out?* she asked, a wave of doubt suddenly coming over her. Even though she'd picked the locks on Nina's and Violet's doors, a prison cell seemed daunting.

*Briana, you seem to be able to do whatever you set your heart on. Just keep us informed. If we need to come down into the dungeons to get you, we will.* Derek paused, then added as an afterthought, *I want you to summon your bow so you have a weapon for protection.*

Brie smacked her own forehead, feeling ridiculous. *I can't believe I didn't think of that. I could have summoned my bow and taken care of Vaylec moons ago.*

*Briana, you are not to kill him,"* Derek instructed sharply. *You're too young to be burdened with that kind of responsibility, and unfortunately, until we understand his connection to the other Blame-*

*less, no one can. Killing him might harm the others.*

*I never would have thought of that. I won't.* Brie paused, debating on whether or not to bring it up. *Derek, there's one more thing. Violet wanted me to tell you something important.*

*We'll discuss it later. The only thing I want you focused on is escaping. There'll be plenty of time to talk on our ride back to Mount Elrad.*

They said their goodbyes with promises to see one another by midnight.

Brie's evening ticked by slowly. Knowing her uncles were nearby was like a form of sweet torture. She alternated between pacing and sitting, finally allowing herself to think about seeing Cassie and Taeo again. She missed them so much, it was painful.

At some point, a small compartment in the bottom of her door slid open, and she was delivered a crusty roll, a chunk of dry cheese, and water. Although she had no appetite, she forced herself to nibble it down, knowing she would need her strength later.

It was impossible to accurately measure the passage of time while in the depths of a dungeon. When everything was quiet and Brie could no longer hear the rotation of guards in the hallways, she decided it was safe to begin her work.

The first thing she did was summon her bow and quiver of arrows from her room in Mount Elrad. They appeared in the blink of an eye, and Brie sighed in relief. She ran her fingers lovingly over the bow, thrilled to have it in her hands again. When she tried to strap it and the quiver to her back, she realized it was impossible while wearing her frilly dress.

With a small thrill of excitement, she summoned her leggings, tunic, and travel boots from her closet in the castle, and hastily changed out of her dress. She heard the lace rip as she removed it. Feeling rebellious, she ripped a bit more out of sheer pleasure, then discarded the offensive garment in the corner of the cell. Maybe the rats would find a better use for it.

After pulling on her comfortable clothes, Brie summoned her scarf, hat, and mittens, and stowed them in her pockets. She paused for a moment, unsure if she should do it, but making a snap decision, she summoned Cassie's notebook and quill. She scrawled one sentence and sent it back.

They're here, and they're breaking me out tonight.

Lastly, Brie retrieved her lock-picking set from the folds of her ruined gown. She had grown accustomed to always carrying it, just as Taeo had instructed. He would be so proud of her. Brie rolled her eyes. Who was she kidding? He would probably be proud of himself for being correct. Brie smirked. She couldn't wait to see the arrogant boy again and share her experiences with him and Cassie.

After one last check to ensure she had everything, Brie finally tiptoed to the door. In the dim light, her eyes searched its large metal expanse for the lock. It was enormous, old, and rusty. Hoping her lockpick set contained the necessary instrument to open it, she shuffled through the ring and selected the largest one. She'd tried it on Violet's door, but it had been too big to fit. Hoping for the best, Brie inserted it into the rusty opening, and it slid inside without resistance. In very little time, she was able to find the sweet spot where the pick snugly fit, and she turned her wrist—but it wouldn't budge.

Brie twisted her wrist again with more force, but instead of unlocking, the door held. A sharp, stabbing pain shot up the arm Vaylec had grabbed to pull her down from her horse.

Letting go, Brie relaxed her arms and shook them out by her sides. Then she took hold of the pick with both hands and twisted it, but the rusty lock was stubborn. She could feel the pick bending, and she worried it would snap off inside the door.

Stamping her foot in frustration, Brie turned the pick with all of her might. Finally, she was rewarded with a very welcome and distinct click.

Relieved, Brie hesitantly pushed on the door and watched as it swung open with a loud and eerie creak. Wincing at the noise, she stepped out into the empty corridor and shut the door behind her.

Brie closed her eyes, placed her hand over her heart, and concentrated on her gift of invisibility. But something felt different this time. No matter how hard she focused, she couldn't connect with the warmth of the sun. She tried for several minutes, but she was unsuccessful. Being underground in a cold, dark prison with the memory of Vaylec's violence toward her was too much of an obstacle. If she concentrated long and hard, maybe she could work her way through it, but it would waste too much time. She would have to try her luck without it.

Navigating through the damp hallways, Brie passed other prison cells and glanced through the bars on the doors to the other prisoners. What crimes had they committed? Were they truly evil people, or had they been wrongfully convicted?

Brie thought about the poor servant girl who had accidently bumped into Violet on New Year's Day. Her clumsiness alone had been the cause of her punishment.

Brie stopped walking.

She wasn't sure about the other prisoners, but she knew without a doubt that the servant girl was innocent. Clumsiness wasn't a crime. If Brie could find her, they could escape together. It would be riskier, and it would take longer, but how could she possibly leave that young woman behind, knowing she would rot away in a cell while her poor child grew up without a mother?

The answer was simple. Brie couldn't.

Retracing her steps, she looked carefully into every cell to make sure she hadn't missed the servant. When she didn't see the girl, Brie proceeded forward and walked down two more corridors, getting closer to the guards as she searched. She could hear them ahead of her, conversing in deep, bored-sounding voices.

Finally, partway down the third corridor, Brie found who she was looking for. With only a few torches hanging on the walls, the lighting was poor, but Brie recognized the woman's slender frame lying on the mattress. She looked thinner, and her clothes were filthy, but it was definitely the same person.

Brie expertly picked her lock, and the servant's eyes opened. This cell was closer to the front of the dungeon, and the lock was well oiled, not rusty. It had likely received a lot more use over the years, and Brie was relieved to find it turned over with ease.

Pulling the door open, Brie slipped into the tiny room.

The young woman sat up in her bed. She rubbed her eyes and looked at the door in confusion. Her mouth dropped open when she saw Brie.

"Princess Briana?"

Brie knelt in front of the woman and whispered, "Yes, it's me. I remember you from dinner on New Year's Day, but forgive me, I don't know your name."

"It's Lyla," the girl whispered, rubbing her eyes and shaking her head, like she was internally debating whether Brie was real or a hallucination.

"We're breaking out of here. Do you have any objections?"

Wide-eyed, Lyla shook her head.

"Perfect," Brie whispered. "Now follow me, and stay quiet."

Brie led the way out of the cell. Together, she and Lyla padded quietly forward, turning the corner onto the last hallway. Ahead, Brie could see an alcove where the guards were stationed, and beyond them was the stairwell that led outside.

Holding hands, Brie and Lyla tiptoed as quietly as possible toward the guards. Two were seated at a table, playing a game of cards, their sword belts resting on the table beside them.

The corridor was narrow, and Brie realized with despair that there was no possible way to sneak past the guards without being noticed. It looked like she was going to have to make use of her self-defense lessons.

As they got closer, Brie could feel Lyla's hesitation, and the servant yanked on Brie's hand, nearly pulling them to a stop. Brie gave the other girl's fingers a reassuring squeeze but tugged gently on her hand, indicating they needed to keep moving forward.

The next thing Brie knew, there was a scuffle of feet and a muffled shriek as Lyla's hand wrenched from hers. Brie turned around and watched in horror as Lyla tripped over her own feet. Lyla flew forward, launching past Brie. Then she landed ungracefully in the lap of one of the guards with an *oomph.*

There was a moment of stunned silence as Lyla and the guard stared at one another in shock.

Brie was the first person to react. She sprinted toward the table and grabbed a sword from it. The guard who was now holding Lyla yelled, "What the bloody hell is going on?"

Brie rammed the hilt of the sword into the temple of the other guard, and he slumped over in his seat, unconscious.

"Get out of the way!" Brie yelled at Lyla.

Finally recovering from her fall, Lyla reached across the table and grabbed a cup of hot coffee, tossing it into the remaining guard's face. Then she jumped out of his lap as he swore and frantically wiped the hot liquid out of his eyes.

With Lyla out of the way, Brie rushed forward and jammed her fingers into the guard's already tender eyes. He screamed in pain and reached toward her blindly, his arms outstretched. Brie grabbed his pinky fingers, bending them as far back as they would go. The man bellowed in more pain and surged out of his chair, knocking the flimsy table over in his haste.

With the table out of the way, Brie kneed the guard in his groin. He bent over in agony. Lyla rejoined the fight and clobbered the man over the top of his head with the blunt edge of a sword, knocking him out cold. They watched in disbelief as he fell face-first onto the stone floor.

Still holding the sword above her head, Lyla said, "I can't believe we just did that."

She and Brie looked at each other, and then burst out laughing.

"Let's get out of here before they wake up," Brie suggested.

As they rushed past the felled guards, Lyla said softly, "I'm sorry, Princess Briana. I'm terribly clumsy, as I'm sure you've noticed."

"You're forgiven," Brie said, "but you might want to consider a new livelihood. Come on; we've almost made it."

They ascended the stone steps together and entered the darkened courtyard. Brie turned to Lyla and whispered, "This is where we part ways. For your safety and mine, please don't breathe a word of what happened tonight to anyone. Do you understand?"

"Yes, I swear to you, I won't," Lyla nodded.

"Go find your child and run far away from Aldestone," Brie commanded.

As they embraced, Lyla whispered, "Thank you, Your Highness. I will never forget your kindness."

They broke apart, and Brie watched as Lyla's slim figure disappeared into the darkness.

# *Freedom*

Brie took a deep breath of the cool night air and blew it out in a rush. Now that she had safely escaped from the dungeon, she could hardly contain her excitement. She scanned her surroundings and saw two guards slumped over on the ground nearby. It certainly looked like her uncles' handiwork.

Spinning around in a circle, Brie searched for them—but she saw no one. She was ready to reach out to Derek telepathically, when arms suddenly grabbed her from behind. A hand clapped over her mouth, and a familiar voice whispered in her ear.

"Who is tall and bossy and has a shaved head?"

Brie giggled in relief and tried to turn around, but the arms tightened, holding her in place as the man continued to whisper. "Who looks and acts like a grumpy grizzly bear but is more resourceful than my grandmother?"

A deep snort came from somewhere behind Brie. Again, she attempted to turn, but hands stopped her.

"Who's your favorite uncle with the dashing good looks who has missed you terribly?"

The man finally loosened his hold, and Brie turned around

to see Kove holding out a yellow rose, sporting a fiercely happy look. He placed the rose in her hair and lifted her off the ground, hugging her tightly, his arms trembling with relief.

"Hello, sunshine," he whispered in a shaky voice.

Brie clung to him, afraid to let go. The joy of being reunited was threatening to make her cry again. "You better have a good reason for why you took so long to get here," she choked out.

Before Kove could answer, Brie was lifted out of his hold and spun around in the air. She squealed in surprise as she landed safely in Flinton's arms.

Brie grinned as she looked at Flinton for the first time in three moons. Kove was right: Flinton did resemble a grizzly bear. His beard had grown since Brie last saw him, and his hair was long and shaggy. Tears fell shamelessly from his eyes, and he sniffed. "You're a sight for sore eyes, short stuff."

"You are too," Brie whispered, hugging his thick neck. She lifted a tangled lock of his hair and dropped it. "But Milly might not agree."

Flinton guffawed and pinched her cheek, then put her on the ground.

Brie finally turned to face Derek. He knelt in front of her. Taking her chin in his hand, he scanned her face. He looked tired and travel-worn, but his eyes were just as sharp and piercing as always. They narrowed. "What happened to you?" he asked, turning her face to get a better view. He gently touched her swollen cheek, and she winced in pain.

Kove and Flinton stepped closer, looking over Derek's shoulder at Brie.

"Vaylec slapped me," Brie quietly told the truth. It was pointless to lie to Derek.

Derek's eyes turned murderous, Flinton let out a dangerous growl, and Kove spewed out several colorful-sounding words. Brie hurriedly added, "It was the one and only time he struck me. Don't worry about it. It barely hurts. Please, just get me out of here."

Derek continued to examine Brie, but he finally nodded. Cradling her cheeks, he leaned forward and planted a kiss on her forehead.

"We've missed you, Briana Rose. Let's take you home."

Derek stood, and they prepared to leave, but the darkened courtyard was suddenly bathed in light. They had been surrounded by a dozen guards with torches.

Two guards split ranks, creating an opening in the circle, and Vaylec strolled forward, accompanied by Eldon, Cecily, Adira, Jarvis, and Torin.

Brie's heart sank.

"No one is taking Briana anywhere," Vaylec said coldly. "*This* is her home."

Brie felt, rather than heard, her uncles arm themselves beside her.

"So Vaylec wants to play," Kove taunted. "But the odds aren't in your favor, Your Filthy Highness. Aren't three grown men a little too much for you to handle? From the looks of it, you prefer to pick on little girls." Kove motioned to Brie.

Vaylec sneered, ignoring the jab. "One of my men sighted you today, and I anticipated you would come. How disappointingly predictable of you. I've been waiting, and you walked right into my hands. I'm curious how you knew Briana would be in the dungeon, though. Lucky guess, perhaps?" He continued without waiting for an answer. "I'll admit, the location is convenient for me, since I plan to lock you up once I'm finished with you."

"You're not as brilliant as you think if you believe a prison cell would keep us captive," Flinton said with a raised eyebrow.

Vaylec smiled. "No, there are other ways to hold a Blameless captive." Keeping his eyes on Brie's uncles, he asked, "Can you sense their presence, Adira?"

Adira took a small step forward. "No, Your Grace, I cannot."

"And why is that?" Vaylec asked. "They are right in front of you."

Before Adira could answer, Derek spoke. "Stop playing games. Shields are amazing things, aren't they, Vaylec?"

A brief look of fear flashed across Vaylec's face.

"As much as we're enjoying this little chat, it's time for us to say goodbye," Derek continued. "You can either let us go peacefully or prepare to be defeated."

Vaylec laughed incredulously. "You can't be serious. You don't think the three of you can fight your way out of this, do you? You're surrounded and outnumbered by both guards and Blameless."

"We don't just think it," Derek said. "We know it."

"We're as serious as a blade to your throat," Flinton challenged. He moved his gargantuan body a few steps toward the middle of the courtyard. A sword appeared in each of his massive hands, and he began to spin them rapidly, crisscrossing them in front of and behind his body in a fabulous display of skill and power. The speed of the swords increased until they became a blur. The muscles in his arms flexed and bulged beneath his tunic, and the expression on his face was deadly. Brie had gotten used to thinking of Flinton as a gentle giant, but tonight she was witnessing a different man. It was the same man who had saved her on the evening of her parents' death: the warrior and protector.

Brie looked past Vaylec toward Adira, whose eyes held a gleam of admiration. *Goodbye, Adira. Thank you for everything. I wish you could come with us.*

At Brie's words, Adira's eyes left Flinton and landed on Brie. A look of longing washed over her, and she nodded, acknowledging Brie's goodbye.

"Very well." Vaylec sneered. "Father, Mother, set the mood."

Cecily and Eldon raised their arms and began to murmur.

A thick layer of fog rose from the ground and wrapped around Brie and her uncles, slowly crawling up their bodies. Brie's gut clenched tightly as the fog quickly reached her knees. They were going to be surrounded by it; it would blind them.

Brie stepped to the side, trying to get away from the fog, but it followed and clung to her. She tried not to panic. A howl rose up into the night, eerily close, causing goosebumps to erupt across Brie's skin. A pack of wolves materialized, as if they'd been waiting in the shadows, and crept up to stand beside the guards, joining the circle.

"Eldon and Cecily, shall I send greetings to my parents and the rest of the Elders?" Kove asked.

Brie wondered why Kove was worried about small talk at a time like this, but Eldon's gaze snapped to Kove and became panicked.

"Kove, do *not* report this back to the Elders!" Eldon begged. "They wouldn't understand. It wouldn't sit well with the Blameless that our son has been the cause of so much chaos. They would question my character, and I would lose my position as an Elder."

As soon as the words left his mouth, the fog began to dissipate.

A wild look of rage entered Vaylec's eyes. Furious, he yelled, "I'm touched that you think so highly of me, Father. Focus on the fog!"

Eldon shook his head as if trying to clear it and raised his arms into the air again. His brows pinched in confusion as the fog continued to thin out instead of grow. He murmured another command, but nothing happened. He stared at his outstretched hands, and a look of realization came over his face.

Eldon sank onto his knees, cradling his head in devastation. "I . . . I can't do it. It won't work." He looked at his wife and said, "I'm sorry, Cecily. I can't bare the shame and dishonor anymore. I hate him."

Cecily kept her hands in the air, but tears streamed down her face.

"For flairs' sake," Kove muttered. "I wanted to distract him, but I didn't want this."

Brie's eyes bounced back and forth, taking everything in, but she did not understand what was happening.

Derek made use of the distraction and attacked. He lifted

his hands, and a ball of fire blazed to life in his palms. It started out small, the size of a stone, and grew into an enormous globe. Then he thrust his arms outward.

The large flame separated into tiny spheres that flew away from Derek and into the chests of several guards, who fell to the pavement. Their torches hit the ground, and instead of going out, they exploded into bigger flames, enveloping the courtyard in smoke and haze.

Chaos descended.

Vaylec shouted orders to the group of Blameless who flanked him, and weapons began to fly through the air.

"Aim to capture but not kill!" Vaylec ordered. "Be careful with the princess!"

Fury rose up inside of Brie, and the need to protect the only family she had left. She removed her bow, drew an arrow, and let it loose. She watched in satisfaction as the arrow embedded itself into Vaylec's left arm. Vaylec cursed and grabbed the arrow, pulling it out roughly, all while continuing to issue commands.

Cecily ordered the wolves to attack.

"Brie!" Flinton yelled. "Onto my back!"

He crouched down, and Brie leapt into the air, throwing the bow over her shoulder. Grabbing his broad shoulders, she circled her legs around his waist—as the fangs of a wolf sank into her calf.

Brie screamed in pain and punched the wolf in the head with her fist, but it did no good. The wolf's jaw clenched down harder, and it began to shake its head back and forth. Brie was nearly blinded by the pain that exploded down her leg. Her grip on Flinton slackened, and she feared she would fall.

The wolf suddenly let go and collapsed. Flinton, Brie's protector, had cut it down with a swipe of his sword. He turned and began to slice through the air at the other wolves, dropping them faster than Brie could keep count.

From her position on Flinton's back, Brie breathed through the throbbing pain in her calf and watched the fight with growing horror.

Derek threw more balls of fire. This time they were directed at Adira, who successfully blocked the flames and returned the attack with a steady rain of knives. Derek's shield was in place, and the knives met an invisible wall around him, dropping.

Brie needed to do something to help. *ADIRA!* She threw her thoughts toward her friend. Adira glanced at Brie, and a small smile crossed her face, like she knew and agreed with what Brie had done. The distraction accomplished its goal. Adira's defenses faltered, and a ball of fire hit her in the chest. With a ghost of a smile still on her face, she fell to the cobblestone ground.

*I'm sorry, Adira,* Brie thought, unsure if she was alive or dead.

Derek's bow and arrow appeared in his hand, and he began to fire off shots at Torin, who had been disappearing and reappearing randomly all over the courtyard.

Kove was everywhere, flipping, kicking, and throwing knives. He was fighting wolves, soldiers, and Blameless alike. He ran headlong into Jarvis, wrapping his arms around the other man's waist and tackling him. Jarvis, who had been wielding a club in his hands, vanished. Kove fell to the ground, wrestling and grappling with the invisible man.

Brie watched in terror as Vaylec turned toward Kove's unprotected back. He pulled the sword from the scabbard at his waist and raised it high into the air, ready to inflict what Brie was certain would be a death blow. She screamed Kove's name in warning.

Eldon, who had been sitting in a useless state of shock, suddenly came to life. He lunged at Vaylec's legs, pulling Vaylec to his knees. Vaylec quickly recovered, his athletic body regaining footing almost immediately. He turned and faced his father with a look of hatred.

"Without your powers, you are no use to me," Vaylec spat out. Then he drove his sword into his father's chest.

Brie couldn't breathe.

Cecily wailed an agonized scream.

The wolves stopped their attack.

Kove ran back to Flinton's side. "Let's go!"

Brie knew it wouldn't take long for Vaylec to rally and lead another attack, and an idea came to her. "Take Flinton's hands," she yelled. "Trust me!" she added desperately.

Derek and Kove grabbed Flinton's hands, one on either side of him.

"Vaylec!" Brie yelled.

Vaylec's eyes snapped to her, angrily, hungrily.

"Your plan will *never* work," Brie shouted. Then, even though it was night, she reached deep and connected with the power of the sun with a fiery resolve she had never before possessed. Heat surged through her, flowing directly to her uncles. There was an explosion of light, a gust of warmth spread through the courtyard, and the four of them vanished.

Vaylec's eyes widened, and his jaw opened in shock. The arm holding his sword dropped to his side as the realization hit him: Brie's magic was very much alive. He'd been waiting for this moment, but his plan had gone horribly wrong. And now Brie and her rescuers were completely invisible.

"Run!" Brie screamed to her uncles.

And they did.

A stream of curses erupted from Vaylec as they fled.

Brie clung to Flinton as he ran out of the courtyard, through the cobblestone streets and past the castle walls. She kept her arms around Flinton's neck and her eyes shut, concentrating with all of her might on maintaining the flow of magic through all four of them. Keeping them invisible was the hardest thing she had ever done. Despite the cool night air, a steady stream of sweat ran down her back from the effort.

"You're brilliant, Briana Rose, just brilliant," Derek said as they raced.

As they neared the forest that surrounded the castle, Brie finally opened her eyes. Four horses came into view, and Brie couldn't believe what she saw.

"You brought Ember?"

"Yes," Kove confirmed. "We thought you would appreciate having your own ride this time."

They reached the horses and broke apart to mount, the cover of invisibility lifting as they separated. Flinton lifted Brie into the saddle, for which she was grateful; she wouldn't have had the strength to mount with her sore arm and injured leg.

The moment she was seated, she threw her arms around Ember's neck and spoke in her ear: "I missed you, girl."

Together, Brie, Flinton, Derek, and Kove spurred their mounts forward and fled Aldestone into the night, just like they had done so many moons before.

As they galloped, conflicting emotions warred inside of Brie. Being reunited with her uncles caused relief and joy to flood through her. For the first time since her capture, she felt like she could finally fully expand her lungs and breathe. She was safe.

But mixed with her relief was concern for the friends she was leaving behind. Brie thought especially of Violet, but also of Adira, Torin, Jarvis, and poor Cecily, who'd lost her husband tonight. She even thought of Odin, Lyla, and the rest of Predonia still under Vaylec's rule. Because of her escape, they would likely be facing his tremendous wrath in the days to come.

Brie didn't know how she would do it, but she vowed to become the queen her country needed her to be. She would devote her time to studying and mastering her magical gifts until she had the knowledge and power to overthrow Vaylec and his reign of terror.

Unsure if she would be heard, Brie had to try one more thing before she left Aldestone. She placed her right hand over her heart, the heart that for some reason had been declared Blameless, and she sent a final message into the night: *Violet, I'm sorry I had to leave you behind. I wish I could have brought you with me, but I promise I'll come back for you. One day, you and all of Predonia will be free.*

# Acknowledgments

Thank you to Robert Pruett and the entire team at Brandylane Publishers, Inc./Belle Isle Books for believing in my manuscript and taking a chance on my story. Thanks to everyone who played a part, great or small, in the publication process. Special thanks to my editor and project manager, Christina Kann, for answering my many questions and holding my hand as an inexperienced author. Your edits and suggestions took my rough work and polished it into something I am proud of!

Huge thanks to my illustrator, Hannu Nevanlinna, for creating a beautiful cover design and bringing my characters to life in such a perfect way.

To my brothers, Matt and Stefan, thanks for your encouragement and the part you played in helping with publication. Eden: thank you, my dear sister, for your unwavering belief in me and *The Blameless.* Thanks to my nephew, Derek, for being willing to have your face plastered on the cover, for being the inspiration for one of my main characters, and for the part you had in supporting my book.

My small group of *The Blameless* fans (you know who you are) must also be mentioned. Thanks for proofreading my work, chapter by chapter, and providing feedback on the story. Your enthusiasm and positive feedback made me believe this book was good enough, and gave me the determination to continue. A special shout out to Carrie. Your developmental edit made all the difference in the world.

To my husband and kids: all of this is for you. Thanks for putting up with my endless book talk and questions, and for being my sounding boards. Thanks for being my earliest and most supportive fans. Each of you touched the story in your own special way. Thanks for putting up with my countless hours of writing, a messy house, and fewer home-cooked meals to bring this book to fruition. I'm so humbled and blessed to be your wife and mother. I love each of you deeply and endlessly.

E.S. Christison

Elisabeth S. Christison's very first job was as a scribe in a library. She was raised by her father, and he passed a love of reading to her, especially fantasy. Elisabeth has passed this same love on to her seven children, and as a result, much of her adult life has been spent in the realms of their make-believe kingdoms, giving her firsthand experience with the whimsical workings of their young minds. She shared her own stories with them at bedtime, but never chose to write them down until an idea she couldn't ignore blazed into her mind. Elisabeth lives with her family in Ohio, and when she isn't busy navigating the seas of motherhood, working as a nurse, or castle-hopping and enjoying fine wine and chocolate with her husband, she can be found writing the sequel to The Blameless or dreaming up other tales.

CPSIA information can be obtained
at www.ICGtesting.com
Printed in the USA
LVHW091330111221
705747LV00018B/1047